▶▶▶ACEL·WORL

THE CARBIDE WOLF

REKI KAWAHARA
ILLUSTRATION BY **HIMA**
DESIGN BY **bee-pee**

IRON POUND

Burst Linker belonging to the Green Legion, Great Wall. Speaks through his fists to Silver Crow, a comrade.

"Anyway, it's been aaaages, this scene."

"A legendary ability that once existed in the Accelerated World... Theoretical Mirror."

ARGON ARRAY

Duel avatar with the role of analyzing whether Silver Crow's Armor of Catastrophe has been purified.

"If it's a trap, I'll kill everyone in the place."

"First, a word of thanks for responding to the sudden request, Argon Array."

KUROYUKIHIME

Vice president of the Umesato Junior High student council. Controls the "Black King," Black Lotus.

"It's to prove my innocence, after all!"

BLUE KNIGHT

Leonids Legion Master. Acts as chair for meetings of the Seven Kings.

HARUYUKI

Boy in the lowest school caste. Member of the new Nega Nebulus, led by Kuroyukihime. Duel avatar: Silver Crow.

UI▷ UNDERSTOOD. WELL THEN, SHALL WE GO TO MY HOUSE? WE MIGHT BE A LITTLE LATE GETTING IN, SO I THINK YOU'D BETTER LEAVE A MESSAGE FOR YOUR HOUSEHOLD.

UTAI SHINOMIYA

Controls a duel avatar belonging to the Black Legion, Nega Nebulus. Fourth grader who guides Haruyuki. Duel avatar: Ardor Maiden.

"You say that, but it's just you getting all hot and bothered by your leg fetish, right? Right?"

NIKO

Elementary school girl and Legion Master of the Red Legion, Prominence. Duel avatar: Scarlet Rain.

"I'm under no obligation to show you any kindness, but...I'll offer you a word in the guise of advice."

MANGANESE BLADE

A senior executive in the Blue Legion, Leonids.

"Just what I expected, Crow. I'd heard about you, but you're much faster than I even imagined."

WOLFRAM CERBERUS

Duel avatar that suddenly appears in the Accelerated World. The strongest and hardest metal color.

"I won't run and hide. Let's settle this with hand-to-hand combat."

LIST OF AVATARS IN EACH LEGION
(Name of Player in Parentheses)

Black Legion, Nega Nebulus
Legion Master: Black Lotus (Kuroyukihime)

Four Elements
Wind: Sky Raker (Fuko Kurasaki)
Fire: Ardor Maiden (Utai Shinomiya)
Water: Aqua Current *Currently retired
Earth: Graphite Edge *Currently retired

Silver Crow (Haruyuki Arita)
Lime Bell (Chiyuri Kurashima)
Cyan Pile (Takumu Mayuzumi)

Red Legion, Prominence
Legion Master: Scarlet Rain (Yuniko Kozuki)
Submaster: Blood Leopard

Red Rider *Exited the Accelerated World
Cherry Rook *Exited the Accelerated World

Blue Legion, Leonids
Legion Master: Blue Knight

Executives
Cobalt Blade
Manganese Blade

Frost Horn
Tourmaline Shell

Yellow Legion, Crypt Cosmic Circus
Legion Master: Yellow Radio

Green Legion, Great Wall
Legion Master: Green Grandé

Six Armors
Third seat: Iron Pound

Ash Roller (Rin Kusakabe)
Bush Utan
Olive Grab

Purple Legion, Aurora Oval
Legion Master: Purple Thorn

Aide
Astor Vine

Crimson Kingbolt *Currently retired

White Legion, Oscillatory Universe
Legion Master: ???

Legion Proxy
Ivory Tower

Acceleration Research Society
Black Vise
Rust Jigsaw
Dusk Taker (Seiji Nomi)
              *Exited the Accelerated World
Sulfur Pot

Others
Nickel Doll
Sand Duct

Matchmaker

Chrome Falcon
Saffron Blossom

Azure Air

Magenta Scissor
Cocoa Cracker

Lagoon Dolphin (Ruka Asato)
Coral Merrow (Mana Itosu)

Aluminum Valkyrie (Chiaki Chigira)
Orange Raptor (Yuko Hori)
Violet Dancer (Kurumi Kuruma)

Zircon Paladin

▶▶▶ACCEL·WORLD

THE CARBIDE WOLF

Reki Kawahara
Illustrations: HIMA
Design: bee-pee

YEN ON

NEW YORK

■ Kuroyukihime = Umesato Junior High School student council vice president. Trim and clever girl who has it all. Her background is shrouded in mystery. Her in-school avatar is a spangle butterfly she programmed herself. Her duel avatar is the Black King, Black Lotus (level nine).

■ Haruyuki = Haruyuki Arita. Eighth grader at Umesato Junior High School. Bullied, on the pudgy side. He's good at games, but shy. His in-school avatar is a pink pig. His duel avatar is Silver Crow (level five).

■ Chiyuri = Chiyuri Kurashima. Haruyuki's childhood friend. Meddling, energetic girl. Her in-school avatar is a silver cat. Her duel avatar is Lime Bell (level four).

■ Takumu = Takumu Mayuzumi. A boy Haruyuki and Chiyuri have known since childhood. Good at kendo. His duel avatar is Cyan Pile (level five).

■ Fuko = Fuko Kurasaki. Burst Linker belonging to the old Nega Nebulus. One of the Four Elements. Lived as a recluse due to certain circumstances, but is persuaded by Kuroyukihime and Haruyuki to come back to the battlefront. Taught Haruyuki about the Incarnate System. Her duel avatar is Sky Raker (level eight).

■ Uiui = Utai Shinomiya. Burst Linker belonging to the old Nega Nebulus. One of the Four Elements. Fourth grader in the elementary division of Matsunogi Academy. Not only can she use the advanced curse removal command "Purify," she is also skilled at long-range attacks. Her duel avatar is Ardor Maiden (level seven).

■ Neurolinker = A portable Internet terminal that connects with the brain via a wireless quantum connection and enhances all five senses with images, sounds, and other stimuli.

■ Brain Burst = Neurolinker application sent to Haruyuki by Kuroyukihime.

■ Duel avatar = Player's virtual self, operated when fighting in Brain Burst.

■ Legion = Groups composed of many duel avatars with the objective of expanding occupied areas and securing rights. There are seven main Legions, each led by one of the Seven Kings of Pure Color.

■ Normal Duel Field = The field where normal Brain Burst battles (one-on-one) are carried out. Although the specs do possess elements of reality, the system is essentially on the level of an old-school fighting game.

■ Unlimited Neutral Field = Field for high-level players where only duel avatars at levels four and up are allowed. The game system is of a wholly different order than that of the Normal Duel Field, and the level of freedom in this field beats out even the next-generation VRMMO.

■ Movement Control System = System in charge of avatar control. Normally, this system handles all avatar movement.

■ Image Control System = System in which the player creates a strong image in their mind to operate the avatar. The mechanism is very different from the normal Movement Control System, and very few players can use it. Key component of the Incarnate System.

■ Incarnate System = Technique allowing players to interfere with the Brain Burst program's Image Control System to bring about a reality outside of the game's framework. Also referred to as "overwriting" game phenomena.

■ Acceleration Research Society = Mysterious Burst Linker group. They do not think of Brain Burst as a simple fighting game and are planning something. Black Vise and Rust Jigsaw are members.

■ Armor of Catastrophe = An Enhanced Armament also called "Chrome Disaster." Equipped with this, an avatar can use powerful abilities such as Drain, which absorbs the HP of the enemy avatar, and Divination, which calculates enemy attacks in advance to evade them. However, the spirit of the wearer is polluted by Chrome Disaster, which comes to rule the wearer completely.

■ Star Caster = The longsword carried by Chrome Disaster. Although it now has a sinister form, it was originally a famous and solemn sword that shone like a star, just as the name suggests.

■ ISS kit = Abbreviation for "IS mode study kit." ("IS mode" is "Incarnate System mode.") The kit allows any duel avatar who uses it to make use of the Incarnate System. While using it, a red "eye" is attached to some part of the avatar, and a black aura overlay—the staple of Incarnate attacks— is emitted from the eye.

■ Seven Arcs = The seven strongest Enhanced Armaments in the Accelerated World. They are the greatsword Impulse, the staff Tempest, the large shield Strife, the Luminary (form unknown), the straight sword Infinity, the full-body armor Destiny, and the Fluctuating Light (form unknown).

■ Mental-Scar Shell = The emotional scars that are the foundation of a duel avatar (mental scars created from trauma in early childhood)—this is the shell enveloping them. Children with exceptionally hard and thick "shells" are said to produce metal-color duel avatars.

When he passed through the automatic doors of the supermarket, a small progress bar appeared in the bottom of his field of view.

The design was simple. A black butterfly at the tip of the bar slowly advanced from left to right, and as the processing rate approached 100 percent, the wings started to tremble. In a mere three seconds or so, the task was complete, the bar disappeared, and the butterfly flew away without a sound. Reflexively, he reached out for it, but the butterfly slipped easily through his fingers. It danced up to the ceiling of the supermarket, exactly like a real butterfly, and then melted into the air.

"As always, Sacchi fixates on the strangest details in the apps she makes, hmm?" The voice came from his right, and he turned his gaze in that direction.

Standing there was a girl wearing her school uniform: a short-sleeved shirt and pleated skirt. The slight breeze of the air conditioning set her long, soft, chestnut hair swaying, and the over-the-knee socks encasing her long, slender legs were a cool light blue. She held a large tote bag in her left hand. The faint smile never left her gentle features, but the meaning behind it changed fluidly depending on the situation. If necessary, it could even become a dispassionate face of anger that was ten times scarier. However, currently present on her face was nothing more than a faint wryness in that smile, topped generously with affection for "Sacchi."

Indicating that he felt exactly the same way via a large grin, Haruyuki Arita answered Fuko Kurasaki: "That butterfly's in all of Kuroyukihime's apps, but when it flies off once it's loaded, you can catch it—if you grab it ultra-fast, with max gentleness."

"What happens when you catch it?"

"You get a point for every butterfly."

Fuko cocked her head even farther to one side. "What happens when you get points?"

"Apparently, something happens when you get to a thousand. But what that is exactly is a secret."

"She really focuses on the details, hmm?" Fuko murmured seriously, a look of real exasperation coming onto her face this time, before she clapped her hands together. "Well then, shall we finish the shopping, Corvus? Children with hungry tummies are waiting upstairs."

"R-right!" Nodding, Haruyuki raised a finger on his right hand and touched the EXECUTE button that was floating where the progress bar had been. Displayed on the right side of his virtual desktop were a ground plan for the supermarket on the first basement floor and a shopping list with ten or so lines on it.

A thin line on the map indicated their route, and blinking dots marked the shelves they would visit, so following this, they headed first in the direction of the fresh-fish area. When they approached a particular shelf, the first line of the list to the right side of the map was highlighted. Written there was "5 potatoes (May Queen) ¥198," and indeed, there was a pile of them on the shelf before his eyes. He picked up a bag, and after checking that the potatoes didn't have eyes or cuts, he pressed the BUY button displayed in his field of view.

He heard a *ching* as 198 yen was taken from the e-money loaded on his Neurolinker. Fuko stretched out the tote bag toward him, opening it wide as she did, so he put the potatoes in it, and the first line of the shopping list was grayed out.

That was when Haruyuki finally noticed: "Oh! I—I can carry that!" he said hurriedly.

"Oh my, could you? Then I'll do the shopping."

He took the bag from Fuko, now five hundred grams heavier, and switched places with her before heading to the next point displayed on the map. On the second line of the list was the row of text listing "2 onions, ¥98."

The shopping list linked with the store map was the app Shopping Optimizer Ver. 2.0, which Kuroyukihime had made. It connected with the store's local net, obtained information about the location and price of the products you wanted to buy, and displayed this on the map. Of course, it wasn't limited just to supermarkets; it allowed the shopper to find a product without randomly wandering through vast, densely packed displays in places such as hardware stores and drugstores.

Store local nets were also equipped with a function to search display location, but almost none of them could connect with a shopping list app, because if they provided that service, customers would quickly sweep through and buy only the things they had already planned to buy and wouldn't pick up extra items as they wandered around the store. What was incredible about Kuroyukihime's shopping app was that it could easily link with data that the store local net should have refused to supply, but he was too scared to ask for the details of how that worked.

Having been assigned to the shopping squad after drawing lots, Fuko and Haruyuki moved swiftly through the crowded evening supermarket following the app's guidance and bought all eleven items on the list, right down to the last line of "Transcendent Curry Sauce/Mild ¥278," in approximately four minutes. Since they had paid via the local net, they passed the register bank's long lines and walked out of the store.

"This is the first time I've used this shopping app," Fuko said as they headed down the central passage of the shopping mall toward the elevators, with wryness in her smile again. "But the design very much reflects Sacchi and her impatient ways."

"Oh. Ha-ha-ha! Apparently, starting in version three, you'll also be able to pay automatically, too."

Fuko rolled her eyes. "So then you'd be able to toss items into your bag as you ran through the store and just leave, I suppose? I'd bet ten burst points the guard at the exit would stop you."

"I—I guess so." He paled slightly as he ran for the door to the residential-wing elevator that had just opened, remembering that Kuroyukihime had asked him to help with the movement test for the next upgrade.

1

Monday, June 24, 2047, 6:30 PM.

In the living room of the Arita household—on the twenty-third floor of B wing, in the mixed-use high-rise condo in northern Koenji, Suginami Ward—the full lineup of friends more important to Haruyuki than anyone else was present: the members of Nega Nebulus.

At the end of the six-person dining table was their master, Kuroyukihime. Sitting alongside each other, on the two chairs closest to the kitchen, were staff officer Takumu Mayuzumi and mood maker Chiyuri Kurashima. On the balcony side were Legion conscience and mascot Utai Shinomiya, as well as its (unintentional) troublemaker, Haruyuki. And directly opposite Kuroyukihime was Legion deputy Fuko Kurasaki.

Since they had met Utai, their sixth member, on the Monday exactly a week earlier, this had somehow become the standard seating plan. However, this day, they had set up extra chairs next to Kuroyukihime and Fuko. There were eight round plates on the table, rather than six.

The sweet smell of freshly cooked rice wafted up from the rice cooker, which had dropped into warming mode earlier, and an almost violently spicy scent drifted over from the large pot on the cooktop. Tortured looks rose up not just on Haruyuki's face, but on those of the other five as well, and the conversation had stopped at some point.

"...I...can't...anymore...," he muttered, shaking his head.

Next to him, Utai weakly moved all ten fingers. UI> IT's ABOUT PATIENCE, C. THIS IS ALSO PRACTICE TO TRAIN OUR MENTAL POWR. Her expression was resolute, but the extremely rare typo showed that she too was reaching her limit.

In front of him, Chiyuri was glaring at the white plate, and Takumu was intently wiping the lenses of his glasses. The terror level of the faint smile on Fuko's mouth was steadily increasing, while Kuroyukihime was very master-like, sitting motionless with her eyes closed.

"...They're late!!" she shouted without provocation, banging lightly on the table. "They are three minutes and thirty seconds late! In the Accelerated World, that's fifty-eight hours!"

"More precisely, that's fifty-seven hours and twenty minutes," Fuko added, grinning.

Haruyuki could almost see the flames rising up behind them, and he jumped in with his usual inertia. "W-well, you know, Kuroyukihime, Master, I—I mean, they say curry gets more delicious the longer you let it sit, right?"

"Oh? Then perhaps we'll leave yours to sit for a good while... Three days or so?"

"We did go to all this trouble. Let's go for the limit and let it rest for a whole week."

"N-no! That's going beyond a different limit!" Haruyuki frantically waved his hands.

In that moment, the sound they'd all been waiting for echoed in their ears. *Ding-dong!* Before the doorbell had even stopped ringing, Haruyuki's right hand flashed like lightning to press the UNLOCK button in the window that displayed his guests.

"W-welcome! I'll come meet you at the elevators, so please— come up to the twenty-third floor!" He almost fell out of his seat in his mad dash toward the door, as the other five stood up behind him.

Kuroyukihime waved her right hand and shot off a rapid series of instructions. "Chiyuri, dish out the rice! Takumu and Fuko, get the salad from the fridge! Uiui, you reheat the curry! Leave the barley tea to me!"

The first thing his visitor said, as Haruyuki guided her into the living room, was, "Ooh! It smells good! I'm starving!"

She turned an innocent smile up at Haruyuki, who could barely move for how he and his guest were being showered in the unified murderous glare of the entirety of Nega Nebulus.

"Where should I sit, Big Brother?" she asked.

Haruyuki hurriedly pushed her red-T-shirted shoulders and led his guest to the chair beside Kuroyukihime. This arrangement made him slightly nervous, but given that the dining table's center seat was seen as the position of honor, they couldn't exactly seat her anywhere else, because the little girl with the red pigtails jumping up onto the chair was of exactly the same rank as Kuroyukihime. She was the Red King, leader of the Legion Prominence—the Immobile Fortress, Scarlet Rain, aka Yuniko Kozuki, in the flesh.

Niko sat neatly beside Kuroyukihime without a fuss, and Haruyuki breathed a momentary sigh of relief. But then their second guest of the evening appeared in the doorway of the living room, without a sound. She had been a few seconds behind Niko because she had to take off her sturdy motorcycle boots in the entryway. She still had long black leather gloves on her hands, which strangely complemented her short-sleeved, sailor-style school uniform. She brushed back the braid hanging over her shoulder.

"Sorry. Kannana accident traffic jam dodge," she explained in a fairly husky voice. It was, of course, the deputy of Prominence, Blood Leopard—"Pard" for short—giving voice to this barest minimum of information.

Haruyuki went to lead her to her seat, but before he could walk over, Fuko, who was closest, stood up.

"Well, that was very nice work. It would have been such a bother if you got caught up in that, Leopard," she said in a gentle tone as she moved to stand in front of Pard.

"Accident traffic jam dodge" happened when a vehicle's control AI applied the emergency brakes because it seemed like the automobile was about to have an accident, and it simultaneously sent out a warning signal to the vehicles around it. When the road was crowded, the warning propagated in a chain reaction to avoid a series of connected collisions, and cars were stopped over a fairly wide range or else forced into slow-driving mode.

And just like that, even in the setting of the Arita living room, invisible sparks shot outward, emitted by the two girls facing each other, bringing Haruyuki to an immediate stop. He swallowed hard as he belatedly connected the dots.

Until the fall of the first Nega Nebulus, Pard, also known as Bloody Kitty, and "Strong Arm" Sky Raker, aka Fuko Kurasaki, had each recognized the other as their greatest rival. He had heard all that before, but apparently the fact that Pard was still sitting at level six, despite being a fairly old veteran, had some deep connection to Raker's semiretirement.

"...Hi, Raker." From the brief greeting Pard offered as she pulled off her gloves, he couldn't tell if the two of them had met before in the real, or if this was actually their first time.

At the very least, they had been reunited in the final stages of the Hermes' Cord race three weeks earlier, and they had to have spoken then as well. But when he thought about it, that had been a multi-team event, so they still hadn't had a direct duel since Raker's return.

...Wh-what if they suddenly start a duel here? Unconsciously, Haruyuki clenched sweaty hands.

But Niko, behind him, cut cleanly through the tension in a voice with angel mode disengaged. "Enough with the standoff. Let's eat already! I can't wait any longer!"

"...You were the ones who kept us waiting, Red King," Kuroyukihime responded.

Fuko took this opportunity to step back and urge Pard to take a seat at the table. The two rivals sat down together, and when Haruyuki had hurried back over to his own seat, Kuroyukihime opened her mouth once more.

"Now then, let's eat. We'll talk after that."

"Let's eat!" the other seven chorused in unison, picking up their spoons and digging into their respective plates of curry at once.

Why had the six members of Nega Nebulus made curry and invited the top two members of Prominence to dine with them? The reason went back to the meeting of the Seven Kings held the previous day, Sunday, June 23.

Chewing on a potato wedge he had selected and peeled, Haruyuki scrolled back twelve hours in his memory, to the moment of judgment when a single wrong move could have ended up with him being given the death penalty by the Kings of Pure Color...

2

Flanked by two beautiful women. Haruyuki wondered if he could actually say that in his current situation.

His duel avatar, Silver Crow, had been made to stand alone atop a raised circular stage, tiers of stairs leading up to it, while two imposingly beautiful female-type avatars stood sharply at attention to either side, one step lower. Unfortunately, however, rather than Crow's guards or attendants, they were there in the role of police officers monitoring a criminal.

"...Um, were you initially equipped with those blades? Or did you find them somewhere?" he asked Cobalt Blade quietly, unable to stand the tension. She was the senior executive of the Leonids, standing to his right.

"The swords are our souls," the female warrior replied in a whisper that sounded slightly indignant, indigo-blue armor clanking as she looked at Haruyuki. "Of course they were initial equipment!"

And then from the left, Manganese Blade—looking almost like Cobalt Blade's twin, her armor having only slightly more green to it—said, "I can't allow that 'find them' to pass. I'll strike you down for your insolence!"

Trembling, he hurried to make his excuses. "Th-th-that's not it.

It's just, I saw a sword that looked a lot like yours in the Unlimited Neutral Field earlier, so I just thought..."

The two warriors looked at each other and then whispered in perfect unison, "Where in the Unlimited Neutral Field did you see it?"

"Uh, um, it was..." Naturally, Haruyuki's recollection was of the straight sword carried by the mysterious blue avatar he had met in the absolutely impenetrable castle towering over the very center of the Unlimited Neutral Field. Its inscription: "The Infinity." The fifth star of the Seven Arcs, the group of the most powerful Enhanced Armament in the Accelerated World.

He couldn't exactly leak such classified information to the executive of an enemy Legion so readily, so Haruyuki brought the index fingers of both hands together to make an X. "Uh, heh-heh," he chuckled nervously. "That's a secret."

Instantly, the eyes of both Cobalt and Manganese flashed, and their hands grabbed hold of the swords plunged into the earth before them like staffs.

But fortunately, a clear voice rang out then, a lazy tone, but still full of a fierce dignity. "Come, come, Cobal, Maga. Don't send him out of here before the investigation's finished."

"Sir!!" the warriors shouted, retaking their original positions.

Haruyuki flinched and pulled his head back. However, he still peered at the owner of the voice from beneath the mirrored shield that made up his own avatar's face.

The platform on which Silver Crow had been made to stand was in the center of a circular plaza about thirty meters in diameter. On the outer circumference of the plaza, seven improvised seats, made by cutting down thick pillars, were arranged in a semicircle. Seated there were the level niners, the rulers of the Accelerated World—the Seven Kings of Pure Color.

From Haruyuki's perspective, on the far right was the leader of Great Wall, the Legion headquartered in the Shibuya area: Nicknamed "Invulnerable," it was the Green King, Green Grandé. This week, like last week, he brought no attendants.

Sitting next to him was Haruyuki's swordmaster and the leader of Nega Nebulus, which held Suginami as its territory; apparently once called "World's End," she was the Black King, Black Lotus. Behind her stood the beautiful Sky Raker, her deputy.

On the third chair was Scarlet Rain, Legion Master of Prominence, who controlled the areas from Nakano to Nerima. Given that she had—naturally—not summoned her army of an Enhanced Armament, her cute little-girl avatar dangled its legs over the edge of the seat. Beside her was the silhouette of Blood Leopard, reminiscent of a leopard standing erect.

And then fourth in line—directly facing Haruyuki—the Blue King sat with an air of composure, acting again as chair for the meeting this time. "Vanquish," aka Blue Knight, was the head of the Leonids, which held as its territory Shinjuku to Bunkyo; the two girls flanking Haruyuki were his executives. This was the very Blue King who had chided them a moment earlier.

Farther to the left, on the fifth chair, sat an avatar with a noble silhouette that immediately brought the word *queen* to mind: the ruler of the Ginza area, "Empress Voltage," the Purple King, Purple Thorn. Behind her, the whip user Aster Vine stood at the ready, a female military officer and the king's close aide. Neither of them so much as twitched, but the pressure they exuded was more obviously focused on Haruyuki than anyone else there.

Occupying the sixth seat was a clown avatar with armor so vividly yellow, it was almost sickening. The head of the Legion Crypt Cosmic Circus, which held Akihabara to Ueno as its territory, the man known as "Radioactive Disturber," the Yellow King, Yellow Radio also hadn't brought attendants, as far as could be seen. His smiling face mask wobbled slowly from side to side like a pendulum.

And then on the far left, in the seventh seat, there was again no sign of the king who should have been there. Instead, there stood an avatar with a tall and thin silhouette that tapered at the end like a pole, one Ivory Tower. That avatar was the proxy for the White King, who ruled over the Legion Oscillatory Universe, which was based in the Roppongi area. Haruyuki had thought that today might be the day that he would meet the only remaining one of the level niners he had not yet seen with his own eyes, but perhaps the White King was surprisingly shy...Or perhaps they had no interest in someone like level-five Silver Crow.

Probably the latter, huh. Even though I'm so curious about them, he murmured to himself, a little dejected, as he moved his eyes even farther to catch a glimpse of the massive palace soaring up beyond the thick fog within this Demon City stage. Naturally, that was the majestic castle, the center of the Accelerated World, but rather than the Unlimited Neutral Field, this was a normal duel field generated by Cobalt and Manganese, so the castle couldn't actually be entered. System-wise, Haruyuki and the kings and everyone else were only connected to this space as the duel Gallery for the two warriors.

In other words, Cobalt and Manganese could not directly attack Silver Crow with the swords they carried, but they could eject him from the space as a Gallery disturbance. Or—and this was unlikely—if everyone present agreed, the duel rules would change to battle royal mode, allowing everyone to be everyone else's enemy.

No, wait. I would totally never press the YES *button. As if I would press it.* Haruyuki hardened his resolve, completely forgetting that he had had the same thought at the last meeting of the Seven Kings, and concluded his examination of the situation.

Ultimately, this place was the grand bench of the Supreme Court, there to pass judgment on the defendant Silver Crow. For the time being, if Black Lotus was his lawyer, then the antagonistic Purple Thorn would have been his prosecutor. If Blue Knight was the judge, then the other four kings were jurors.

Although these players were all lined up, there was a uniform silence as they awaited the appearance of the last player in the case—the "witness" who would check whether Silver Crow was clean or not with a special ability. At one word from her (or him), the fate of Haruyuki's life as a Burst Linker would be decided.

Of course, Haruyuki was certain of his innocence.

The immediate reason that he had been made to stand in this place as a suspect was that in the Hermes' Cord race, he had summoned the cursed Enhanced Armament, the Armor of Catastrophe, Chrome Disaster. Haruyuki, the sixth owner—no, host—of the armor that had caused enormous calamity over and over since the dawn of the Accelerated World, had been permitted a week's deferment. If he hadn't managed to purify the armor from his avatar in the seven days since the last meeting of the Seven Kings, an enormous bounty would have been placed on his head. Given that he was still only (and finally) at level five, this was equivalent to a death sentence.

Thus, Haruyuki and his Legion comrades had made every effort during that week to get rid of the armor parasitizing Silver Crow. They rescued Ardor Maiden—who had the Purify ability—from the altar of the God Suzaku, faced the memories of the two Burst Linkers who had generated the armor, untangled the logic hidden in the presence that was Chrome Disaster, and finally succeed in removing the entire curse.

The two Enhanced Armaments that were the armor's original form—the great sword Star Caster and the full-body armor the Destiny—had already been cut away from Silver Crow through Maiden's purification power and left to rest forever in a certain place in the Accelerated World. With nothing parasitizing Haruyuki's duel avatar anymore, there was no reason for anyone there to censure him.

Or that's what he believed, but he wasn't completely free of worry about whether or not that would be easily recognized. Because he didn't really know what kind of Burst Linker this witness everyone was waiting for was. Kuroyukihime and Fuko talked as though they had some idea, but they really didn't seem like they trusted this person completely.

In other words, if, for instance, in the worst case, the witness had been brought over to the public prosecutor's side, the witness might ignore the results of their own analysis and declare him "Dirty!" and Haruyuki would have no evidence to deny this. If he simply stood there silently thinking about this, he would only get more and more worried, so he felt the sudden urge to talk to the warriors on either side of him.

"Um, Manganese?"

His interlocutor turned annoyed eyes on him. "...What is it now?"

"Are you and Cobalt sisters in the real, too?" he asked in a whisper. "Or are you maybe even twins?"

"...We're twins."

"W-wow! But then, you each have different 'parents'? Is that it?"

"Oh, that's a good question, kid," Cobalt muttered from the opposite side. She brought her face in closer and continued in a somewhat self-satisfied tone. "You know that Neurolinkers identify the user based on characteristic brain waves. So then what do you do when you have two people with essentially the same brain waves?"

"Huh? Shared Neurolinker?" He cocked his head. "B-but you both accelerate at the same time like this..."

"Heh-heh-heh," Manganese Blade laughed quietly. "If you want to know the rest of the story, transfer to Leonids and perform your devotions. If you're not useless, we might make you our spear carrier."

"That actually depends on the direction of today's meeting, though. Heh-heh-heh."

"Huh? Um! No, I'll pass this time..."

"What?!" The two grabbed the hilts of their swords again, and Blue Knight (seated directly in front of them) shook his head in exasperation, about to chide them once more.

Just as he was on the verge of doing so, a strangely bright voice echoed through the foggy circular plaza:

"Hey! Sorry I'm late, yo! I accidentally came out on the total other side of the castle!"

*   *   *

The tapping of fleet feet against the hard ground of a Demon City stage. Judging the sound to be from behind, Haruyuki quickly turned around. A second or two later, the warriors flanking him followed suit.

Through the thick veil of fog, he could make out a single silhouette: a small, slender, female-type avatar. Her head alone was disproportionately large, making her look unbalanced, but she came straight toward them, seemingly unconcerned with the glares she was getting.

"She's here, Maga."

"Don't let your guard down, Cobal."

Sensing the excessive tension in the voices of the warriors in this brief exchange, Haruyuki was confused. If this had been the Unlimited Neutral Field, an approaching duel avatar would have required the greatest amount of caution, but this was a normal duel field. It was true that at the present moment, the restriction preventing members of the Gallery from coming within ten meters of the duelers had been turned off in the options, but even so, the basic principle of the Gallery not having any attack power whatsoever was unchanged.

Unfortunately, he didn't get the chance to ask them what on earth they were on guard against. The visitor casually cut through the fog, passing immediately by Haruyuki, and stopped before the Seven Kings.

Her armor was a very light lavender. She had no distinctive parts on her limbs or body, and her form was supple like a female type. But, indeed, what stood out more than anything was her head. Of her approximately 160 centimeters, her head took up more than thirty. Haruyuki couldn't immediately determine from behind whether the fan shape was hat-type armor or her actual head.

She put a hand on her right hip and bowed slightly, while the Blue King stood up from his seat.

"First, a word of thanks for responding to the sudden request, Argon Array."

"Whaaat? No biggie. I got my reward and all. Ha-ha-ha!" The reply from the Burst Linker—apparently named Argon Array—was relentlessly bright. Haruyuki couldn't sense even a hint of nervousness at being before the Seven Kings. "Anyway, it's been aaaages, this scene. How many years has it even been since I saw all you kingies lined up together!"

"Oh my!" The first one to react was Yellow Radio. "You do say the strangest things, Quad Eyes. As I recall, after we started to be called kings, there was just the one time we all came together… that time when the previous Red King was caught in a surprise attack and exited this world. And yet you speak as though you happened to be present there?"

He spoke as though he were interrogating Argon, but it was obvious to anyone there that his actual intention was to challenge the Black King. Haruyuki gritted his teeth hard, but Kuroyukihime and Fuko both let it slide, pretending not to recognize Radio's words for what they were; in the end, he managed to endure it somehow.

Argon was also not perturbed. She cocked her head exaggeratedly and shrugged. "Yeah, I guess yer right. My memory's real terrible, y'know? 'Cos I've known little Radio since you were just a wee one this high, huh?" She indicated the level of her own chest with her right hand before answering herself: "Obvs, that's not true, though!" When even the Yellow King fell silent, she struck the final blow. "Aah, it's no good!! Just for ages, every time I see little Radio, I end up wanting to go eat some o' them little fried radio balls. Whaddaya think? Join me? There's a tasty little place in Iidabashi. 'Course, they're only good in Tokyo! Ha-ha-ha!"

"…Always the fast talker," Yellow Radio muttered, baffled and shifting in his seat, before Blue Knight began to speak once more.

"All fine and good to renew old friendships, but it's about time to get to the point. We've got other matters on the agenda after this, after all."

"Ah, yeah, I came to 'look' an' all. 'Kay, I'll just take a peek, then." Having had her back to Haruyuki all this time, Argon Array now whirled around.

So it's a hat was Haruyuki's first thought. The top half of the face mask with its exposed mouth—as sometimes happened with female types—was covered by lens-shaped goggles. And above those, he could see two round parts, but they were hidden by a cover. The abnormal size of her head was apparently a result of the additional armor sitting on her actual head.

These thoughts absently racing through his mind, Haruyuki stared hard at Argon as she approached him. Paying no attention to Cobalt and Manganese stepping back bit by bit to either side of him, he simply continued to stand there.

Argon slowly climbed the first, then the second step of the dais staircase before stepping onto the third step, where Haruyuki stood, all seemingly without hesitation. Once she had climbed that far, there wasn't even twenty centimeters between them; her large lens-shaped goggles gleamed immediately before him. Unconsciously, Haruyuki peered into them, but they were filled with darkness, and he couldn't see through to the other side.

"...Hmm. So this *boyo*'s the Corvus of legend, huh?" As she spoke, she turned her face toward him, and the reflection of light made it look like her two lenses blinked. "So the story I heard is you went an' cut that armor out your own self? My buddies and me, we're all high-fiving you, boyo. So, like, this'll be great, y'know."

"O-okay," Haruyuki replied, shrinking back, and Argon Array laughed throatily.

He didn't know much about this Burst Linker acting as the witness. He'd only heard that she had the power to see everything about another duel avatar's status, and that she was able to determine the existence of a parasitic object; her nickname was Quad Eyes Analyst.

From the way she spoke, he could imagine that she was a fairly old hand, but since he had only just learned her actual avatar name that day, it was of course his first meeting with her. From her nickname, he'd thought she would have four eyes, but there were just two lenses covering Argon's face. He wondered where the other two were as he stared intently at her petite form.

Snap.

Somewhere deep in his mind, he felt a small spark bounce up. If he had to say, it was like the circuit was connected for a mere instant to a memory that shouldn't normally have been there. *Somewhere...*, he thought, but he couldn't call up any more information. A hazy silhouette flickered on a screen filled with noise.

As he stood there stock-still, Argon pulled her body back and looked back and forth between Cobalt and Manganese on either side of him. "Right! You wanna get started? Boyo and me are Gallery now, so if I'm gonna use my ability, I'm gonna need you ladies to pull us into your duel."

"...We're aware of that," Cobalt replied in a hard voice, opened Instruct, and made some quick movements. Soon enough, a small window opened before Haruyuki and Argon. The message in English read You have been invited to Battle Royal mode. Yes/No.

Argon said "Yaap" and quickly hit yes, but Haruyuki couldn't stop his head from spinning. Participating in Battle Royal mode meant that he would be raised up—or maybe lowered?—from safe spectator to dueler, complete with health gauge. If the samurai sisters Cobalt and Manganese got it into their heads, they could carve Haruyuki to pieces in minutes with their two swords—

For the first time since they had arrived at the meeting space, Black Lotus spoke, albeit quietly. "It's all right, Crow. If it's a trap, I'll kill everyone in the place."

Behind her, Sky Raker followed up with, "Naturally. We'll hang them all from Skytree."

At this not-insignificant utterance, the temperature started to drop to about minus one hundred, when the Red King, Scarlet Rain, sitting beside them, dropped an additional bomb:

"Whoa, whoa, Lotus. Lemme just say this, Promi's just an observer! If you're gonna hang anyone, just do those sickly-looking kids over there."

"Those sickly-looking kids" clearly indicated blue and purple and the rest, and even if the adult Blue King stayed calm, the auras around Purple Thorn and Aster Vine flared up. If this kept up, a second super war among the Seven Kings was certain to break out.

Haruyuki hurriedly reached his right hand out to the window. "I-it's fine! It's to prove my innocence, after all!" Firming up his resolve, he pushed the button.

A message flashed saying he was taking part in a Battle Royal, and his own health gauge dropped into existence with a metallic *tink* in the upper right of his field of view. The gauges of the other three were compressed and displayed to the upper right.

Cobalt and Manganese were both level seven, a rank befitting the close aides of the Blue King. However, a new surprise was that the level inscribed to the right of ARGON ARRAY was eight. She really was quite the veteran, and powerful. With this, he could understand the familiar tone she took with the Yellow King, as though she had known him forever.

However, Argon herself was relentlessly light. "Wohkay! Time for work. Gonna take a real hard peek at you. You ready, Corvus?" She sidled up to him.

Reflexively, Haruyuki stood at attention. All he could say in response was "Please."

"'Kay, here we go." Two round panels equipped on Argon Array's hat—which he had thought of as a part of her head until then—opened up with a *klak*.

Inside were lenses about one and a half times the diameter of those in the position of her actual eyes. The four lenses—no, the four eyes—peered at Haruyuki from extremely close up.

Next, he heard a whining from inside her large head. Warm air

was vented from the slits on the side, and then all the lenses lit up a dazzling purple. The light shot out straight ahead like a searchlight or a laser, penetrating Silver Crow's body in four places.

"...!!" Unconsciously, his body froze, but there was not the slightest sensation of damage. When he glanced up at his health gauge, it was still full. That said, he did definitely have the strange sensation of something piercing through to the core of his avatar.

"...Mm-hmm, mm-hmm. Your storage is totally empty, yeah?" Argon said abruptly in a quiet voice. Her words meant that she had seen into his item storage, which, as a general rule, was invisible to other people. "And you don't have any Enhanced Armament equipped, either. No sign of fraud with some kind of buff or item, either..."

The sunshine of Argon's voice had faded at some point, and in its place, a businesslike cool had appeared. Her voice had not a shred of interest in the subject individual; it was at best analyzing as an object of observation.

Snap!

Another spark in his head, this one a little stronger than the last. In his actual field of view, another scene floated up to overlay it.

Many human figures standing around the edge of a steep cliff, looking down at him. They were not real humans, but duel avatars. He was sure this was a scene he had seen somewhere a long, long time ago. No, not a long time ago. A dream. A scene he had seen in a dream a few days earlier?

Haruyuki held his breath and tried desperately to call up the hazy memory. The chronology was confused because the scene was from a distant past he had witnessed only in a dream. And it was not even his own memory, but one etched into a certain Enhanced Armament that no longer existed. The memory of the lone Burst Linker who had generated that Enhanced Armament in the first place and who had long since left the Accelerated World.

He mustered every ounce of his concentration and, bit by bit, cleared away the noise that filled the screen. What he had thought was a cliff was actually a curved surface, a large craterlike hole. One of the avatars standing on the edge had four eyes shining in an excessively large head. A faint, halting voice jumped into his ears.

"...ge full recovery...No depletion...attack gauge...about it, it's Main...overwrite through...circuit."

A voice he'd heard somewhere. A cold voice, as if reading off data, followed by a voice responding.

"It seems...deepening of concentra...indeed...phenomenon... fast. Although...controlled...different issue."

The source of these words was a tall, thin avatar standing beside the large-headed avatar. But "tall and thin" wasn't quite right. More like several thin panels lined up vertically. The first voice began again:

"True, true. And...with a Mental-Scar Shell strength...beyond... into metal..."

As Haruyuki almost squeezed out his own soul to somehow replay the information up to that point, he heard a quiet voice in the real world around him:

"Hmm, just like a metal color, y'know. Mental-Scar Shell's thick; I can't see too easy beyond that."

Instantly, an incredible impact shook his consciousness, and the screen of his memory shattered into tiny pieces. But right before it did, all the noise disappeared, burning into his mind a scene so sharply defined, it was like a photograph.

They were the same. The silhouette with four eyes looking down from the top of the cliff in *his* memory, and the female-type avatar analyzing Haruyuki with four eyes in that very moment—they were the same.

And the layered avatar of thin panels that had been standing next to the four-eyed avatar had appeared before Haruyuki three times to torture him and his friends with strange abilities. It was the vice president of the Acceleration Research Society, the "Restrainer," Black Vise.

Which meant—

Which meant...

Haruyuki froze, as the voice continued, getting back a little of its sunniness. "So then, not a single parasitic object. You kin relax, boyo. You're not possessed by that armor no more. Quad Eyes here'll swear it!"

Instantly, Cobalt and Manganese relaxed slightly on either side of him. Before him as well, Kuroyukihime and Fuko nodded at each other, their huge relief apparent, and Niko slapped a fist into her open palm. Pard gave him a slight thumbs-up as if to say "GJ," while the Green King dipped his head faintly.

The Yellow King, seated on the opposite side, spread his hands in a sort of "oh well" gesture, and the Purple King merely shrugged, but Aster Vine (behind her) snapped her coiled whip. The White King's proxy, Ivory Tower, showed absolutely no reaction, while the Blue King, seated in the center, nodded deeply before standing up, cloak flapping.

But Haruyuki could hardly focus on the reactions of the kings and their aides. In the back of his mind, a single phrase was repeating over and over like a siren: *It's her. It's her. It's her!*

The Quad Eyes Analyst aka Argon Array was—

Black Vise's comrade.

A core member of the Acceleration Research Society.

Beneath his slightly downturned helmet, his teeth chattered in fear and horror. If that had been the real world, rivers of sweat would have been pouring out of his entire body and his eyes would have even been blurred with tears.

"Naaaah, were you that nervous, boyo?!" He heard a smiling voice. From the top part of his field of view, Argon's four eyes, the light almost completely gone from them, were peering at him. "Relaaaax. No one's gonna be putting any bounties on yer head—" She cut herself off there.

The light in her four lenses, which had started to disappear, increased slightly in intensity. Blinking them like actual eyes, she got close, closer.

He couldn't let her notice. She couldn't find out what he had realized. If she saw through him, Argon would go against her previous words and declare that Haruyuki was still parasitized by the Armor of Catastrophe. Silver Crow would be found guilty and would be chased through the field as a wanted man— No, Cobalt and Manganese would undoubtedly take his head off before he had the chance to run. He had to somehow make it out of that place and tell Kuroyukihime and the others the knowledge he had gained.

Intently fighting the urge to fly back, Haruyuki stood quietly as Argon stroked his helmet with a gentle finger. And then, ever so faintly, so quiet that only the two of them could hear her voice:

"Boyo...you. Know me...?"

If Silver Crow's face hadn't been entirely hidden by his mirrored helmet, she might have seen through the look on his face. But he forced himself to turn his stiff head toward her, cocking his head questioningly.

Perhaps it was fortunate he didn't—couldn't—speak, because Argon didn't push him any further.

"Nah. Just my imagination, I guess," was all she said before pulling her face away. She patted the top of his helmet and stepped down the stairs.

He couldn't let his relief show. He mustered up the last of his mental strength and pretended to stand there blankly. As expected, Argon turned around when she got to the bottom step and favored him with one final laserlike look. But he apparently passed this test as well, because the light in her four eyes disappeared.

The Analyst put her hands on her hips and turned to face the Blue King as he stood. "I said it before, but no parasite stuff is attached to Corvus there. Plus he's totally naked of anything like an Enhanced Armament. Which means he can't be the Disaster, basically."

"I'm relieved to hear it, Quad Eyes. To be honest, I was concerned I'd have to fight that thing again."

The Yellow King laughed at the Blue King's straightforward words. Knight sent a glare his way that said "you're no different," before making the heavy armor covering his body creak as he loudly declared, "And that is the first item on the agenda resolved—"

"Er, may I speak?" The owner of the interjecting voice was the representative of the White King, Ivory Tower. They had been entirely silent, their miniature tower body motionless, until that point. The avatar raised its long and slender right hand, like a second tower, and continued in a flat, featureless voice, "I understand the matter of Chrome Disaster being detached from Mr. Silver Crow. However, in that case, wouldn't the Armor then be sealed in an item card once more? Where did that card go, pray tell?"

Haruyuki's head was full of the truth about Argon Array, but he could not fail to turn his mind to this observation. The cards for the two items that had been removed from Silver Crow through Ardor Maiden's purification ability were currently resting safely in the home of the two Burst Linkers who had been the items' owners in the past. Because he had left the key to the house inside with the cards, no one would be able to see the house, much less enter it.

But he couldn't explain all that in this place. Because there might have been a secret way of breaking into another person's house in the Accelerated World that no one in Nega Nebulus knew about. If the Yellow King or one of his ilk managed to get hold of the Enhanced Armament again—although there should no longer have been any way to fuse the two into the Disaster—he had no idea what they would get up to.

Bathed in the stares of the kings, Haruyuki was at a loss for words, but the Black King stood up on his behalf.

"The item cards were sealed in a form that will not allow anyone to get them ever again. Even I and Crow can no longer touch them. Are you dissatisfied with this answer, Ivory Tower? Or... do you wish to know the method of sealing and the place?"

At her cool voice, the avatar patterned after a tower and the color of an elephant's tusk moved their head from left to right. "No, no, your answer is sufficient, Black King. I apologize for my interjection, Blue King." And then they brought their hand down and fell silent, an ornament once again.

When Black Lotus sat down, she waved her right hand lightly, as if to encourage Blue Knight to continue. The Blue King nodded and then began speaking again. "That resolves the first item on our agenda. Quad Eyes, good work. And apologies, but now that you've become a dueler, you can't burst out right away. Could you wait a bit until the end of the meeting?"

"No big, no big. I'll just watch from a corner." Argon Array moved to the left side of the plaza.

Haruyuki followed her quietly with his eyes. He was now certain that the girl, also known as Quad Eyes Analyst, was a member of the Acceleration Research Society, a disturbance to the Accelerated World...and at a senior-enough level to be able to stand alongside the vice president Black Vise. But since his proof was the extremely vague "I had a vision," even if he did say something here, he couldn't expect that he would be able to make the kings believe him.

Unfortunately, there was only one thing for him to do in that moment—to not make Argon suspicious again. He would have to somehow make it through the rest of the meeting and then report to Kuroyukihime and Fuko as soon as they burst out.

Haruyuki steadied himself and took a deep breath. "Um," he said, raising his right hand. "Is it okay if I get down from here, too?" Miraculously, his voice came out without shaking or stammering.

The Blue King glanced at Haruyuki and nodded, signaling the direction of the Black King with his thumb. After Haruyuki bowed in return, he stepped down one stair and then also bowed neatly to the sister guards behind him. Turning around, he leapt down to the ground and trotted over to the Black King's seat, being careful not to fall or break into a run.

He felt sure he had managed to move fairly normally, but even so, the instant he was standing by Fuko's side, he felt such an enormous sense of relief that his knees threatened to give out under him. But this was not the time to be letting his guard down; he snapped his back straight and glanced at the opposite side of the meeting area—at Argon Array, standing behind Ivory Tower.

The Analyst had already closed the two eyes on her hat. Hands on her hips, toes tapping out a rhythm, she didn't look anything like one of the leaders of an evil organization. But he couldn't be careless. Just like Silver Crow's mask, Argon Array's lens-shaped goggles hid the direction of her gaze. Although she looked like she was standing lazily, she might have been secretly observing him.

Keep it together, keep it together, he chanted to himself.

Sky Raker, to his left, brought her face close to his and murmured, "Welcome back, Corvus." The brief statement held all the kindness of the master whom Haruyuki adored, and his heart filled to the brim.

Without a moment's delay, Black Lotus, who was sitting right in front of him, looked back at Haruyuki. "Nice work, Crow," she said kindly, and real tears threatened to pour out of his eyes.

But the human being known as Haruyuki Arita was finally learning that it would be a huge mistake to lose his focus here; he simply nodded two, then three times. During this exchange, Cobalt and Manganese also descended from the dais, cut across the plaza, and took up their positions behind the Blue King.

"Fifteen minutes left, hmm? I'll hurry, then. The second item on the agenda, the information provided by Great Wall about Midtown Tower." He cut himself off there and glanced over at the

Green King, who was sitting calmly on his chair at the far right end. "Maybe you could explain, Invincible?"

All eyes turned to Green Grandé, who—naturally—maintained his silence, moving his right arm only the slightest bit. As if this was a signal, a silhouette slid out of the fog behind him. Dark green armor with a metallic luster. Round headgear up top, large gloves on both hands...

"Oh, it's Pound," Haruyuki murmured.

The level seven who occupied the third seat of the Six Armors—the executive group of the Green Legion—"Fists of Steel" Iron Pound nodded at Haruyuki. He walked past his leader and approached the center of the plaza without the slightest hesitation. "I will be explaining the situation on behalf of our king."

Given that he had once been a rival of "Strong Arm" Raker, Pound was himself a fairly old hand. And it seemed that he had already met basically everyone in the venue, as he began to talk without bothering to introduce himself. "I'm sure some Legions have already confirmed this themselves, but at Tokyo Midtown Tower in the west of the Akasaka area in the Unlimited Neutral Field, the Legend-class Enemy Archangel Metatron has appeared. Judging from this and other information we've obtained, we believe an object corresponding to the main body of the infectious ISS kit Enhanced Armament that has been plaguing the Accelerated World is on the top floors of the tower."

For the next three or so minutes, Iron Pound neatly summed up a great deal of information for the kings: The fact that if you got within a range of two hundred meters of Midtown, you would instantly be evaporated by the super-powerful laser that Metatron released. That the only way to cancel out Metatron's invincibility was to wait for the Unlimited Neutral Field to change into a Hell stage. And that they had waited for several months of inside time for that chance, but in the end, no Hell stage had appeared.

Once Pound was finished explaining the situation, there were a few seconds of silence, broken first by the Purple King, Purple Thorn.

"Well, that's quite understandable. I could count the number of times I've seen a Hell stage in a normal duel field, much less in the Unlimited Neutral Field." Her voice was a little boastful, and if he had to say, on the sweet, cute side, but it hid a will like a super-high-voltage current. She sounded as though, if she only got the chance, she would most certainly take the Black King's head.

"Hell in the Unlimited Neutral Field really is hell, after all. All the Beast-class monsters turned into Devil-class Enemies? No, thanks." This from the Blue King. The other kings and retainers nodded, as if in absolute agreement.

"Hmm, I just have an eensy question?" The high-pitched voice of Yellow Radio cut into the heavy silence. "I'll accept that you can't approach Midtown Tower from the outside. But in that case, what about from the inside? If you go up to the top floor of the tower in the real world and use the Unlimited Burst command, couldn't you slip past Metatron's attack range and infiltrate the tower?"

"Oh!" Haruyuki cried out unconsciously. It was just like the Yellow King said: Since the coordinates where you appeared in the Unlimited Neutral Field were based on your location in the real world, if you went up the real Midtown Tower and accelerated, it made sense that you would be instantly inside the enemy camp.

However, the idea Haruyuki thought was so brilliant was rejected out of hand by the Red King, sitting to his immediate right. "Now look, Radio. Grandé thought about that ages ago already. If the enemy base were inside Roppongi Hills, that might work. 'Cos you can ride to the very top floor for five hundred yen if you're in junior high. But, like, I checked into it, too. A large part of Midtown Tower is a fancy hotel. Anyone not staying there is totally shut out."

"Oh!" Haruyuki cried again.

In the center of the plaza, Iron Pound also nodded and added,

"And the cheapest twin room is thirty thousand yen for one person for one night."

There was a collective gulp. Even though the most powerful warriors—the Seven Kings of Pure Color and the senior members of their Legions—might have been Burst Linkers in the Accelerated World, in the real world they were a group of junior high and high school students whose only income was their allowances. Thirty thousand yen was not a sum of money any of them could casually shell out. At the very least, if they had a guarantee that they would definitely be able to destroy the ISS kit main body on their first infiltration, they might have been able to pool their money to scrape together the cost of staying there and send in attack personnel. But the first visit would probably end with reconnaissance. And thirty thousand yen for just that was tight. So tight it hurt.

A ponderous silence filled the venue once more, cut through this time by Black Lotus's swordlike voice. "Trying to do something about problems in the Accelerated World with real money is heresy. It can't possibly be that those fellows in the Acceleration Research Society saved up their money to move Metatron out of the Contrary Cathedral. We, too, should face this situation as Burst Linkers."

"Oh-ho! Quite impressive, wonderful!" The Yellow King clapped his long, thin hands together. "That said, Black King, are you saying you have some sort of plan? Your specialty of surprise attacks won't be effective on Metatron, I'm sure?"

At this very obvious challenge, Haruyuki and Fuko took a half step forward. But Kuroyukihime replied, as cool as ever: "Similarly, your special smoke screens and bribes won't work either, hmm? Now sit back and listen. Grandé has no doubt thought of something, given the fact that he's gone out of his way to bring along someone to explain."

Radio narrowed his eyes unhappily, but he simply adjusted his position on his seat without saying anything further. Once again, all eyes were turned to Pound in the center of the plaza.

Indeed, if it were just an explanation of the situation, it would have been enough to simply send a text mail to the anonymous addresses that served as the contact for each Legion. The fact that the Green King had not left it at that and had instead brought along additional personnel he had not brought to the previous meeting surely meant he had some kind of proposal.

Haruyuki swallowed his breath and waited for Pound to continue.

However, in the next instant, the steel-colored boxer-type avatar turned his gaze straight ahead, so Haruyuki threw his head back unconsciously. He whirled his head around, looking to the left and the right, but it did appear that Pound was indeed focusing his attention on Silver Crow.

Oh, I have a bad feeling about this.

Pound nodded gravely, as if reading Haruyuki's mind. "We do actually have just one plan to break this deadlock. Silver Crow...I know you've just gone through purifying the armor, but could you do a bit more work for us?"

"Huh?! Um! B-b-b-b-but—" Haruyuki shook his head quickly as he inched back. "M-M-M-Metatron's laser has perfect range in the air too! I-i-i-if I fly in, I'll just get shot down! For sure!"

"Mmm, that's true," Pound agreed readily. "But this time, we're not counting on your flying ability. It's your other uniqueness... your silver metal color."

"C-c-c-color? I-it's true, I am silver, but there's nothing really special about that...Basically, strong against poison, at most."

"Right now, that's true. But you are the only person here with a certain possibility." Here, Iron Pound stopped once more and then continued in an even more serious tone:

"The possibility of acquiring a legendary ability that once existed in the Accelerated World...one that has an absolute resistance to all kinds of light techniques: Theoretical Mirror."

3

"Unh, I ate so much, I'm so full. I ate so much, I might just turn into a yellow type." Groaning, Niko set her spoon down.

Having finished eating a few minutes earlier, Haruyuki waited for their score from the Red King with sweaty, clenched hands. The curry was Chiyuri's mother's own original recipe, and while Chiyuri and Utai had been in charge of preparation for the most part, with Haruyuki's role simply being to peel the potatoes he had bought, he was still feeling nervousness on par with opening mail containing the results of an academic aptitude test.

In the silence that filled the living room, Niko closed her eyes for a while, but then finally opened them with a snap. "Eighty-five percent!" she shouted. "Just barely passed!"

Instantly, the members of Nega Nebulus let out a long sigh of relief. Pard added a brief "GJ" to the rating.

They quickly cleared away the dishes, moved to the sofa set, and then all eight of them faced one another once more.

The sofa was really only meant for six people, but since Niko and Utai had less than half the mass of Haruyuki, they could all fit if they squeezed in a bit. The sight of the sixth-grade girl and fourth-grade girl sitting alongside each other and drinking iced tea was actually rather charming. Haruyuki had been an only child for fourteen years, and he absently daydreamed about how it would be nice to have little sisters like this. But in the Accelerated World, one of them was a powerful king, while the other was the Shrine Maiden of the Conflagration, controlling super-high-temperature flames. Now that he thought about it, they were both red types specializing in long-distance attacks, and if, hypothetically, they were to go up against each other, it would surely be a spectacular duel.

"So, ah...? Is this maybe your first time meeting Niko, Shinomiya? Oh! Of course, in the real, but even in the Accelerated World?"

The two elementary school girls glanced at each other and shook their heads at the same time. Niko opened her mouth first.

"I became a Burst Linker just a little bit before the first Nega Nebulus disappeared, but I did see Maiden any number of times in the Territories back then."

Next, Utai tapped nimbly at her holo keyboard. UI> ALTHOUGH, BECAUSE WE'RE BOTH RED TYPES, WE BASICALLY ONLY SHOT FIREPOWER AT EACH OTHER FROM A DISTANCE.

"But this one time, big sister Strong Arm there, she threw Maiden right into the middle of our base, okay! She fell down right in front of me."

UI> I DO VERY MUCH APOLOGIZE FOR THAT.

Even during this exchange, Fuko simply tilted her glass to one side, feigning ignorance. A chill raced up Haruyuki's spine.

"Right," he said, musing aloud. "Back then, we must have fought in the Territories against Promi like we do everyone else. It'd be great if we could get to the point where we can do that again."

Currently, the new Nega Nebulus that Haruyuki belonged to had a cease-fire of unlimited term with Niko's Prominence and thus did not fight them in the Territories. Given that Negabu had only six members at the moment, they had their hands full with the Leonids, who came faithfully to attack them every week, and Great Wall, who sent in smaller teams about every other week, so the cease-fire agreement was a huge help. But at the same time, it did get in the way of the fun of Brain Burst as a game.

A series of complicated expressions flitted across Niko's face before she turned her gaze toward Kuroyukihime, sitting to the left. "...Lotus. This prob'ly isn't for me to say or anything, but...to be honest, shouldn't your priority be getting your Legion back to full strength instead of joining the Midtown Tower mission just 'cos Knight and Grandé asked you to? I mean, your other two Elements haven't come back yet, right...?"

After a moment's pause, the Black King nodded. "Yes. Both Aqua and Graph are still sealed inside the four gates of the castle. Naturally, I would also like to set out on a plan to rescue them right away. However...the fact that we were able to bring Maiden back from the altar of the God Suzaku was essentially a miracle. It would have been no surprise if we had lost even Crow along with her."

Her words were certainly true. Although Haruyuki had succeeded in recovering Ardor Maiden, they had failed to escape and had plunged into the castle. If they hadn't met the mysterious avatar Trilead Tetroxide deep within the main building, escape from that place would have been impossible.

Of course, they hadn't explained all of this to Niko, but she got the basic idea. She didn't push the issue any further, but simply nodded and added, briefly, "That so? Then I'll just say this. Pard and the others in the Triplex are waiting for the day when they can go head-to-head with Negabu in the Territories, just like in the old days."

Pard also nodded shortly.

"When that time comes, I'll be sure to drop Maiden on your head once more, Red King," Fuko responded, smiling.

Instantly, Utai faced downward, and Haruyuki and Takumu shrank back with a small "Eep." But Chiyuri laughed boldly and said, "Ah-ha-ha, sister Fuko! Throw me with her! Being tossed into the base, that sounds super fun!"

"Hee-hee, you're so hard, Chiko, it would probably be worth-while to throw you."

"But in that case, we won't have much fun all by ourselves in the base. How about it, Haruyuki? Want to carry me in a special attack on the enemy camp?"

"M-Master, if you do that, there'll only be me left to protect *our* base!" Takumu cried out, and everyone laughed together.

Once the laughter subsided, Kuroyukihime composed herself and cleared her throat once. "I believe that day will become reality at some point—perhaps even in the near future. But to that end, naturally, Nega Nebulus will have to recover its strength, but first, we must kick these evildoers out of the Accelerated World."

"The Acceleration Research Society, right," Takumu murmured.

Kuroyukihime nodded. "The ISS kits both grant the user a dark Incarnate technique and control their mind. It's only been a week since they appeared in the Accelerated World, and yet the kit infection is spreading at a terrifying rate. Right now, we've managed to just barely contain it within the borderlands of Setagaya, Koto, and Adachi, but when it reaches the city center, all the rules of the Accelerated World will no doubt break down. I've been called the destroyer of order, but I cannot accept sully-ing even the spirit of the duel, absolutely not." Her words held a deep anger and anxiety.

Niko picked up where she left off: "I am one hundred percent in agreement. We've confirmed that the kit infection has spread from Adachi Ward to Kita Ward these last two days. After that, it'll be Itabashi, and then Nerima. If we don't smash the source this week, we won't be able to avoid seeing some people infected in Promi, too."

"The situation is the same for Suginami, coming after Setagaya," Kuroyukihime said, and then paused.

Actually, Nega Nebulus had already had someone infected with the ISS kit the previous week: Takumu—Cyan Pile. He had gone off to the Setagaya area in order to make himself a guinea pig for the kit destruction and was given an ISS kit by a Burst Linker

known as Magenta Scissor. Although the kit was still in the form
of a sealed item at that point, Takumu was almost immediately
attacked in the real by Supernova Remnant, the most ferocious
PK group in the Accelerated World, and to fight them off, he had
opened and equipped the kit.

The power of the dark Incarnate was incredible, and Takumu
defeated Remnant in a single blow, but due to the intense mental
interference, his will was pulled to the dark side. Understanding that he might turn his sword on his friends if he continued
like that, he went to try to get information from Magenta Scissor
about the kits, prepared for her to strike him down as well.

However, Haruyuki had seen Takumu's crisis and raced home
from school. They had a direct duel where they pitted their Incarnate and their wills against each other, and Takumu had managed painfully to come back to himself. That night, Chiyuri had
joined them in this very room, and sleeping together in a huddle,
the three of them had had a mysterious dream.

Waking up inside the Brain Burst central server—also known as
the Main Visualizer—the whereabouts of which were completely
unknown, Haruyuki and Chiyuri chased after the sleepwalking
Takumu and witnessed a strange sight:

In one corner of the central server (which resembled a swirling galaxy), a large object—an inky-black brain—had been
constructed, and countless ISS kit owners were connected to
it with blood vessel–like cords. Understanding that thing was
the kit main body, Haruyuki manifested a long-distance Incarnate attack, Laser Lance, and severed the blood vessel connected to Takumu. They then returned to the real world with the
now-awake Takumu. When they opened their eyes, the ISS kit
lodged in Takumu had completely disappeared.

That fact indicated if they destroyed the ISS kit main body, all
the terminal kits would also disappear. But to infiltrate the central server while still themselves, they would need to meet the
extremely difficult condition of sleeping while directing with a
kit user. In reality, that was impossible. But the kit main body

that existed inside the server was a shadow. The ISS kit main body existed somewhere in the Accelerated World's Unlimited Neutral Field as a "real" object.

Haruyuki had chased after a mysterious luminescent body that had escaped when the kit terminal was destroyed within the Unlimited Neutral Field. Its destination had been that tower soaring up into the air, Tokyo Midtown. Haruyuki had tried to charge in, but he was stopped by the Green King and his subordinate, Iron Pound. They had long been monitoring the tower from the roof of the relatively nearby Roppongi Hills Tower. It was they who had told Haruyuki that Midtown Tower was guarded by the Legend-class Enemy Archangel Metatron, completely invincible outside of a Hell stage…

Having taken a brief moment to reflect on the situation thus far, Haruyuki held his breath and waited for Kuroyukihime to continue.

"Already, last week, in Suginami Area Three, Crow and Maiden fought Bush Utan and Olive Grab, both equipped with ISS kits. Utan apparently managed to break free of the kit's control after that, but Olive appears to still be connected. If we're seeing infected within the ranks of even GW, then we have less of a grace period than we imagined. Taking part in the tower mission is to protect our Legion and territory, while also responding to the call at the meeting of the Seven Kings."

"…Well, Promi's basically the same there. We owe you for the whole Fifth Disaster thing, and we got no problems with helping Negabu. But, like"—Niko crossed her arms and stared hard at Haruyuki with eyes that shone green in the light—"say your plan works, this crow here turns into a serious joker for us, you know! Promi's got the most light technique users of any of the seven Legions."

"Which is why we mobilized everyone to carry out the incredibly difficult mission you indicated! After taking a second helping, *now* you say you don't want to—"

"Got it! I get it! And I said you passed, didn't I? But, Lotus, if you're ranking curry as incredibly difficult, you're not much of a cook, huh?" the Red King said, grinning.

A look of anger still on her face, Kuroyukihime's cheeks flushed, and Utai and Fuko had a strange coughing fit.

"Y'know, Niko…if it's Kuroyukihime you want to know about, she peeled the onions—" With an easy smile, Chiyuri began to divulge top-secret information, but fell silent halfway through at the activation of the long-dormant Super Cool Kuroyukihime Smile.

Niko cackled with laughter for a while longer before composing herself and nodding once. "Well, I promised, anyway. I'll go along with you for three bowls of curry—on this plan of yours to get the Theoretical Mirror ability for Silver Crow."

Right.

At the meeting of the Seven Kings the previous day, the kings had requested that Haruyuki act as the first lance in the strategy against Archangel Metatron. According to Iron Pound, if he managed to acquire a certain rare ability, he might be able to resist the absolute, insta-death laser emitted by Metatron.

To obtain this ability, Theoretical Mirror, the assistance of a Burst Linker with a very powerful light technique was essential. But there were no light users among the other five members of Nega Nebulus. If Haruyuki had to say, at first glance Takumu's level-four special attack Lightning Cyan Spike appeared to be a light attack, but according to the owner himself, it was a "technique that changes the pile to plasma and launches it," a physical attack categorized as heat/piercing.

Of course, Haruyuki still hadn't learned the definitions of plasma or lasers in his science class in the real world. But in the Accelerated World, a plasma technique was an attack manipulating a flow of super-high-temperature particles (a companion to flame attacks, as it were), while a laser technique was at best an attack using light concentrated into a straight line. A sword could cut through plasma, but it couldn't cut the massless laser.

Ultimately, Takumu's technique was a counterfeit laser, so if they were going to look for the help of a light technique user, they would have to look outside of Nega Nebulus. After the meeting of the Seven Kings was over, the six Legion members had a heated discussion in a dive call before finally making a decision. They would get the help of the Burst Linker with the most powerful laser technique they knew of: the Immobile Fortress, Scarlet Rain.

To this request, the Red King had put forth an unexpected condition: "You make me happy with homemade curry, and I'll help you out."

By the time the glasses in front of them were empty and everyone had taken turns going to the washroom, the time was seven thirty PM.

Of the eight of them, Niko had the strictest curfew, given that she lived in a dorm at her elementary school. But as usual, she had apparently given them a story of some kind and gotten permission to spend the night elsewhere, so there was no problem. Next was Utai, but her curfew was nine PM, a relatively—almost impossibly—late hour for an elementary school student, so they still had an hour before they had to think about moving. The master of the house, Haruyuki's mother, wouldn't be home before the date changed.

When they were all seated once more on the sofa set, they used the multicolored cables Chiyuri and Takumu had brought from home to connect their own Neurolinkers to the XSB hub that was connected to the Arita home server. Kuroyukihime had brought said ten-port hub, which was sitting silently on the glass table. If anything happened, someone just had to turn off the power on the hub, and all of them would instantly burst out.

"...Huh? But why a safety when we're dueling?" Haruyuki belatedly asked, and looked at Kuroyukihime as he was on the verge of inserting the end of the cable into his own neck. He had assumed that at that moment, he (seeking the ability) and Niko (provider of the light technique) would duel, and the other six would be in the Gallery. If it was a one-on-one duel, then it would end in thirty minutes of inside time, 1.8 seconds of real time, so there shouldn't have been any need for an emergency disconnection safety.

But Kuroyukihime stared at him blankly before blinking slowly, as if she had realized something, and then broke out into a grin. "Well, it's obvious, Haruyuki. We're not going to a normal duel field. We're diving into the Unlimited Neutral Field."

"Huh? Up there? It's not going to be a normal duel?" Haruyuki asked, brushing aside a creeping bad feeling.

The answer to this was also extremely simple.

"Mmm, that won't do. One death likely won't be enough for this mission. In my estimation, it will take five at minimum—no, perhaps ten."

Without missing a beat, Pard remarked, "You do it in twenty, GJ."

I don't waaaaannaaaa.

Haruyuki kicked and screamed, and Takumu and Chiyuri grabbed hold of him from both sides.

"You can totally do it, Haru."

"We're right here with you!"

They offered these extremely reassuring words as they popped the cable into his Neurolinker.

Striking the final blow was Fuko: "If you make us wait inside… well, you understand, yes, Corvus?" When she smiled gently, escape was already impossible.

For the sake of Utai, who had difficulty calling out the acceleration command, Kuroyukihime set a countdown to start in twenty seconds. As Haruyuki counted with her, he thought, *Let it be what it may. It won't kill me.* And then, with his friends, he shouted, "Unlimited Burst!"

It was only after the thundering sound of acceleration ripped through his ears that he realized, *No, it will kill me. Twenty times, too.*

4

"…Got kinda lucky with the stage."

At the sound of Niko's voice, he opened his closed eyelids. What he saw through his half-mirrored helmet were countless neon signs in primary colors glittering in the nighttime city. A Downtown stage. It resembled Akihabara Electric Town some-how, so Haruyuki definitely didn't hate it. But the highs and lows in the terrain were extreme, and there weren't many wide-open spaces, so it wasn't really suited to practice or events with a num-ber of people.

"Why lucky?" he asked.

The bright-red girl-type avatar moved her head from side to side, shaking the two antenna parts. "With, like, a Storm or a Drizzle stage, you get a minus correction on laser techniques. And with underwater stages like an Ocean, you can't even use lasers."

"…Makes sense." He nodded.

Kuroyukihime and Fuko strolled up, having apparently gone to take a quick look at their surroundings.

"We can't see any other Burst Linkers in the area," Kuroyuki-hime noted.

"There was a largish Beast-class Enemy a little south of Kan-nana, so if we're going to move, north would be best," Fuko added.

"Oh, okay then, let's finish the day off by hunting that guy! Crow's gonna lose some points. Gotta top him up again!" Niko's thoughtful consideration sent a chill up his spine.

The eight of them had appeared on the roof of a skyscraper that corresponded to Haruyuki's condo in the real world. Entry into buildings was not permitted in the Downtown stage, so their coordinates when they dived had been moved up here. It was a large condo, so the roof was also fairly large.

Haruyuki looked around once more before proposing, "If we need a big space, isn't this already good enough? Even if there are other Burst Linkers, it won't be easy for them to get up here from the ground or anything."

"That is exactly as you say, but..." A little ways off, the shrine maiden–type avatar, clad in the two colors of unbleached cloth and scarlet, cocked her head to one side. "If we use very showy major techniques in a place as high up as this, the battle effects will be visible from a fair distance. A blue hunting party might come over from Shinjuku."

"If they do come over and try to interfere." Raker grinned. "Well then, you and I will take care of them, right, Uiui?"

Maiden shrank back as she murmured, "...I suppose."

"'Kay! So we'll give it a go here! The mission to get Silver Crow the Theoretical Mirror ability starts now!" Niko shouted, with the enthusiasm of a children's educational program, and Pard, Takumu, and Chiyuri clapped. The Red King nodded thoughtfully and then continued in a teacherlike tone, "So until Crow dies— Wait, before we get into it, if you have any questions, ask 'em now. Anyone."

"I do!" Chiyuri raised her hand right away. "Um, I don't really get it yet. How is an ability different from a special attack? I actually only know that you can use an ability without shouting the name."

"Oh, good question. And the answer is...from the teacher in charge of system explanations, Black Lotus."

"Wh-what? Me?!" Startled at being called up so suddenly, Kuroyukihime cleared her throat once before beginning to talk, moving the sword of her right hand as a pointer. "The most basic difference is that an ability is essentially a passive skill, while a special attack is an active skill."

For Haruyuki, who had been a Net gamer since before he could remember, the terms were very familiar, but Chiyuri appeared not to have heard them before.

"Passive?" She cocked her triangle hat to one side.

Kuroyukihime would have to explain the explanation. "A passive skill is, in other words...a receptive— No, that's not it. Let's see...." She struggled for a moment, but then readily abandoned the exercise and turned the point of her sword to one side of Chiyuri. "We'll hear the rest from Professor in Times of Trouble, Cyan Pile."

Having served as a Legion officer for long years, Takumu nodded as though he had known it would come to this, and stepped forward to stand beside Kuroyukihime. "In Brain Burst, passive skills are powers that are targeted on yourself and always activated, or activated for as long as your gauge lasts. Active skills are defined as powers that are mainly targeted externally that use up your gauge and have a momentary effect." He spoke smoothly, as one would expect of someone known as the Professor.

However, perhaps this was still too difficult for Chiyuri. "Always on you. Momentary externally," she murmured.

Takumu turned the Pile Driver Enhanced Armament equipped on his right hand up toward the night sky and launched the pile inside with a sharp metallic rasp. The pointed spike instantly stretched up more than a meter, and then began to be reloaded, spinning as it moved.

"This technique of mine looks like a special attack at first glance, but it's actually a passive skill that's always available, given to me by this Enhanced Armament. In other words, it's an ability. I don't need my special-attack gauge to use it. Your swords are the same, right, Master?"

Kuroyukihime looked down at her own glittering obsidian arms and nodded. "Mmm, exactly. The ability name is Terminate Sword. And of course, it's always activated."

"Oh, I get it. I think I understand!" Chiyuri shouted, and snapped the index finger of her right hand out at Haruyuki. "Haru, your flying ability is a passive skill, but it's not always activated. It's the limited activation kind where you use up your gauge when you use it. Ash's Wall Riding and Sister Raker's Boost Jump are like that, too."

"O-oh, right." The things he had simply understood had been neatly put into words for his friend. He was impressed; Chiyuri was basically a newbie when it came to games, but her ability to absorb things since she had become a Burst Linker was honestly astounding.

"So then this Theoretical Mirror ability, if you can get it, maybe it'll be always activated. So that would...maybe make light techniques ineffective forever?" Chiyuri mused.

Haruyuki gulped hard beneath his helmet before lifting his head with a thought. "Huh? But everyone's been talking about getting it...but can I even do something like that? I mean, can't you only get special attacks and abilities as level-up bonuses? I-I'm not going to be able to make it to level six for a while." He tentatively looked around at everyone, and Kuroyukihime looked back with a face that he could tell was exasperated, even through her goggles.

"Look, Crow. There are limits to your forgetfulness. Try to remember. The time when you awoke your flying ability."

How was it exactly? He crossed his arms and thought before finally realizing it.

Right. The duel avatar Silver Crow hadn't been a flying type right from the start. At the time he was born into the Accelerated World, he had been just a plain old metal color without wings.

But in the final stages of a fierce battle with Cyan Pile, when he had tried to stand up one last time, wounds covering his body—on his back, where there had been no protrusions until that point, ten shining silver metallic fins were generated and then guided Haruyuki into the sky. In other words, he obtained his flying ability not at the time when his avatar was born, not when he went up to level two, but...

"It was...in the middle of a duel," Haruyuki murmured.

"Right." Kuroyukihime nodded deeply. "You can only get special attacks when you level up, but that's not necessarily the case for abilities. They sometimes manifest through some sort of trigger during a normal duel or while diving in the Unlimited Neutral Field. Like how in the very old RPGs, a new technique would flash in the middle of battle. If you had the Instruct menu open in the moment when your Flight awakened, you would have seen a new ability written there...Of course, it is an extremely rare phenomenon."

"E-extremely rare?" he repeated reflexively, and then realized that that was not the important part. "No, um, the trigger. What exactly is it?"

"Mmm...Right. It's a bit difficult to put into words." Kuroyukihime closed her mouth.

"Adversity." Blood Leopard, silently watching the proceedings up to that point, picked up the thought on Kuroyukihime's behalf. At this one word, the high rankers all nodded together.

Fuko, standing beside Pard, smiled and added, "That's just it. To call up a new ability, you need adversity, and the will to fight it. In that sense, the process is a little similar to acquiring Incarnate techniques."

"Incarnate techniques are slowly refined through the imagination, while abilities are, in the end, activated instantaneously as a behavior trigger. Thus, Haruyuki, no matter how strongly you imagine a mirror, you will not be able to obtain the Theoretical Mirror with mental strength alone."

ALWAYS-ACTIVATED ABILITIES

Passive skills that do not use the special-attack gauge.
Skill acquisition possible not only when leveling up, but also during duels.

CYAN PILE
Thrust with Pile Driver

BLACK LOTUS
Brandish with Terminate Sword

LIMITED ACTIVATION ABILITIES

Passive skills that use the special-attack gauge.
Skill acquisition possible not only when leveling up, but also during duels.

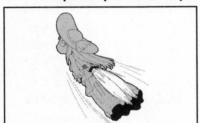

SKY RAKER
Boost Jump with Gale Thruster

ASH ROLLER
Wall Riding with Night Rocker

SPECIAL ATTACKS

Active skills that use up the
special-attack gauge. Can be obtained
only through leveling up.

LIME BELL
Citron Call with Choir Chime

INCARNATE ATTACK

An ability that overwrites phenomena without
using the special-attack gauge. Acquisition rare
but possible through deepening of Image.

SILVER CROW
Laser Sword with Incarnate Sword

Kuroyukihime concluded the explanation and then turned her gaze toward Lime Bell. "Chiyuri, is that good enough for the difference between abilities and special attacks, and Incarnate attacks, while we're at it?"

"Yeah. I totally get it now, Professor!" she responded enthusiastically.

Haruyuki nodded. If he wanted to get a new power, an ability, he would have to fight adversity and take a step forward. Just like he had eight months ago in the hospital room where Kuroyukihime was sleeping. That was exactly why he needed the help of the Red King and her powerful light techniques. He had to take the lasers she fired with his whole body, fight back, and move forward. If he could do that, the Theoretical Mirror ability should definitely show up in Silver Crow.

Finally hardening his resolve, Haruyuki stared at the small avatar of Scarlet Rain and the gun-type Enhanced Armament shining at her hips. "I don't have any more questions, Niko. Let's get started."

"Oh, that's what I like to see! Hardly ever get to see that attitude. 'Kay, how about we start with the actual technique?"

Grinning, the Red King turned around and began to walk toward the center of the wide roof. Faced with that strong back, half to encourage himself, Haruyuki called out to her, "No point holding back, Niko. Keep firing that laser gun until you run out of bullets."

It's settled, he said to himself.

In that moment, Niko turned around, a few dozen meters away from him, and looked at the guns on her own hips with a slight "Huh?" She then shrugged and said, rather unexpectedly, "Oh, I can't use these. They're not lasers. Real bullets."

"Huh?" Now it was Haruyuki's turn to be confused.

"I've got just one light technique. Hold on a sec. I'll call it now." She tossed her head back to the dark sky. "Equip Invincible."

She gave the voice command dryly, and in the next instant, several enormous polygon blocks appeared from behind her, together with a low rumbling. They immediately grew more detailed, transforming into machine guns and missile pods, thick armor plating and hover-thrusters.

The minimal-sized girl avatar was in the blink of an eye surrounded by armament containers, until finally, two enormous main armaments fused onto her from either side. With a mechanical growl, the entire thing shuddered and landed, white smoke pluming from all the exhaust ports, as it radiated a sense of overwhelming presence on par with a large Enemy. This was the Red King's true form—the true nature of the one also known as Immobile Fortress.

"Wh-whoa, whoa! So huuuuuuge!" Chiyuri cried, reeling at beholding for the first time the sight of Scarlet Rain and the entirety of her Enhanced Armament fully deployed.

Niko glanced over at her, only her head and shoulders peeking out from the center of the containers. "You guys should get back a little more. You might get caught with splash damage," she instructed, kindly yet terrifyingly.

Once Chiyuri and Takumu had retreated to where Kuroyukihime and the others were standing along the southern edge of the roof, Niko looked straight at Haruyuki once more. "'Kay then, you wanna go ahead with the first blow?"

Hearing this, Haruyuki finally recovered from his mentally stunned state. "Huh? Um, you can't, uh…your light technique, is it maybe that…?"

"No maybe about it. This is it." She whirled the right main armament, which made a cool whining vibration sound and caught Haruyuki dead center in the sights of the enormous barrel.

"No way. No. Hold on a sec. Is there, like, maybe, something a little milder at first, like a test course?"

"I told you, didn't I? This is the only light technique I have. Relax. I'll use the normal firing rather than the special attack."

These thoughtful words were nearly drowned out by the sound of the cooling fans whirring at the rear of the armament. Sparks raced and snapped along the long barrel, and in the depths of the darkness of the mouth of that barrel, a crimson light flickered irregularly.

"Here we go. Firing in three, two, one…" The merciless countdown began, and unable to do anything further, Haruyuki crossed both arms in front of his body and took a defensive pose. "Fire!"

Zrrsssshooon! The sound of firing was also fierce and cool—but before that, Haruyuki's field of view was colored a pure red. A strange sensation enveloped his body. The pain from damage taken in the Unlimited Neutral Field was double what it was in the regular duel field, but more than painful, this was hot. And because that heat was so intense, it actually felt cold, too.

Believe! Create an image! Haruyuki shouted in his heart, as he fought back against the current of concentrated light energy. *My armor is silver. Of all the metal colors, silver is the most reflective. Bounce back that laser. Become a mirror. A Theoretical Mirror, enough to bounce back all light.*

From the center of his crimson field of view, a pure white light radiated outward and raced past his surroundings. The pressure and the heat receded somewhere, and his consciousness alone floated up.

…Ahh, Niko, the light…I can see the light… In his wandering thoughts, Haruyuki felt like he heard Niko responding in her angel mode.

…Yeah, I know, Big Bro.

…But, uh, Big Bro…? You're melting.

"Huh?" A brief cry slipped out of his mouth.

A tenth of a second later, there was a *shhhf* sound, and Haruyuki evaporated.

Ten times he was assaulted by the main armament of the Red King. Ten times he died, ten times he came back to life.

At first, Kuroyukihime and the others kept an eye on him from nearby during the sixty minutes they had to wait for him to regenerate, but around the third time, they started to get bored, and he couldn't chide them for being heartless when they went to hunt Enemies together the fifth time. If he had been in their place, Haruyuki would have gotten bored, too. In fact, he was actually grateful they faithfully came back to the rooftop every hour.

"...Um...," Niko said, the tenth time he came back to life, looking at him with slightly pitying eyes. "...What d'you wanna do? Keep going? The curry was pretty great, so I'll hang out with you for another ten times or so, but, like..."

Haruyuki was dejected and spent, his mouth turned down at the corners.

"Mm-hmm," Kuroyukihime replied on his behalf, also sounding a little evasive. "Well, I did think that if we just kept going, at some point...but like this, I also feel like we need to approach this from a different direction. How about it, Raker?"

"I suppose so. What if we increase the extent of the adversity a little more?"

"Oh? For instance?"

"He could get hit with both of the Red King's main armaments at once, or instead of her normal attack, the special attack."

Haruyuki had no sooner heard that much than he was lifting his drooping head and shaking it vigorously. "N-no, that's— please pick a slightly different approach!"

"Mmm. I see. But, well, different, hmm."

Okay, so the real thing. Actual training with Archangel Metatron's incredible laser.

Haruyuki was ready to flee the instant anyone put forth this idea. However, fortunately, as if reading his mind, Takumu threw him a life raft.

"Master, just doing this is not working, so maybe that means just the action is not enough."

"Meaning?"

"Maybe a level of understanding of the image—the mirror—is required?"

Haruyuki joined Black Lotus and the others in cocking his head to one side. "But like, Taku, a mirror's a mirror, right? Just a panel that reflects light…"

"It is in the real world. But what about in the Accelerated World? Just like the silver color of Haru's armor is a metaphor for Haru's internal world, if a perfect mirror exists in this world, then surely…"

"It's a metaphor for some kind of concept?" Kuroyukihime murmured, and appeared to sink deeper into thought.

Silence followed for a few seconds, this time broken by Chiyuri raising her hand. "I just thought of a question, a little late, I know, but…"

"Mmm. Go ahead."

"There was someone before Haru who mastered this Theoretical Mirror ability he's trying to learn, right? Go get them to teach—or maybe, can't we just have them go up against Metatron?"

Haruyuki opened his mouth, gaping. Now that she mentioned it, this idea made perfect sense. It was precisely because there existed a Burst Linker who had acquired this ability that it had been given that name, so why hadn't they even considered him or her up to that point? Or rather, why had Kuroyukihime and Fuko ignored that direction all this time?

Takumu likely felt the same doubt. He stared at the Legion Master hard, together with Haruyuki and Chiyuri.

Faced with their combined gazes, Kuroyukihime uncharacteristically lowered her head as if to avoid them and glanced to her right, at the shrine maiden avatar standing a way off.

Also unusually, Ardor Maiden curled her normally ramrod-straight back and hid her face beneath her bangs. And now that he was thinking about it, Haruyuki realized belatedly that Shinomiya hadn't been talking very much that day, although he didn't know the reason for that.

"Let's save that matter for next time." Fuko nodded gently at the confused threesome. "It's just as Pile says. Rather than continuing this harsh training any further, I also think we should try to approach it from the theoretical side. Red King, Leopard—I'd like to end things here today. What do you think?"

The two members of the Red Legion exchanged a look and then nodded together.

"I got no probs with that."

"NP for me, either."

"Well then, shall we all move to the leave point in Koenji Station? There was a slightly largish Wild-class Enemy along the way, so how about we hunt that and replenish the Burst points Corvus lost?"

5

Pushing back against the gravity of the real world, Haruyuki raised his eyelids. The Arita living room didn't appear to have changed a bit from before the dive. Which was only natural. The approximately twelve hours they had spent inside was only the passage of forty or so seconds on this side.

However, Haruyuki couldn't stand up right away because of the feeling of exhaustion pressing heavily on his shoulders. This was perhaps the first time since he'd become a Burst Linker that he had died that many times in a row. Because the laser emitted by the Red King's armaments was almost too powerful, evaporating Silver Crow in a matter of seconds, the pain and the shock actually hadn't been that bad, but he couldn't help but be embarrassed at the fact that there had been absolutely no difference between the first time and the tenth time in how long the evaporation took.

When he stayed buried in the sofa, head hanging dejectedly, Kuroyukihime, having plucked the XSB cable from her Neurolinker, turned a kind smile on him from the opposite sofa. "Nice work, Haruyuki. You really tried your best out there. Sorry you had to have that terrible experience."

"Huh? No, I mean. It's just…I didn't learn the Theoretical Mirror ability, after all…," he mumbled in reply.

Kuroyukihime, Fuko, Niko, and Pard all exchanged a brief glance, and then Niko opened her mouth on behalf of all.

"Now, look, Crow. To be blunt, we all thought the possibility of you suddenly awakening the ability in today's training was fairly low."

"…Huh?"

"The job Lotus asked me to do wasn't to help you get Theoretical Mirror—it was to make you feel with your body what a light attack was. Because you're so good at seeing what comes next and dodging in duels and the Territories and stuff, you only take hits from homing missiles or super-barrage machine guns."

"Uh, yeah, well…" It was true that Haruyuki had recently become able to dodge pretty much all single-shot, direct, long-distance attacks—in other words, laser and rifle types—while flying. His rivals also knew this and had thus begun to ready anti–Silver Crow firepower, like Niko said, so his chances of being hit by a laser decreased even further.

"Whaaat? So that was the goal right from the start, huh? So then, Haru, how was it? You see some kind of secret to light techniques?" Chiyuri asked, leaning forward.

Haruyuki shrugged, grinning wryly. "I mean, it's a secret, you know. It was totally different from even the other big red techniques, like the ones where they shoot shells or release flames and stuff, but…"

"Hmm. How was it different?" This time, the question came from Takumu, looking very interested.

"Hmm, right, okay. There was no explosive impact, and there was no smell of fuel burning. At best, it's this flow of pure energy coming at an incredible density. My armor reflected the flow for just the first instant, but it quickly burned red and then melted and evaporated…I guess that's what it felt like."

"I see…In the real world, at least, I'm pretty sure that of all the metals, silver has the greatest reflectivity. Um, what percent was it exactly?" Takumu quickly moved to flick at his virtual desktop.

But before he could, Pard said, "Average of ninety-five percent of visible light."

"...Why d'you know that?" her Legion Master asked.

The senior executive in her sailor-style uniform answered seriously, "I thought this might play out like this, so I looked it up. I don't like waiting for Net searches."

"...I see."

How very like this impatient alien, they all thought.

Takumu cleared his throat before continuing. "S-so in other words, this metallic mirror reflects basically all wavelengths of light. Put another way, that's why it's the color silver. Metals look metallic because they have a low reflectance in the blue light region. But the reflectance of silver's not one hundred percent. The light it can't completely reflect, a mere few percent, heats Silver Crow's armor and evaporates him."

"Ooh, I get it. So, basically, Crow's not shiny enough, right?" Chiyuri noted, and Takumu stopped for a moment before nodding. And then, of course, came: "So let's polish him. If that's it, then we just have to polish him! Like with cleansers or something, until Silver Crow's all shiny!"

After imagining the scene of everyone joining up to roughly polish his avatar, Haruyuki hurriedly shook his head from side to side. "N-no way! That will totally hurt like crazy! And it's not like there's cleanser or anything in the Accelerated World..."

"Well, it's not that there *isn't* any." Kuroyukihime nodded with a straight face, freezing Haruyuki, but fortunately, she followed up with supplementary words negating this comment. "But no matter how much we polish him, his reflectance likely won't reach a hundred percent. Even supposing we could get it up to ninety-nine percent, he still wouldn't be able to withstand Rain's armaments. The force of that remaining one percent would melt his avatar."

"...In other words, that's also how amazing Niko's light attack is." Chiyuri sighed, apparently giving up on the polishing idea.

The Red King twitched her nose proudly. "Well, it's so-so, y'know. But Crow's the first one who's ever been able to withstand a direct blast of my guns at that level for almost five seconds. You should be more confident."

"True. Showered in that for a mere one second, the armor all over my body was burnt." Kuroyukihime was referring to the time they went to subjugate the fifth Armor of Catastrophe together and Niko had lost her temper, shooting Lotus together with Disaster with her laser canon.

"Tch! What's done is done. And anyway, you're black to start with, so it's no big diff if you get a little burnt," Niko snarled.

Kuroyukihime was quick to retort. "So then, given that you're red already, you have no issue with being boiled in tomato sauce, hmm? We'll have spaghetti arrabbiata at the next dinner party."

"H-hey, look, this isn't about the real world! I'm basically no good with spicy pasta! If we're gonna do tomato, then a regular spaghetti sauce is good enough!"

"I'll just say this now. I'm not good with squid ink spaghetti."

"No one said anything about squid ink!!"

If he didn't step up and say something, the two kings were likely to work themselves up to a direct duel, so Haruyuki hurriedly stuck his body between them. "W-well, if you're both okay with tomato sauce pasta, I'd recommend Chiyu's mom's special pescatora. It's full of seafood; it's seriously the best!"

"...Oh."

"...Huh."

Perhaps imagining the taste, they both fell silent, and he was able to bring the conversation back on track.

"Um, so then, Taku, my—Silver Crow's—armor has a high level of reflectance, but it's not perfect, which is why it can't invalidate a super-powerful light attack?"

"Mm-hmm. That's what I think." The brains of the Legion went on to suggest, as his frameless glasses caught the light, "So then what could bring the reflectance rate of a metal up to the impossible one hundred percent is the Theoretical Mirror ability in question, I'm sure of it. I said this on the other side, too, but adversity and action alone are probably not enough to get it. An image arrived at through knowledge is also an essential trigger. Put simply, you need to know more deeply what a mirror is. That's about all I can guess right now."

"Know a mirror, huh?" Haruyuki murmured, as if digesting the idea, and then looked again at his good friend's face. "Thanks, Taku. I feel like I can kinda see the way now."

"You do? We're counting on you, Haru. We need your power to cut the roots of those ISS kits taking over the Accelerated World."

"Yeah. When I was swallowed up by the armor, lots of people helped me out, so now it's my turn to fight."

He and Takumu nodded sharply at each other.

"Yeah, yeah. Sorry to butt in on this little love fest, but it's about time to call it a night," Chiyuri interjected, clapping her hands together.

"It wasn't a love fest!" Haruyuki hurried to protest, and when he spotted a hint of glee in the sulky face of his other childhood friend, he felt even more awkward. He began tidying up the cables on the table to hide his embarrassment, and for some reason, Kuroyukihime and Fuko and the others laughed out loud in bright voices.

The shared mission between the two Legions was adjourned there for the time being. And there was a reason he hadn't brought up the subject of Argon Array aka Quad Eyes Analyst at the gathering that day.

Naturally, Haruyuki had reported to Kuroyukihime and Fuko that Argon Array was a core member of the Acceleration Research Society as soon as the meeting the previous day had ended. They had both heard his story with the utmost seriousness and said they would begin an immediate investigation, but at the same time, they decided that the information should stay within Nega Nebulus; they could not tell the two members of Prominence yet. The reason for this was that if Niko or Pard was to act independently, the malice of the Acceleration Research Society might be turned against the Red Legion—in fact, the possibility of that was extremely high.

It wasn't that they didn't have faith in Prominence's investigative abilities or fighting power. But unlike Nega Nebulus, it was a large Legion, with a general force of more than thirty people. It wasn't possible to always be up-to-date on the status of all its members, and worming their way in from the edges of a Legion was the Acceleration Research Society's specialty.

Thus, Haruyuki turned toward Niko and Pard as they got ready to head home and stood to see them off, while apologizing to them in his heart. He tried to see them to the outside door, but at the entrance to the living room, Pard said, "Here's good," and stopped him. Guessing that it would take her a while to put on her riding boots at the doorway, he bowed his head without protest.

"'Kay, see ya! Thanks for the curry! Make sure to call us when you're doing the pescatora!" Niko called before shutting the door to the living room, and the sound of two sets of footsteps receded down the hallway. A minute and a half later, the door lock/unlock dialogue popped up in his field of view. Another few minutes after that, Kuroyukihime, Fuko, and Utai, all going home together in the same car, stood up and slipped out the front door—Haruyuki saw them off there this time—and then finally, Chiyuri and Takumu went home to the different floors of the same condo complex.

The second he was alone, a profound sadness washed over him, and he let out a thin sigh. Despite the fact that this was his own familiar home, the white wallpaper and hard resin flooring had quickly taken on the face of a distant stranger. Takumu and the others had helped clean up, so there was not a trace of the commotion of only a half an hour earlier.

When he glanced at the analog clock on the wall, it had just hit eight fifteen PM. On his virtual desktop, Haruyuki turned off the air conditioning and lights in the living room, gently closed the glass door, and returned to his own room at the end of the hallway. The wall to his left in his thirteen-square-meter Western-style room was taken up by a sliding bookshelf, while the right side was occupied by a semi-double bed. Neither furnishing seemed very suitable for a boy in junior high school, but he was simply using the things his father had left behind long ago when his parents got divorced.

As he increased the illumination of the LED ceiling lights slightly, set to a warm color, he moved to his writing desk, which faced the southern window, and then sat down in the mesh office chair that had also been his father's. Although the desktop had been far away when he first started using it, even when the chair was raised to the highest setting, now it fit him perfectly, as if it had been made to order.

He set his arms down on the desk and launched the reminder app, another original from Kuroyukihime. He had one piece of homework for the next day, but he had taken care of it with the help of Takumu and the others over the course of the evening, so it was marked completed. Other than that, he had one task related to the Umesato Junior High School festival, which was coming up the following Sunday. The deadline for applications to bring guests, including parents and guardians, was in two days, but there was no way his mother would come, and he had no friends outside of school he wanted to—

His thoughts had gotten that far when several faces flitted across the back of his mind: The two members of the Red Legion he had seen just half an hour earlier. And Haru's old rival in the Green Legion. Strictly speaking, Fuko Kurosaki and Utai Shinomiya weren't Umesato students, either, but he was sure Kuroyukihime would invite them.

But could he really invite Burst Linkers from Prominence and Great Wall to a school festival that had absolutely nothing to do with Brain Burst? The relationship Haruyuki had with those girls was at best through the intermediary of the Accelerated World. He had met them several times in the real, including that day, but every time, the sole matter of business had been something related to Brain Burst.

After thinking about it for a while, he decided to table the matter until the following day and wiped away his virtual desktop with his hand. All the windows disappeared, and the icons quickly retreated to the edge of his field of view. He leaned back in the office chair, reclining leisurely, and his thoughts turned toward one more piece of homework.

"...A mirror, huh...?" he murmured to himself.

Wait, do I have one? he wondered, pulling open his desk drawer. It was filled with a jumble of things—memory cards of unknown content, cables of mysterious origin—but it didn't seem like there was a hand mirror in there anywhere. And he didn't have a wall or full-length mirror in his room. He found a chrome card case and pulled that out instead. After he polished it with the hem of his T-shirt, he looked closely at the glittering silver—

"Whoa, whoa, at least have a hand mirror or something. Geez."

He heard a voice from behind. Half unconsciously, he retorted, "N-not too many junior high school boys have something like that, you know."

"Huh? From what I've seen, Pile's got one, though."

"No matter how you look at it, Taku's one of the few—" After conversing normally up to that point, he finally realized it: This was not a voice call via Neurolinker. It was a conversation using real mouths and ears. Which meant, in other words, the distance from which this real voice was reaching him...

"—?!" Haruyuki and the chair whirled around at an incredible speed, the force of which spun him all the way around once before he could get a look in the six o'clock direction.

A light-gray blanket covered the substantial, semi-double bed. Poking out from beneath that, torso leaning up against the extra-large pillow, face plastered with a grin and red pigtails swinging, was definitely the leader of Prominence, who had supposedly gone back to the Nerima area on a large electric bike earlier. It was Scarlet Rain, Yuniko Kozuki.

"Wh-wh-wha-ah-ah?!" *Why are you here?!* Haruyuki stammered the line like a broken audio file playing, flapping his mouth open and shut.

Even if, hypothetically, she had once again gotten a hold of an instant key to the Arita house through some means or another, a warning would have been displayed in Haruyuki's vision the moment the entryway door was opened. But he hadn't seen anything like that since everyone went home. So then how had she opened the locked door…?

"…Oh…! N-n-no way! Did you not leave right from the start?! You closed the door when you left the living room, and then only Pard went toward the entryway, while you snuck into my room and hid under the blanket. That's it, isn't it!" Famed detective Haruyuki called out with all his might upon discovering the trick to the locked room.

"No other way, is there?" Niko readily assented. "But I mean, you shoulda noticed when you came in the room. This blanket's so thin, it was totes obvious I was under it."

"Unh! …I-it's just, I didn't actually think anyone was here or anything…"

"You're the sort that gets killed in the first ten minutes of a horror movie."

"Y-you're one to— Hey, that's not the point!" Panting as he collected his thoughts, he finally happened upon what he should say next. "Wh-why?! Obviously, Pard was helping you, right? S-s-s-so why would you do this?!"

"Like I said, I fed them this story about staying out for the night, so I can't go back to the dorm today. And it's all because of you asking me for help, so only natural you take responsibility," she told him, the look on her face saying it was the most obvious thing in the world, and he actually started to feel like it *was* only natural. He nodded unconsciously before shaking his head frantically once more.

"B-b-b-b-but my mom's coming home today! What am I supposed to tell her?!"

"Although it would be fun to have you introduce us, we can do that next time. She won't find out as long as I stay in your room. Oh! But let me use the bath first. And I need a change of clothes."

"Find out...Bath...Clothes..." Almost belatedly, the cooling mechanism for the circuit of his thoughts could no longer keep up, and he simply parroted her words back to her, while Niko peeled the blanket away and sprang out of the bed to the floor. She opened the closet on the north side on the room and rummaged through the ten or so T-shirts on hangers there.

"You got terrible taste. No red? Red...Oh! This'll work." With a clattering sound, she pulled out a large, bright-red shirt with the logo of an Italian motorcycle manufacturer on it and headed for the door.

"'Kay, gimme about twenty minutes. If your momma comes home before then, you just take care of it."

Kachak! She opened the door, and then Haruyuki was left alone in his room.

That was an illusion for sure—no, wait, the real issue is, how am I supposed to 'take care of it'? I'll just have to use the Cousin Tomoko Saito strategy again—his mind raced until, finally, there was flashing in the edge of his field of view to indicate that the bath was in use.

If, hypothetically, he pressed that small icon and then activated emergency mode from the home server operation window that opened, it would be possible to call up a bath monitor window, but of course, he would never think of—well, he would just think of it and then reject the idea. Haruyuki let out a sigh so long it lasted at least ten seconds.

Fortunately, he supposed, even though Niko's bath stretched out five minutes longer than she said it would, the catastrophe of his mother returning home during that time was evaded.

"Foowheee, that bath of yours really is huuuge!" the Red King commented as she returned to his room.

Haruyuki went to toss her the bottle of mineral water he had just taken out of the refrigerator, averting his eyes. His aim was off, and Niko caught it just as it was on the verge of crashing into the bookshelf.

"Watch out! You gotta look where you're throwing stuff!"

"A-as if I could look! You gotta actually get dressed before you come in here!" he shrieked back.

"I am dressed." Niko looked down at herself and spread her hands out as if to say "What are you talking about?" And she was indeed wearing clothes, but just the single T-shirt she had commandeered from his closet, her thin, pale bare legs stretching out from beneath the hem. Although the T-shirt was large enough to cover her to the knees, since she was carrying in her right hand the T-shirt and cut-off jeans she had been wearing, he was forced to know what was under the shirt.

"Th-that's not enough, is it! I mean!" Haruyuki shot back, covering 70 percent or so of his field of view.

Niko chuckled as she pulled the hem of the shirt up three centimeters. "You say that, but it's just you getting all hot and bothered by your leg fetish, right? Right?"

"N-no—! I-I'm not into that!"

"So what are you into?"

"W-well, that's—" He froze, and a screen in the back of his mind came on. The image shown there was for some reason the sword legs of Black Lotus, Sky Raker's legs in their high heels, Blood Leopard's animal-shaped legs, and he waved his hands—*What is this, anyway?!*—and wiped the images away.

Seeing Haruyuki like this, Niko smiled for some reason in full-fledged angel mode and sang, "Brother's acting stra~ange! ♪" This was followed by "Thanks for the water!" as she twisted the cap off the plastic bottle and drank deeply.

Without realizing its intensity, Haruyuki felt his heart pound hard at the sight of the girl with her hair casually down, the ends still damp, as he repeated to himself like an incantation, *That is the Red King, that is the Red King.*

After emptying half the bottle in one go, Niko exhaled heavily, set the bottle down on the sideboard, together with her clothes, and then flopped backward onto the bed. On top of the adult-size bed, she looked extra small, making Haruyuki's heart skip a beat in a different way than it had before.

Arms and legs splayed, Niko closed her eyes for more than a minute. Just when Haruyuki was starting to worry that she had already fallen asleep—in which case, where would *he* sleep—she abruptly spoke in a quiet voice. "...If you don't want to, you can step down, y'know."

"...Huh? Wh-what?"

"From the vanguard in the Metatron strategy. To be honest, I'm annoyed at the kings. They were all shouting about putting a bounty on your head up to today, and now, as soon as there's no basis for that, they're all, 'go get the Theoretical Mirror ability.' Too convenient, no matter how you look at it. Those guys, 'specially Purple and Yellow, they don't care at all if you end up in unlimited EK fighting Metatron, y'know..."

Her tone was restrained, but he could sense the deep indignation in it—and a note of apprehension. He wasn't able to reply immediately.

Abruptly, a faint voice came back to life in his ears. Right, after the meeting of the Seven Kings the week before, too, Niko had suddenly shown up at his house. And when she was leaving, she'd said to him, *Look, Big Brother Haruyuki. If one of us—or maybe both of us—lose Brain Burst, we'll probably forget everything, everything about each other, you know. So promise. That when we find a name we don't know in the address book of our Neurolinkers, before we erase the data, we'll send one mail. And then maybe, one more time...*

"...Niko." Haruyuki finally opened his mouth, and the girl on the bed lifted her eyelids slightly. As he stared at her eyes, shining a deep green, he added, "Um...Th-thanks. But it's okay. I've seen Metatron's laser with my own eyes. It's too powerful for me to get close enough to end up in unlimited EK. And Iron Pound asking me to be in the vanguard…I feel that pressure, but I'm also a little happy, actually. So I mean, I mean…"

While he fumbled and searched earnestly for the right words, he noticed that Niko had at some point turned her gaze directly on him. On her youthful face, innocence and a deep discretion coexisted, making him aware all over again of the fact that she was also a king.

"…I mean, they say I'm the only completely flying type in the Accelerated World, so basically, I'm a foreign body. Regardless of the fact that I'm a member of Nega Nebulus, for a lot of Burst Linkers, I'm just this irregular someone they have to figure out how to attack. In a way, I'm sort of like an Enemy. But I think Pound spoke to me yesterday as an equal Burst Linker. I was pretty surprised, 'cos, like…it was amazing. That's why… That's why I…" He had somehow stammered and faltered this far in explaining himself, but he couldn't find the words that came next.

Here's what I thought. I thought maybe, if I actually carried out my role as the vanguard in this mission against Metatron, then just maybe, that might be an opportunity for the five kings and Kuroyukihime—who've been so antagonistic for so long—to take a step toward each other. The way you and Kuroyukihime became friends.

"Right." As if she had completely seen through into Haruyuki's heart full of these thoughts, Niko smiled gently, clearly, and a tiny bit sadly. "Well, if you've thought it through, then I won't try to stop you. But, like…just be careful. Metatron's not your only enemy."

"Huh? What does that mean…?"

"You remember what I said last week?"

Haruyuki blinked rapidly a few times at the sudden unexpected question, before replying in an unintelligible voice, "Uh, um. Yeah. Like…if I found a name I didn't know in my Neurolinker address book—"

Suddenly, Niko's face became as red as the T-shirt she was wearing, and the large pillow whizzed as it flew through the air at him. Taking it squarely in the face, Haruyuki heard a high-pitched shriek.

"N-n-not that! W-well, you do have to remember that, too, but—not that, the part before that!"

"B-before?" Cradling the pillow in his arms after it fell from his face, Haruyuki searched his memory once again. A single strange word came back to life in his mind. "Oh, uh, that? Um, that the Ori—Originators are monsters or something?"

"Right, that." Niko already had her serious face back on, and Haruyuki gulped, still clutching the pillow. "At the meeting last week, pathetically, I freaked. But today, I carefully measured the information pressure of all the kings. It's not like I have special abs like the Analyst or anything, but like any good red type, I got a bit of a scanning function in these eyes, okay?"

Haruyuki very nearly reacted to "Analyst," but managed to control himself somehow, and asked about something different. "S-scan...? Like...you can see through things?"

"Idiot. Like a thermal scan or wind direction scan. If I really put some muscle into it, I can see the amount of memory info a Burst Linker's built up, too. It's like...how a ton of gravity'll distort space. And at that meeting, radiating an information pressure that was an order of magnitude different from the others was first of all...the Green King, Green Grandé." Niko raised one finger as she announced the name.

To a certain degree, Haruyuki had expected it. That evening four days earlier, while he was fused with the Armor of Catastrophe, Haruyuki had crossed swords with Green Grandé. In that instant, part of the vast amount of time the king had spent in the Accelerated World poured into Haruyuki, albeit just the smallest amount. "Yeah. I kinda got the sense too that the Green King was a little different from the other kings."

"He doesn't talk, much less duel." A faintly wry smile crossed

Niko's face, and she quickly resumed her serious look before raising another finger. "And the second person was...the Blue King, Blue Knight."

"Huh? Him? I kinda thought he was maybe the easiest of all the kings to get along with."

"Because his tone and attitude are fairly informal. But, like... kinda so-so on whether that's his true self, y'know? You hear stuff about him." After showing the slightest hesitation, Niko lowered her voice and continued. "When Lotus took the head of the previous Red King, it was the Blue King who went craziest. Apparently, he rampaged like he was a totally different person, cutting through not just the buildings and stuff in the stage, but the earth itself."

"Th-the earth is fundamentally indestructible."

"That's why, like, it's a rumor at best. But it's not sure if that lighthearted chairman from yesterday's meeting is the real knight. He's probably like the Green King, a Burst Linker with no parent—in other words, an Originator."

"Origin...ator?" Haruyuki quietly repeated the word he had heard not only from Niko, but also from the mouth of the Green King himself. The parent-child relationship was the first bond a Burst Linker had. The parent told the child everything they knew, and the child worked to live up to the parent's expectations. It was precisely because of this bond that Burst Linkers were able to love the Accelerated World—that was Haruyuki's understanding. Because if you had no parent, then right from the start, every Burst Linker other than yourself was an enemy.

"My parent's gone now, but even still, even now, I'm glad I'm Cherry's child. Because all the many important things he taught me when I was still a chick are the reason I'm here now," Niko half murmured, and she beat at the chest of the red T-shirt with her right hand. "But that's exactly why I can't even imagine it. What kind of place is the Accelerated World for the first Burst Linkers—for the Originators? What would it be like with no parent, no Legion, all you can do is fight and take points from each other, like..."

Naturally, Haruyuki was also unable to truly imagine that situation. But he could vaguely picture it. Because the Armor of Catastrophe he had been fused with until just a few days earlier was itself a product of the depth of the love and sadness of two Originators.

"In a world like that," Haruyuki said, almost muttering, as he stared hard at Niko sitting cross-legged on the bed, "even in a world that was only fighting like that, I'm sure there were Burst Linkers who could understand each other through the duel. Like the way you and I did, you know?"

"..." Niko made a face like she was wavering between shouting and launching another long-distance attack, and then she smiled slightly, wryly.

"Guess so. Maybe there were one or two like you in those Originators...Anyway, we got off track there. From what I saw, the Green and Blue Kings aren't really putting it out there. In fact, Purple and Yellow are actually way more up-front."

"So then...the only Originators at that meeting were those two?" Haruyuki asked.

Niko glanced down on her own right hand, index and middle fingers still standing up, and then moved her thumb a couple times as if hesitating to add to that number.

"Yeah, probably. But, like...maybe..."

"Huh...?"

"Nah, it's nothing. Anyway, what I'm trying to say is watch your back when you go up against Metatron. It's not just Purple, who's obviously hostile to Negabu. We don't know what Green and Blue are thinking in the depths of their hearts."

"R-right. Got it. Thanks for worrying about me, Niko." Haruyuki bowed his head, and the redheaded girl grinned and rolled her small body over onto the bed. After a long yawn, she waved her right hand in the air.

"I'm going to sleep. Gimme the pillow back."

"Y-you're the one who threw it..." Grumbling, Haruyuki stood up from the chair and placed the pillow under Niko's raised head. Which brought him back to his question of a few minutes earlier. "So then where'm I supposed to sleep?"

Niko used both hands to fix the pillow under her head as she rolled over to the left. Just like that, she closed her eyes and said, "'Night, Big Brother."

This necessarily generated space on the right side, but still, there was the question of whether he could charge in there.

"Uh, um...A-anyway, I'm gonna take a bath, too." Mumbling, he set aside the issue of the bed and hurriedly escaped from the room.

When he returned from the bathroom twenty minutes later, Niko was already fast asleep, complete with adorably soft snoring.

He picked up the half-empty bottle of water from the side-board and drank down the lukewarm water before considering the optimal situation. Taking another blanket and going to sleep on the sofa in the living room would have been the gentlemanly solution, but his mother would naturally find him there when she came home. If she asked him about it, the only excuse he could think up was "There was a monster in my room," and he certainly could not believe she would accept that. That said, it would be too painful to sleep directly on the floor of his room.

"Even if she *is* in another Legion, that's still the order of a king and all," he whispered, overcoming the logical and moral hurdles somehow to mentally brace himself and kneel on the edge of the bed. Keeping the maximum distance from Niko, he smoothly shifted to a position lying on his back and turned the LED lights to night-light mode.

The instant he was blanketed in the dim orange gloom, his eyelids abruptly grew heavy, despite the situation he found himself in. Just as he was about to drift off into sleep, he heard the small voice of Niko, whom he thought was already dead to the world.

"I wasn't sure if I should, but I'll tell you this."

"Huh…? What…?"

"The person who had the Theoretical Mirror ability you're trying to get."

Half in a dream, Haruyuki waited for what she would say next.

"His name is Mirror Masker. He's Ardor Maiden's…parent."

6

"Yeeeeeaaaaaahooooooo!!" The shrill cry came at him from behind, accompanied by the roar of a V-twin engine.

Haruyuki didn't even have time to look behind him, but he felt the heat of the tire spinning a few centimeters behind his toes. He reached his arms out straight ahead, mustered up thrust in his wings, and fled.

It was Tuesday, June 25, 7:50 AM.

In 1-choume Minami Koenji, Suginami Ward—also known as Suginami Area No. 2—a duel was underway, customary for this place. Ash Roller of the Green Legion versus Silver Crow of the Black Legion—abbreviated to "Ash-Crow." Obviously, it wasn't every day, but at some point they had reached an agreement where the one who won the previous round would challenge the other every other day—working out to Tuesday, Thursday, and Saturday mornings.

The duels between the biker Ash and the flying Crow often played out as a high-speed battle on the ground for the first half, and then, once their special-attack gauges had built up, it turned into 3-D combat in midair in the second half. There were a lot of highlights, and the fighting was fairly showy visually, so the regular Gallery for these matches had been increasing lately. When Haruyuki thought about the people making a detour to watch the duel on their way to school, he always worked hard to give them a passionate, bright, fun fight.

However, things had been a little off since the duel started that day. Ash Roller was, for some reason, excessively fiery—or rather, he was in berserker mode, to the point that steam was coming out of the mouth of his skull helmet.

"All riiiiiiight! You just wait right there, you damned crow!" a raging voice chased at him from behind.

"N-no!!" Haruyuki responded with a high-pitched cry. "If I wait here, I'll be in a traffic accident!!"

"You think you'd get off that easy?! Traffic fatality's minus nine points! Yaaaah!!"

"Y-you're the one who'd lose points on your license!!"

The pair flew around, bantering like this, on the single-lane road that ran west from Kannana Street. Church on the right, library on the left—neither a real building, of course, but rather transformed into something strange: an assemblage of countless metal pipes—the fighters raced past them, just barely above the ground. The twenty or so members of the Gallery who had set the automatic follow mode for these battles appeared one after another on the rooftops of the buildings out front and disappeared again once Crow and Ash had passed them.

Visually confirming a largish intersection up ahead, Haruyuki leaned his avatar to the right and entered a sharp turn. Veering toward the left, he slalomed down the road before kicking against a telephone pole ten meters in front of the intersection and using the reaction to turn on a dime. Sparks shooting off the tips of his wings against the road surface, he slipped through the intersection to the right.

"Ngaah!"

The outer wall immediately closed in on him, so he frantically pulled his chin and stomach in to fight against the centrifugal force. With a margin of mere millimeters, he cleared the corner and heaved a sigh of relief as he returned to flying in a direct line.

That was a satisfying turn, even for him. Given that Ash was several times heavier when counting the motorcycle, he wouldn't be able to turn with the same speed. Haruyuki could pull away here and get the fight back on track after being basically forced into close combat in the opening—

Whoooaaaaa!!

The cheer of the Gallery interrupted his thoughts, and Haruyuki twitched and looked back. What he saw was a large building crumbling, flames shooting up, and the silhouette of an American motorcycle racing fiercely through those flames. It swerved to the left and right, dodging chunks of falling building, and merged with the road Haruyuki was flying down with basically no damage. Most likely, Ash had seen that he wouldn't be able to make the turn and had instead destroyed the building ahead of him, tearing open a shortcut.

"Wh…Wha—?!" Haruyuki shouted incredulously before hurriedly accelerating again. But having relaxed momentarily, he couldn't immediately get back up to top speed. The roar of the engine charged up behind him, and this time the front wheel did touch Crow's toes. *Skreeeenk!* A grinding noise rang out, and his health gauge dropped.

"Hot, hot, hot! Wh-wh-why are you so serious todaaaaaay?!" Haruyuki nearly shrieked the question.

Ash Roller flung back an unexpected reply. "Obviousooooo! You! My adorable baby sis!! You axed her from the curryyyyyy paaaaaartyyyyyyyyy!!"

"H-huuuuh?!"

In his great surprise, he lost focus, and once more, the tire ate away at his toes. He was almost dragged down to the road surface, but he endured it desperately, and somehow managed to open up a gap between them once more.

Passing by the ostentatious temples stretching along to his right, Haruyuki earnestly set his brain to work. The "curry party" Ash was talking about had to have been the gathering with the homemade curry held at the Arita house the previous evening.

And similarly, the "adorable baby sis" indicated Ash Roller in the real, Fuko Kurasaki's child, Rin Kusakabe.

As to why Ash referred to his own real self as his little sister, the situation was extremely complicated, and even Haruyuki still didn't grasp it completely. Roughly speaking, the girl Rin had two Neurolinkers, and the one with Brain Burst installed was the Neurolinker of her older brother who had been in a coma for several years after a motorcycle accident, Rinta Kusakabe. She could only become a Burst Linker when she was using her brother's Neurolinker. But the personality lodged in the duel avatar known as Ash Roller that appeared in the Accelerated World was not conscious of itself as Rin for some reason, but rather as her older brother, Rinta. Haruyuki couldn't even begin to guess at what kind of logic was at work there. The one thing he could say was that older brother Ash doted on his little sister, Rin, and in that very instance, he thought that Haruyuki was bullying her, and so he was now furious.

"Y-y-you got it wrong!!" Given that they were moving at such high speeds, their conversation shouldn't have reached the ears of the Gallery, but even so, Haruyuki lowered his voice as he desperately tried to defend himself. "P-p-people from another Legion came yesterday! I couldn't exactly invite your little sister!"

"Excuses! No thank yooooouuu!! So then you move the time and you no-problemo it!!"

"W-we didn't have that kind of leeway! A-and Master explained the situation to your sister, and she said it was okay, though!"

"You! Maybe you got the go-ahead! But her heart was in tear-time! You totally don't get iiiiiiiit!!"

An ominous metal sound drowned out the last of his roar of anger, and Haruyuki glanced back to see thick cylinder parts on both sides of the front fork of the American motorcycle. One was already empty. But the other was still loaded with a tapered dual surface-to-surface, surface-to-air ordnance—a missile. And the red lens on the head of it was blinking, locked onto Haruyuki.

"Eee! Eeeeeeee!!" Haruyuki let several screams slip out and paddled both his hands like he was swimming in midair.

If he could ascend straight up and fly into the black clouds blanketing the sky of the stage, he could shake free of the missile. But he couldn't do that, because this was a nature-type, wind-based Thunder stage. Lightning shot out in all directions in the clouds, and not only that, increasing altitude even slightly meant that he would be hammered mercilessly by lightning bolts. It was one of the stages that Silver Crow—a flying type and with silver armor that had maximum conductivity—was least compatible with.

Naturally, if Ash hit Silver Crow with a missile at this close range, he wouldn't make it out unscathed, either. But he had 70 percent left in his health gauge in contrast with Crow's approximately 50 percent. Given that big brother Ash could take some blowback damage no problem, these calculations probably weren't even in his head.

Since it's come to this—!! Haruyuki focused his ears on the beeping lock-on sound behind him and waited for the right time.

"Yeah, you fly, you damned Crow!! Howling Paaaaaaaanhead!!" Ash howled the name of the technique.

Haruyuki flipped up and around, spreading his arms out, flying upside down. "S-s-s-special attack! Stop a sword in my haaaaands!" he shouted, his voice cracking, and caught the missile between his palms immediately after it was launched. An instant before the missile could generate any thrust, its fuel ignited, he forced the seeker lens straight up. He immediately released his hands, and the missile shot vertically, trailing white smoke. The Gallery erupted in cheers at the unexpected sight.

This was his chance for a counterattack, but Haruyuki accidentally chased after the ascending missile with his eyes. Ash and the Gallery were similarly looking up at the sky. Showered in the countless gazes, the white missile—or rather, rocket now—quickly drew near the black clouds in the sky above. Several bolts of lightning rained down to strike it and scattered in all directions.

"...Ah," Haruyuki murmured.

"...Oh," Ash groaned.

Bolts of lightning chased the fragments of falling missile, charging at the earth to wrap the two Burst Linkers directly below in purple flashing.

"Hngyaaaah!!" Their shrieks rang out over the stage, their skeletons flickering in their silhouettes.

"...Phew..." The duel over and now returned to the real world, Haruyuki leaned back against the guardrail of the pedestrian bridge over the Koenji intersection and let out a long sigh. "...Well, a draw at that point, it was a good fight, huh..."

As he told himself this, Haruyuki added what he had learned that day to the "duel notes" he kept in his head: In a Thunder stage, it was possible to guide the thunderbolts by throwing an easily breakable object up into the sky. And it was possible to change the trajectory of a missile-type weapon immediately after it was launched.

"...I really have so much to learn still..."

About duel techniques, about the history of the Accelerated World... Adding this in his heart, Haruyuki sighed once more.

That morning, the Red King Niko had boldly marched right past the room where his mother was sleeping and returned home to Nerima, leaving that lone piece of information she had dropped in Haruyuki's mind as he was on the verge of sleep.

The Burst Linker Mirror Masker, the pioneer of the Theoretical Mirror ability, was the parent of Ardor Maiden, one of the Four Elements of Nega Nebulus...It was a difficult story to swallow at first. If that was true, then why hadn't Kuroyukihime, Fuko, and Utai told Haruyuki and the others right away? But when he thought it over, they had actually been a little evasive the previous evening. If there had been some kind of circumstance making them reluctant to speak, it would have to have been deeply connected with the Legion's—no, with Utai's—personal past.

"I'll ask Shinomiya herself today," Haruyuki resolved out loud.

If there was a reason to stay quiet about it, Niko wouldn't have said anything to him to begin with. By announcing the information to him, she had to have been giving him a push.

Looking at the time display in the edge of his field of view, he saw that it was almost 7:55. It wasn't time for him to start worrying about being late just yet, but even so, he descended the pedestrian bridge at a trot before spotting a large EV bus racing north on Kannana Street and stopped once more.

There was a possibility that the real Ash Roller, Rin Kusakabe, was riding in that bus. She had apparently discovered Silver Crow's true identity by always looking up at the pedestrian bridge through the window of her bus immediately after an Ash-Crow duel and spotting Haruyuki standing there any number of times. It was such an idiotic way of being cracked in the real, but now that he had been cracked, there was no point in running and hiding.

Still standing in the center of the pedestrian bridge, he stared at the bus drawing near on the road below. It would be nice if the brother's rage from the duel before had melted away even a bit, he mused as he waited for it to pass by. And then the left turn signal of the bus started flashing, and the vehicle came to a halt at the bus stop a little north of the intersection. The Koenji overpass stop was not near any stations or schools, so buses almost always went right past it. When he looked over with curiosity, he saw the bus quickly pull out again. A single girl had gotten off, and the uniform she was wearing looked familiar to him.

"Ah! R-r-r-ri—" A panicked cry leaked out of him.

The girl looked straight up from the ground and waved her right hand slightly. She started to move at a trot, so Haruyuki also hurriedly headed toward the escalator on that side. He ran down it, almost falling forward, and when he landed at the base of the pedestrian bridge, the girl had also picked up speed. She stumbled once as she ran over and flailed both arms to get her balance before stopping in front of him.

Although they were only about a meter apart now, suddenly

he had no words. *Um, I guess first I should say something about the duel, or maybe apologize for not being able to invite her to the curry meeting yesterday, or no, wait, first, I should say hello—* Round and round his thoughts went.

"Oh! Um. Before, my brother. Was really rude." The thin voice came from the girl's mouth, and her slightly curly hair was thrown forward as she bowed.

"Huh? No, not at all. I mean, I should be the one apologizing for yesterday!"

They both bowed low, and the crowns of their heads brushed against each other. Panicking that this was no longer an apology, but an attack, Haruyuki yanked his body back upright and moved to take a step back.

The girl grabbed onto his schoolbag, and after she, too, righted herself, Rin Kusakabe smiled faintly, eyes teary.

The reason she had gotten off the bus was apparently because she wanted to apologize for the way Ash Roller had been acting in the duel. Naturally, she would have to get on the next bus heading to Shibuya, so Haruyuki suggested they go back to the bus stop and talk.

"Um, are you okay? For time?"

"I'm fine. I've still got plenty of time before they close the school gates." As he spoke, he checked the bus information displayed in his field of view. According to the schedule, the next bus would arrive in four minutes. They wouldn't be able to talk for very long, but it was enough time to apologize again.

He turned to Rin again, still clutching his schoolbag, and carefully lowered his head once more. "Kusakabe, I'm really sorry about yesterday. I wanted to invite you, too, but...I couldn't exactly make you meet the senior members of Prominence in the real..."

"N-no, Master explained. The situation to me, and I. Agreed. But my brother just went ahead and. Did that." Her eyes grew increasingly teary as she spoke. Around her neck was a largish metallic gray Neurolinker, a long crack like a lightning bolt in the exterior shell.

It was the Neurolinker her older brother Rinta, the motorcycle racer, had used. She could only duel as a Burst Linker when she was wearing it. When she took it off and put on her own Neurolinker immediately after the duel, her memories of the duel time gradually grew hazy and all but disappeared within half a day, becoming something that had happened in a dream. Put another way, only now could Rin could remember the fine details of what Ash had said and done in the duel.

"Ah, ha-ha-ha! He's a good brother. And a serious duel like that is fun sometimes, too. It ended with that big show, too, so the Gallery was pretty pleased."

"R...eally?"

Faced with her teary, dubious gaze and upturned grayish eyes, Haruyuki couldn't stop his respiration rate, pulse, and temperature from all spiking dramatically. A mere five days earlier, Rin Kusakabe had told him clearly, pressed completely up against him so that there was no room for him to have misheard: "I like you."

W-well, that was because I was on the brink of vanishing from the Accelerated World together with the armor. Basically, talk under martial law goes back to civilian control when things are normal.

The ambiguous declaration calmed him to some extent, and he bobbed his head up and down. "R-really. I'm always the most excited about duels with Ash. The win rate's exactly fifty-fifty, and I can think of all kinds of strategies in advance because he's an opponent I know really well."

"You. Can?" Head hanging deeply, Rin's lovely lips moved in the shape of "I'm so happy," and his heart once again skipped several beats.

However, the problem was when Rin's emotions swelled, her older brother Ash in the Accelerated World remembered it with fairly high fidelity. If they stayed here facing each other like this, he might go into berserker mode again—"You damned crow! Touching my baby sis!"—in the next duel. Although Ash had gotten angry this time at the fact that Haruyuki had stayed away from Rin, not inviting her over for curry, so either way it was ridiculous...

His thoughts had reached this point when he remembered something. "Oh, right! Kusakabe?"

"...Yes?" Rin lifted her face.

"My school festival's this Sunday, so...if you have time, do you want to come?" he asked, working hard to sound as casual as possible. "I have some extra invitations."

Instantly, Rin's face lit up, although her voice became even weaker for some reason. "Are you. Sure? Um, I do. Want to go, I really. Want to go."

He nodded and smiled in return, but a cold sweat abruptly ran down his back. Inviting a girl anywhere was, for Haruyuki, the most difficult mission in the real world. Even asking Chiyuri, whom he had known since they were born, to tag-team with him in a duel after school required thirty minutes of advance mental preparation.

Fortunately, with perfect timing, an icon popped up to notify him of the bus's arrival. When he looked up at the road, the light green body of the vehicle jutted out from the row of passenger vehicles.

"O-okay, I'll mail you the details later. Say hi to your brother for me." That last part was for both Ash Roller in the Accelerated World and Rinta Kusakabe in the real world, whom Rin went to visit in the hospital every day after school. Apparently understanding this, Rin nodded and reluctantly let go of Haruyuki's bag.

She started to turn toward the approaching bus, but then stopped and said, unexpectedly, "Um. Next, I'm thinking of. Putting four missiles on the. Motorcycle."

Gulp.

Shrinking back into himself, Haruyuki somehow managed to answer with a smile. "Th-that'll be nice, won't it? Really nice."

A bright grin instantly spread across her face, and after waving lightly, she got on the bus waiting before them. He watched as the large vehicle drove off accompanied by the low whine of the motor, and then he let out another long sigh.

He had wrestled a little the previous night with whether or not to invite Rin to the school festival when it had absolutely nothing to do with Brain Burst; but when he thought about it as easing Ash's anger, he could maybe attach a real reason to the invitation. Maybe. At any rate, Ash was a solid member of the large Legion Great Wall, and maintaining friendly relations was a critical mission. Definitely.

If there was one problem, it was that the school festival at Umesato was not just displays and presentations in the real-world classrooms and gyms; they were also working hard on a full-dive event on the local net. A connection to the local net was essential to truly enjoy the school festival, but giving a Burst Linker from another Legion that permission was a bit of an issue in terms of the security of the entire Legion.

"But, well, Kusakabe already knows all of us in the real anyway." So that "no-problemo'd" it, Haruyuki decided, climbing the escalator back up to the pedestrian bridge.

He slipped through the gates five minutes before they closed, and when he entered eighth grade class C, Takumu and Chiyuri were already in their seats.

The kendo team and the track team were coming up on tournaments in the middle of July, so they both left for school more than an hour earlier than Haruyuki did for morning practice. After school, they also took part in Legion missions when practice was over, and Haruyuki honestly worried that they were pushing themselves too hard.

However, they said the experience of the Accelerated World was useful in their team activities. And naturally, though not in the sense that they would use acceleration in the middle of a meet. The ability to concentrate, the intellectual aspects—in

other words, the positive mental effects—were nothing to sneeze at. Taku often said that when he remembered the battle with Dusk Taker, he didn't flinch in the face of any opponent, even if that opponent was a champion. However, the fact that Dusk Taker, Seiji Nomi, still trained hard with Takumu as a seventh-grade member of the Umesato kendo team...Haruyuki did actually have some complicated feelings when he heard about that.

At any rate, it wasn't as though Haruyuki didn't want to make use of whatever it was he learned in Brain Burst out in the real world, but given that he was in the Animal Care Club, rather than a sports team or some cultural club, it was fairly difficult to do that. In fact, he had actually learned mental preparedness when flying in the Accelerated World from Hoo, the northern white-faced owl in the animal hutch.

That's okay, though. My goal is the same as Kuroyukihime's: to see the ending of Brain Burst. All the duels, all the time I spend in the Accelerated World is for that purpose. I can't forget that the objective to gain the Theoretical Mirror ability, attack the Archangel Metatron, and destroy the ISS kit main body in Tokyo Midtown Tower is, in the end, connected to that horizon, he told himself as he took his seat just as the first bell rang.

His homeroom teacher, Sugeno, came in through the door at the front, and the student on classroom helper duty that day gave the order to stand and bow. Haruyuki's thoughts, which threatened to wander off into the Accelerated World, were pulled back, and he called out "Good morning" with the rest of his classmates.

7

Snap open.

Peek, snap shut.

After repeating this series of actions ten or so times, Haruyuki groaned quietly. He was sitting on a wooden bench placed just that week in front of the animal hutch at the western edge of Umesato's rear yard. It wasn't new—for more than ten years, it had gone without use in the storeroom of the second school building, but it was solidly built. Her Excellency the vice president of the student council had neatly manipulated the list of furnishings on the school server and bestowed it upon the Animal Care Club. The branches of a camphor tree stretched out above his head, so he wouldn't get wet in a little rain shower.

He had already finished changing the paper spread out in the animal hutch and cleaning the water tub, and the owl Hoo was drowsily sitting on the perch on the other side of the wire mesh. After glancing at him, Haruyuki went again to open the thin tool in the palm of his hand...

"Prez, sorry. You done cleaning already?"

The voice suddenly flew into his ears, and he snapped to attention on the bench. The object in his hand tumbled to the ground in reaction, and a pale hand scooped it up before he could. Unable to immediately accept the proffered item—a small mirror with the Umesato crest on the case that he had bought at the school shop over lunch—he blinked rapidly for a moment.

"What's wrong?" Still holding the mirror, speaking in a doubtful voice, was another member of the Animal Care Club, eighth grade class B's Reina Izeki. Just as the long hair with ringlets, the sharp eyeliner, and the decorated Neurolinker indicated, she normally belonged to a caste far, far away from Haruyuki.

Why's someone like you got a mirror? He had unconsciously expected her to say something like that, but Reina simply cocked her head. Thinking that if he was asked that question, he would say that it was to send an SOS by reflecting sunlight if he were shipwrecked, Haruyuki moved his stiff right hand to take the mirror.

"Th-thanks, Izeki," he said hoarsely, and quickly tucked it away in the pocket of his uniform.

"Yup," she responded briefly before turning toward the hutch and waving brightly at Hoo. The owl conscientiously flapped its wings restlessly and deliberately and returned the greeting.

"Oh yeah, so what're we gonna show at the school festival?" Reina turned around and asked.

It took him a second and a half to realize that by "we" she meant the Animal Care Club. "Oh...Y-yeah. I thought we'd borrow an empty classroom and have the visitors take a look at Hoo, but he only just moved here. So I figured maybe it would be too stressful to be seen by a bunch of people, and I gave up on that for this year."

"Hmm, that's our prez." She nodded as if agreeing with him, and then took a few steps before dropping down on the bench. She stared at Haruyuki out of the corner of her eye, a strangely meaningful smile crossing her face. "So why were you staring at that mirror? Maybe you've got a date after this?"

"N-n-n-no!" Waving both hands wildly, he seriously considered whether or not he should put into practice the excuse from before.

But before he could, Reina nodded as if to say "I won't tell anyone," and then added, as if it had just popped into her mind, "But the mirrors they sell here are acrylic, so I wouldn't really recommend them, you know."

"Huh? A-acrylic? What's that?"

"Like…it's obviously plastic. Here, lemme look."

Having been thus told, Haruyuki had no choice but to pull the mirror out of his pocket and open it.

"Here." Reina tapped the surface of the mirror with a long-ish fingernail. "If this is acrylic, it distorts, and the color kinda changes, too." She dug around in her bag, which was sitting at the base of the bench, and pulled out a portable mirror that was clearly top quality. Deftly flipping it open with one hand, she offered it to Haruyuki. "This is high-precision colored glass. See how they're different?"

Obediently, Haruyuki looked back and forth between the mirror with the school crest in his left hand and the one with the brand-name logo in his right.

The reason he had been opening and closing the compact mirror over and over a few minutes earlier was because when he tried to look at the mirror, he necessarily saw his own round face. But for the moment, he forgot that fear and compared the round face that appeared in the two mirrors.

"Oh…Wow, they're totally different." The quality of the images on the left and one on the right were so different that it made him cry out involuntarily in admiration. The mirror on the left had a cheap coloring to it, like it was coming through colorless sheet plastic, while in contrast, the mirror on the right was so clear, he could almost believe that he was looking at the real thing with his own eyes.

While he looked back and forth between the two, Haruyuki got a prickly sensation in the core of his head like he was approaching something really important. In other words, a mirror was—the more the mirror…

But when he had managed to get that far in his thoughts, the sensation disappeared from his head. He lifted his gaze, and Reina explained further.

"It's, like, different, right? I mean, forget the distortion. You don't want the color to be different when you're putting on makeup. Those huge mirrors at salons and stuff, they cost like fifty thousand."

"...I—I get it." This made a deep kind of sense and also reconfirmed that he really had no need for something like this. He returned the expensive mirror in his right hand to Reina.

"So, Prez, who's you going out with?"

"I—I told you, it's not like that!"

"Oh, maybe the super prez?" The "super president" Reina referred to was the president who surpassed the club president, just as she noted—in other words, the legitimate owner of Hoo and the shadow ruler of the Animal Care Club. "Hmm, I dunno. Like, fourth grade's kinda dodgy?"

"N-n-n-n-n-n-n—!"

"Oh, here she is."

He jerked his head up and saw a small form walking across the rear yard from the direction of the school gates. He didn't need to see the white uniform dress, the brown backpack, and the right hand carrying a bag to know that it was the Super President of the Umesato Animal Care Club, Utai Shinomiya.

"Heeeey, super prez! So, like, just now, the prez..."

"No— Nooooooo!"

At the same time as Haruyuki shrieked, Hoo, detecting Utai nearby, began to beat his wings loudly.

Once the highlight of the club work—feeding time—was over, Reina signed the log file and headed home. "'Kay, you guys take your time!"

UI> What does she mean "take our time"? Utai typed, in curiosity.

"M-maybe uploading the log? I mean, like the school net traffic, it's like, you know," he tried to explain awkwardly as he wiped the sweat from his brow.

Perhaps kind enough to be fooled by this, Utai nodded with an ambiguous look on her face and started to clean up the cooler she had set on the bench.

As he watched her small back, a voice came back to life in his ears: *His name is Mirror Masker. He's Ardor Maiden's...parent.*

Haruyuki had thought he would ask Utai directly about what Niko had told him once the work for the club was done that day. But now that he actually had the chance, he couldn't quite manage to bring it up.

When he thought about it, he had come all this way not having the slightest idea about the parents of the three veteran Burst Linkers in Nega Nebulus—Kuroyukihime, Fuko, and Utai. Kuroyukihime had told him before that she would talk to him about her parent when the time came that she could, and he had made an effort to never touch on it again. But he hadn't even thought about discovering the parents of Fuko and Utai, much less ask about them.

One thing he could say was that if they were still close with their parents, it wouldn't have been particularly strange for them to introduce him to them. Given that not only had he not been introduced, he hadn't even been told their names, there had to have been a reason why they couldn't or why they didn't want to. Thus, Haruyuki continued to hesitate for a long time as he stared at Utai's back.

Almost as if she sensed this, Utai stopped her cleaning and looked back at him. With eyes that had a faint hint of crimson racing through the irises, she looked directly into his eyes.

"Um..." As if he'd been sucked into those clear eyes, brief words spilled from his mouth. "Shinomiya, your..."

But he didn't give voice to the rest. Utai kept staring quietly at his face, and then finally, she moved her small hands, and text scrolled slowly across his virtual desktop. UI> ARITA, YOU ALREADY KNOW, DON'T YOU? ABOUT MY PARENT.

Swallowing his breath and not letting it out again for a while,

Haruyuki steadied himself and nodded. "Yeah. The Red King told me yesterday. She said your parent was the creator of the Theoretical Mirror ability."

Utai didn't react immediately. After a silence of five seconds or so, a faint smile crossed her peach-colored lips.

UI> NIKO WAS BEING CONSIDERATE OF ME. AND SACCHI AND FU, TOO. PLEASE DON'T BLAME THEM FOR NOT SAYING ANYTHING YESTERDAY. THEY WERE WAITING FOR ME TO MAKE A DECISION. AND NIKO, THROUGH YOU, IS GIVING ME A LITTLE PUSH.

Unable to immediately grasp the meaning of this, Haruyuki reread the text displayed on his virtual desktop several times. And then he finally understood: Utai did actually have a thick, high wall in her heart when it came to her own parent. Naturally, Kuroyukihime and Fuko had guessed at this situation, but Niko had, too. She had struggled with it, and then made a decision. By telling Haruyuki the truth, she would make Utai take a step forward.

Pursing his lips, Haruyuki waited.

After another few seconds, Utai tapped at her keyboard with resolute fingers, but the text she sent to him was far heavier than anything he had expected.

UI> MY PARENT, MIRROR MASKER, IS ACTUALLY MY OLDER BROTHER. BUT MY OLDER BROTHER IS NO LONGER IN THE ACCEL-ERATED WORLD. She paused momentarily.

UI> NOR IN THE REAL WORLD.

After putting everything away, Utai sat Haruyuki down on the empty bench and then sat down next to him. The slightly over-cast sky was colored a pale orange. The voices of the baseball team echoed faintly from the grounds. And although there were still a large number of students in the school busy with preparations for the school festival, that activity didn't reach the rear yard.

Dropping his gaze to the mossy ground, Haruyuki couldn't decide what to say—or even if he should say anything at all. The text Utai had typed out a few minutes earlier was still displayed in the chat window on his virtual desktop. No matter how many times he read it, the meaning was clear: Utai's parent Burst Linker was her real older brother, and he was no longer alive. And not in the sense of losing all his points and exiting the Accelerated World. He had really died in the real world.

Haruyuki was fourteen that year, but he had never experienced the death of anyone close to him. The closest thing he'd experienced to it was the time Kuroyukihime had sustained serious injuries the year before, protecting him from a car running wild. Just remembering the night he had spent in the hallway of the hospital praying for her recovery made his heart beat faster and sweat ooze from his palms.

But what if...He didn't want to think about it, but what if they hadn't been able to save her then? Haruyuki couldn't even imagine where he would be now. At the very least, he wouldn't be laughing and having fun with duels every day like he was now.

UI> I AM SORRY.

A single line of text scrolled across the chat window abruptly, and Haruyuki blinked. Before he could muster some kind of reaction, Utai's fingers were tapping at the lap of her white skirt once more.

UI> I KNEW THAT IT WOULD ONLY TROUBLE YOU IF I DIDN'T SAY SOMETHING. BUT IN MY HEAD, EVERYTHING WAS SUCH A JUMBLE.

"Th-there was no rush. I mean, if you didn't want to, you didn't have to say anything." The words fell from Haruyuki's lips. "I mean, I'm sorry for not saying anything. I'm four years older, but...I couldn't say anything..."

UI> WELL THEN, I AM TWO LEVELS HIGHER, AFTER ALL.

He unconsciously turned his gaze toward her at this about-face; on Utai's face was the usual gentle smile. But beneath it, a faint desolateness seemed to bleed through.

Abruptly, a certain scene came back to life in Haruyuki's mind. It was the time he and Utai had charged into the Castle in the Unlimited Neutral Field. When they had slipped past the eyes of the patrolling soldier Enemies and successfully infiltrated the inner sanctuary, Ardor Maiden had said, "It's just that since we got here, I've steadily felt more and more like I could rely on you, C. Almost like…my older brother." To this, Haruyuki had responded, "Mei, you have an older brother? What grade's he in?" But Utai hadn't answered; she'd just smiled sadly instead.

As if she had seen through with her wide eyes to the memory that Haruyuki called up, Utai moved her fingers gently.

UI> WITH YOUR ARMOR COLOR, YOU REALLY DID RESEMBLE HIM QUITE A BIT THAT TIME. MY OLDER BROTHER, HE ALWAYS GUIDED ME, GENTLY BUT FIRMLY…MIRROR MASKER. WHICH IS EXACTLY WHY…I WAS FEARFUL PERHAPS. OF YOU APPROACHING MY BROTHER ANY FURTHER BY OBTAINING THE THEORETICAL MIRROR ABILITY.

"Shinomiya…"

UI> ONCE AGAIN, I MUST APOLOGIZE TO YOU, ARITA. I KNEW RIGHT FROM THE START. THAT SIMPLY EXPOSING YOURSELF TO A POWERFUL LIGHT TECHNIQUE WOULD NOT ALLOW YOU TO GAIN THE POWER YOU SEEK. BECAUSE THE MIRROR THAT WAS IN MY BROTHER'S HEART IS NOT A PHYSICAL PRESENCE MADE OF GLASS AND SILVER.

The instant he read this, Haruyuki felt something spark deep in his head. He caught hold of the tail of the thought that had begun to form when he compared the mirror he bought at the shop and the mirror Reina Izeki had lent him maybe half an hour earlier, and pulled on that thought cautiously.

"Yeah…I think I get that, sort of. A mirror…the more perfect it is, the less it's a 'thing.' I mean, if there was a mirror that could completely reflect all light, you wouldn't actually be able to see it, right? You'd just see the other things reflected there. So then… um, uh…"

Once again, he reached the limits of his verbal prowess, but Utai opened her eyes slightly wider, a smile with a different nuance crossing on her face.

UI> I'm surprised. You've managed to reach that point all under your own power, hmm?

"Huh…? Th-that point? What point?" he unconsciously asked the stupid question, but Utai's fingers didn't move for a while, the smile still lingering on her lips.

Finally, she nodded, as if having made some kind of decision, and tapped on the lap of her skirt. *Tak, tak, tak, tak.*

UI> Arita. Do you want to see with your own eyes? The mirror that my brother had lodged in his heart?

The question was abrupt, and it was hard for him to grasp entirely what it meant, but Haruyuki nodded deeply. "Yeah. I do. I feel like if I saw it, I could make it there."

UI> Understood. Well then, shall we go?

"Go?" Haruyuki asked. "To the Unlimited Neutral Field?"

Utai was briefly puzzled and then shook her head decisively.

UI> No. To my house in the real world. We might be a little late getting in, so I think you'd better leave a message for your household.

8

Roughly speaking, Tokyo's Suginami Ward was a diamond shape that leaned downward to the right. The Koenji area, where Haruyuki's condo and Umesato Junior High were located, sat on the eastern corner of the diamond. If you went west from there, you reached the Asagaya housing complex where Kuroyukihime lived. To the southwest was the Matsunoki area, where the elementary school Utai attended was. He was pretty sure that the Omiya area, to the south of that, was Utai's home address.

Walking alongside her in her white uniform on the brick promenade that stretched south from Umesato, Haruyuki remembered that they had done the same thing on the day they first met. That time, when they entered the Omiya area, they sat down on a bench placed along the promenade and had a tag-team duel. Their opponents had been Bush Utan and Olive Grab from the Green Legion. In the middle of the battle, Utan had activated the power of the ISS kit, pushing Haruyuki to his wits' end, but Utai had repelled Olive, who was using the same power, and emerged completely unscathed before calling up an enormous storm of flames and burning Utan to a crisp.

The same thing couldn't possibly happen again today. The thought flickered through his mind, but fortunately, that day, she didn't say PLEASE SHOW ME YOUR ACTUAL ABILITIES, but instead continued walking. Haruyuki was carrying the bag with Hoo's dinner set in it, but even taking that away, Utai's pace was so quick you almost couldn't feel the difference in their heights. Her back was perfectly straight, and the way she moved her feet smoothly forward, it looked as though she had had some kind of footwork training.

The address display on his virtual desktop's navigation map changed to Omiya 1-choume, and once they had gone another two hundred meters or so, they veered east off the promenade. Around them was a residential neighborhood full of old houses, and marks indicating shrines and temples popped up all over the place on the map.

"This...is totally different from around Koenji," Haruyuki murmured unconsciously, and Utai nodded sharply.

UI> WHEN I WAS LITTLE, I USED TO BE AFRAID TO WALK AROUND HERE BY MYSELF AT NIGHT.

And now that Utai, who was currently around ten years old, had said this, Haruyuki, being four years older, couldn't very well say, "It's scary walking with even the two of us." However, the way the ancient trees rustled in the warm breeze beyond the walls running along both sides of them—the noise of the tree-tops honestly made him nervous, like in a Graveyard stage.

Even though it was still only six, there wasn't a soul on the road. If there hadn't been the evenly spaced row of streetlights, which doubled as social camera pillars, he would have wondered if he hadn't been sucked back fifty years in time. The pair walked silently along the road that wasn't quite straight, and finally, right around the time when Haruyuki's sense of direction was starting to get screwed up even with the navigation map, ancient-looking *sukiya*-style gates appeared on the right side of the road.

Made of dark, natural wood, the gates had traditional clay tiles on their roof. The doors were closed tightly, so that there was no way to peek inside. But as proof that this was no ordinary citizen's home, a large sign hung on the pillar on the right side.

Since Utai stopped in front of the gate, Haruyuki also came to a stop and looked up at the sign. The characters, in a magnificent black block style, read SUGINAMI NOH.

"Suginami...Noh?" he read aloud, and Utai nodded sharply.

UI> THIS IS MY HOUSE. PLEASE COME THIS WAY, she quickly typed out, before she walked over to a metal inset-door apparently for general use and waved her left hand. Naturally, she was operating her virtual desktop, but it looked almost like she gave an order using supernatural powers; the heavy sound of the door unlocking echoed in the air.

She pushed open the door and urged Haruyuki through it. Getting nervous at this late stage, he slipped through the door with a quick "Thanks for having me"—only to have his first glance at what lay on the other side make his jaw drop.

It was almost like the Castle inside the Unlimited Neutral Field. Well, of course, it wasn't on the same scale, but the way the stately Japanese-style mansion spread out beyond massive trees that were who knew how many hundreds of years old seemed highly otherworldly. And there were even two buildings! On the right was a bungalow residence. And on the left, a great hall soared up, one that at first glance looked like a shrine. That was probably the Noh stage noted on the sign out front.

The door locked once more, and Utai came up beside him.

"Shinomiya—so, like, 'Noh'...um...is that like Kabuki and stuff?" Haruyuki asked reverently. The question was exceedingly vague, but Utai smiled and nodded.

UI> IT IS INDEED SIMILARLY A TRADITIONAL ART LIKE KABUKI. I'M SURPRISED YOU KNOW IT.

"S-sorry, that's about all I know," he apologized, shrinking into himself, before timidly asking another question. "So what's the difference between Noh and Kabuki?" Obviously, if he secretly searched online from his virtual desktop or something, he could have found a page explaining this, but pretending to know anything using this sort of stopgap information would have been deeply pathetic if he was found out. Or rather, he had no doubt he *would* have been found out by Utai, and right away at that. Better to simply confess his ignorance, he decided.

UI >THE BORING ONE IS NOH, AND THE SILLY ONE IS KABUKI, IS WHAT FU SAYS. Seeing Haruyuki's dumbfounded expression, Utai exploded into soundless laughter like a gentle breeze and quickly continued typing.

UI> I'LL PROPERLY EXPLAIN THE DIFFERENCE ON THE STAGE. COME THIS WAY.

The "stage" she mentioned was indeed the wooden hall standing on the west side of the site. As they approached, he saw that it was actually a fairly strange structure. The two different-size buildings were connected by a passageway, but the larger building was open on three sides, and there was a magnificent painting of pine trees on a wooden wall directly to the back. Overall, it was quite old, and it gave the impression of not being used very often. A passageway with a roof stretched out about ten meters diagonally from the left inside the building and connected with the smaller building.

They passed through the garden, which was like a deep forest, and then went around to the back of the small building, where there was a sliding door entrance. Utai took an old-fashioned metal key out of the pocket of her uniform and unlocked it. She quietly pulled it open using both hands and nodded at Haruyuki.

"Th-thanks for having me," he said for the second time, and slipped through the entryway. Utai followed him and firmly closed the old-fashioned sliding door before turning on a light switch on the wall.

The instant the white incandescent lights—also old style—on the ceiling came on, Haruyuki gasped. It was such a luxurious space. It couldn't have been more than ten square meters, but the ceiling, walls, floor, and all the furnishings were polished natural wood. Perhaps this had been normal back when the building had been built, but if someone wanted to build the same room new now, it would have cost some real money.

Taking her shoes off at the step up into the room, Utai took two pairs of slippers out of the shoe caddy to the side and offered one pair to Haruyuki. He thanked her and stepped up into the room.

The furnishings included an old-fashioned bureau against the right wall and a backless seat on the floor; and directly in front of him, a large piece of furniture, the true nature of which was unknown to him. To the left, there was a stand of closed-up folding-screen panels, and it seemed that it alone was fairly new, when compared with the other objects.

As he whirled his head around the room, text flowed slowly across the chat window. UI> THIS IS THE STAGE'S *KAGAMI NO MA*, OR MIRROR ROOM.

After staring at this one sentence for a while, Haruyuki turned to face Utai and asked quietly, "Mirror...room?"

UI> YES. I'LL SHOW YOU NOW. PLEASE HAVE A SEAT ON THAT CHAIR.

He did as she urged and took a few steps to lower himself onto the round wooden stool. Immediately before him was the large mysterious furnishing. Utai walked toward this, undid the metal clasp on the side surface, and then pulled the panel immediately in front from the right to left, opening it. Next, she opened the panel beneath—from the left to the right—and stepped back behind Haruyuki.

So that's not furniture; it's a door, maybe? he wondered for a brief moment. He understood it wasn't a door the instant he locked eyes with the junior high school boy with a round face sitting before him. Reflexively, he threw his head back, and the boy in front of him tilted his body in exactly the same way. Both of them simultaneously were supported from behind by an elementary school girl, thus narrowly avoiding falling off their chair.

There couldn't have been more than one of these stupid, round-type junior high students. Which meant that what Haruyuki was looking at was also Haruyuki. The mysterious furnishing was an absurdly large, three-sided mirror.

Although normally he couldn't stand to look at his own self in the mirror for more than a second, at that moment alone,

Haruyuki was so surprised that he continued to stare intently. He had never before seen such a large, impressive mirror. The biggest mirror in the Arita household was the full-length mirror in his mother's room, but this was easily more than ten times as large as that. It was almost like a small room where three of the walls were made of mirror.

"......"

After staring soundlessly for more than ten seconds, Haruyuki finally realized that its size wasn't the three-sided mirror's only distinct feature. Its quality as a mirror—the clarity of the surface glass, the reflectance of the silver layer substrate—was incredible. The quality was greater than even the high-precision mirror that Reina Izeki had lent him at school. In fact, rather than a mirror, it seemed like an entrance to another world, one where left and right were reversed.

UI> THERE ARE A VARIETY OF DIFFERENCES BETWEEN NOH AND KABUKI, BUT... The text appeared soundlessly in the holo window, the only thing this mirror didn't reflect. UI> ONE OF THE BIGGEST DIFFERENCES IS THAT WHILE KABUKI ACTORS PAINT THEIR OWN FACES TO PERFORM, IN NOH, THEY WEAR A MASK CALLED AN OMOTE.

After taking a few seconds to digest this text, Haruyuki murmured, "Oh, really? So then that's the Noh mask you hear about, huh?"

UI> THAT'S EXACTLY RIGHT. THE NOH ACTOR WEARING THE OMOTE BLENDS HIS CONSCIOUSNESS WITH THE MASK TO BECOME SOMETHING NOT HUMAN AND DANCES AND SINGS. TO REACH THAT STATE OF MIND, THEY FOCUS THEIR MENTAL ENERGIES HERE IN THE MIRROR ROOM. THE LARGE MIRROR YOU'RE LOOKING AT IS THE BOUNDARY BETWEEN THIS WORLD AND THE OTHER WORLD.

"The boundary..." That sensation assaulted him again, the certainty and impatience that he was getting quite close to something important. Unconsciously, he stood up from the chair and took one step, then another toward the mirror.

The figure of himself approaching in tandem shimmered

like the surface of water. Before he knew it, standing there was his other self, body wrapped in silver armor, face hidden by an opaque helmet: Silver Crow. Haruyuki raised his right hand, and Crow similarly moved his. The tips of their fingers gradually drew near each other, and just as they were on the verge of touching, his shirt was yanked from behind, and Haruyuki came back to himself with a gasp.

During the time it took him to blink once, the duel avatar in the mirror disappeared and the pudgy junior high boy returned. Turning around, he saw Utai smiling as she clutched his shirt. She deftly typed with just her right hand.

UI> You've looked at this enough. We'll continue this conversation in my room.

Leaving the mirror room, the two of them slipped through the grove of trees once more and headed for the main building on the east side of the site. While they walked, the spacey feeling in his head faded, but in its place, he felt the sharp pain of tension in his stomach. If they ran into Utai's family, how on earth should he introduce himself? A fourth grader and an eighth grader were separated enough in age that if they were understood in the worst possible way, he could be reported or even arrested.

As he ran various simulations in his head, Utai noted, as if seeing through him, UI> It's all right. Grandfather and Father are both out. When they have a big performance, they don't come home very often.

"P-performance? A Noh play?"

UI> Yes.

At this response, he belatedly understood. Given the fact that she had a large Noh stage at her house and that her grandfather and father were both Noh performers, Utai Shinomiya wasn't simply taking Noh lessons or anything; she was the child of a Noh house. And her late brother—Mirror Masker—was, too.

Haruyuki fell silent once more, and Utai didn't attempt to say anything else, but rather silently opened the door to the main house.

The room she led him to didn't actually have wooden walls and floors, but it was still a rarity, a Japanese-style room with tatami mats. The furnishings were basically a wooden Japanese-style writing desk, a bureau, and a bookshelf; there was no bed. Which probably meant that Utai spread a futon out and slept on the floor. For Haruyuki, it was a completely unknown sleep environment.

Utai set her backpack down on the shelf and offered him a floor cushion before saying—well, writing—PLEASE EXCUSE ME A MOMENT and leaving the room.

When he thought about it, he probably hadn't used a proper floor cushion for the last few years. Although he tried to take on the challenge of sitting formally on his knees, he got the sense of serious damage in his legs after ten seconds. Distributing his weight to the left and right, he endured the pain, but fortunately, Utai returned in about three minutes with a tray.

The moment she saw Haruyuki's posture, she appeared to stifle a laugh. She first set down the tray on the desk and then moved both hands. UI> PLEASE MAKE YOURSELF COMFORTABLE.

"R-right. Well, then I'll gratefully accept your...kindness— Ow, ow..." His numb legs quickly crumpled into a cross-legged posture, and he let out a sigh of relief. Before him, Utai sat neatly in the formal kneeling position. Her movements were also neat and contained as she set out the cold tea poured into faceted glasses and the small plate of *mizuyokan* sweet bean jelly.

"Th-thanks."

She urged him on with a gesture, so he brought the cold tea to his mouth. Apparently, it was green tea made with real tea leaves and then cooled; there was a faint sweetness to the drink even in the midst of its crisp bitterness. He enjoyed the flavor, so totally different from tea from a plastic bottle, for a while before he realized something.

The calm that this girl Utai Shinomiya possessed, very uncharacteristic of her ten years of age, was not something that was only cultivated by her being a Burst Linker. The fact that she had been born and raised in this large, traditionally Japanese house had given form to the girl now and to the duel avatar Ardor Maiden. Once he understood this, there was only a single thing this house had in common with his own home on the twenty-third floor of a skyscraper condo in northern Koenji: It was quiet. The lonely silence of no one to say "welcome home" when the child returned from school.

"Um…Shinomiya. What about the other people in your house?" he asked timidly.

After taking a sip of her own tea, Utai typed on the desk. UI> I MENTIONED THIS BEFORE, BUT MY GRANDFATHER, FATHER, AND OLDER BROTHER ARE CURRENTLY RESIDING IN KYOTO FOR A PERFORMANCE. MY MOTHER ALSO WORKS, SO SHE DOESN'T COME HOME UNTIL VERY LATE AT NIGHT.

"Huh…So then it's just you right now?"

UI> THERE IS SOMEONE WHO TAKES CARE OF THE HOUSE, BUT THEY'LL BE GOING HOME SOON.

"Th-they will?" He had been totally swallowed up by the atmosphere until that point, but putting aside all the various special circumstances, this was basically nothing other than being alone in a house with a girl, wasn't it? As he belatedly realized this, his breathing and heart rate started to accelerate, but he managed to summon his fighting spirit to maintain the status quo. The night before, not only had he been alone with her, but Niko had snored softly in the bed right next to him. And a few days before that, he had also stayed over at Kuroyukihime's house. He should have accumulated enough experience points not to panic here and now. Probably.

Unaware of this turmoil within him—or if she was aware of it, she didn't show it on her face—Utai brought some *mizuyokan* to her mouth with a bamboo teaspoon. When Haruyuki did the same, the chilled, smooth jellied dessert slipped down his throat and cooled his thoughts.

In her explanation before, Utai had typed *older brother*. Which meant… "Do—did you have two older brothers?" he asked quietly, and the ponytail swung lightly.

UI> Yes. The oldest is nine years above me, so we didn't really play together very much. And the younger one... my brother Kyoya, who taught me about the Accelerated World, he was four years older than me. He passed away three years ago...I was seven and he was eleven.

A typing master far beyond Haruyuki, Utai still tapped her fingers at the desk, awkwardly this time. Her head was hanging, and he couldn't see the look on her face. He tried to stop her with a "that's enough," but before he could, her slender fingers started moving again.

UI> In the world of Noh theater...And it's the same in Kabuki and Kyogen as well. children born into families who perform are not given a choice.

"Choice?"

UI> Whether to go into the world of entertainment or not. The child cannot choose this. From the time you can remember, you are in contact with the art of your parents and siblings and relatives. It's close to you, you study it, and then at a mere four or five years of age, you first step onto the stage as a KOKATA child actor. Everything up to this point is already decided when you are born into a Noh family.

"F-from the time you're that little?" Haruyuki asked, dumbfounded. He tried to remember what he had been doing when he was four years old, but he only had a hazy memory of racing around the playground of his kindergarten.

Utai lifted her face for a mere instant and showed him a faint smile before continuing. UI> Naturally, not all children proceed like this down the path of Noh performer. In fact, the children who continue are actually in the minority. You can perform as a KOKATA until around the time you start junior high, but I think more than half the children leave the stage before that time. But my older brother did not stop. And Kyoya and I also had no

INTENTION OF STOPPING. ACTUALLY, MY BROTHER AND I LOVED THE WORLD OF NOH. THE TINY UNIVERSE OF THE STAGE....

Haruyuki continued to silently look at the cherry-pink characters spelled out haltingly. It wasn't as though he had immediately understood the world of Noh. He hadn't seen a play live, and he felt like he had glanced at a 2-D image in his social studies class, but maybe not. That was about it. And although it was quite belated at this point, he realized something:

When the shrine maiden of the conflagration, Ardor Maiden, activated her Incarnate technique, and therein danced and sang, that figure was itself Noh. Utai Shinomiya's form and abilities in the Accelerated World were intimately linked to the Noh performances she had been learning since before she could remember.

Once his thoughts had proceeded to this point, Haruyuki ran straight into a huge question. The duel avatar was the manifestation of mental scars. In which case, the crimson-and-white shrine maiden that was Utai's avatar had to have been generated from her own wounds. So that meant Utai's wounds were linked to the world of Noh that she so loved.

UI> WHEN I WAS THREE YEARS OLD, I STEPPED ONTO THE STAGE AS A *KOKATA* FOR THE FIRST TIME. I WAS STILL AN AGE WHEN I WAS MORE A BABY THAN A CHILD, BUT EVEN SO, I CLEARLY REMEMBER THE TENSION AND EMOTION OF THAT DAY.

Utai resumed her typing, and Haruyuki chased the text wordlessly.

UI> FROM THEN ON, I BELIEVED THAT I WOULD BECOME A NOH PERFORMER LIKE MY GRANDFATHER AND MY FATHER, AND I WORKED HARD IN MY LESSONS EVERY DAY. HOWEVER, THE DAY I STARTED ELEMENTARY SCHOOL, MY FATHER TOLD ME THAT I COULD ONLY BE A *KOKATA*. THAT ONCE I GREW UP I COULD NO LONGER ASCEND TO THE STAGE.

"What? Why? That's—" Haruyuki cried out unconsciously. That was awful. It was just too much, dragging a child into the world of entertainment whether she liked it or not, with no choice of her own, and then forcing her to quit after a few years.

But Utai smiled again as if to reassure him, and moved her fingers calmly. UI> It can't be helped. Because Kabuki and Kyogen...and Noh are the world of men. Did you know, for instance, that there are no women Kabuki actors?

When she said that, he realized the actors who played women in Kabuki were called *onnagata* precisely because they were not women.

UI> In recent years, there have been more than a few women Noh performers, but that depends on the school. In the school that our Shinomiya house belongs to, women are not allowed. Naturally, I was very sad when I learned this. Given that I would at some point no longer be able to stand on the stage, I considered giving up my lessons. But from the time I was little, this is all I've ever known, so I didn't know what else there was for me. It was then that my brother Kyoya showed me another spirit world. He was already a Burst Linker at the time, and he gave me Brain Burst.

She paused for a moment, and then her lithe fingers began to dance again.

UI> The mental scars that are the origin for Ardor Maiden...I myself can't put them clearly into words. But there's simply one thing: I believe that Maiden was born clad in the two colors of light crimson and white because there were two worlds, two selves within me from before I became a Burst Linker. It was the same with Kyoya's Mirror Masker. He possessed silver and white.

The "light crimson" in the middle of the text caught Haruyuki's eyes. Because the scarlet coloring of Ardor Maiden's lower half was actually a dark red. But the second half of her statement quickly pulled his attention away from that. "Silver...and white. So then...just his lower half was a metal color? So that can happen too, huh..."

UI> I ALSO HAVE NEVER SEEN IT ON ANYONE OTHER THAN MY BROTHER.

Utai's agreement sent him into thought. If Mirror Masker, the avatar with the Theoretical Mirror ability, was such a special avatar, then it seemed uncertain as to whether or not Silver Crow—who was also silver, but just a regular metal color overall—could actually acquire the ability. Just when he was about to hang his head dejectedly, Haruyuki shook it off. He had to focus on Utai's story at that moment, not himself. When he brought his attention back to the ad hoc window on his virtual desktop, the cursor began to move again with perfect timing.

UI> UNTIL THEN, I HAD ONLY HAD MY LESSONS EVERY DAY, SO I HAD NO FRIENDS WITH WHOM TO PLAY. SO FOR ME, THE ACCELERATED WORLD, WHERE I COULD MEET SO MANY BURST LINKERS, WAS A FUN, THRILLING PLACE. EACH DAY, THE PART OF ME THAT IS ARDOR MAIDEN COULD PUT ON THE *OMOTE* AND DANCE TO MY HEART'S CONTENT.

"Um. At the time, you were in first grade, right, Shinomiya? Weren't you…scared of dueling?" Haruyuki unconsciously interjected, and the girl, currently in fourth grade, grinned.

UI> IN NOH, THERE ARE A GREAT NUMBER OF PROGRAMS WITH HAUNTINGS AND KILLINGS AND TRANSFORMATIONS AND DISAPPEARANCES.

"I—I guess so."

UI> THE DUELS WERE FUN, AND EVERYONE I MET WAS SO KIND TO ME. BUT…CONTRARY TO MY BROTHER'S IDEA, THE MORE I DANCED IN THE ACCELERATED WORLD, THE STRONGER MY THOUGHTS ABOUT ANOTHER DIFFERENT WORLD, THE NOH STAGE, GREW. FOR ME, THE TWO WORLDS WERE THE SAME IN A CERTAIN SENSE. MY DESIRE TO EXPRESS ON THE NOH STAGE THE THINGS I NOTICED IN THE ACCELERATED WORLD, THAT I LEARNED, THE MENTAL STATE I REACHED, SIMPLY GREW.

"Right…In a way, your duel avatar is a perfect match, huh?"

UI> YES…I SUPPOSE SO. KYOYA ALSO SEEMED TO HAVE NOT ANTICIPATED IT WOULD BE TO THAT EXTENT. HE HAD GIVEN

ME BRAIN BURST TO MAKE ME FORGET THE STAGE, BUT HE SAW THAT IT HAD THE COMPLETE OPPOSITE EFFECT. AND HE TRIED TO TAKE RESPONSIBILITY FOR THAT. IT WAS A SUMMER DAY A YEAR AFTER I BECAME A BURST LINKER...SO IT WOULD HAVE BEEN THREE YEARS AGO NOW...

Here, Utai's fingers froze.

At some point, the sky beyond the window had grown red, and the color of the evening sun sneaking into the room also bled into her white uniform. The light wasn't on, so the room was increasingly gloomy, and the trees in the yard rustled like the sound of waves.

Head hanging deeply, Utai didn't so much as twitch for a long time, but then abruptly, she lifted her head and stared at Haruyuki with those eyes with traces of red running through them. Her ten fingers danced loosely, followed by black shadows.

UI> MY BROTHER KYOYA. HE WENT TO THE MIRROR ROOM I SHOWED YOU EARLIER TO ASK OF MY GRANDFATHER, THE HEAD OF THE SHINOIYA HOUSE OF THE KANZE SCHOOL, THE SEVENTH SEIGORO SHINOMIYA, TO PLEASE ALLOW ME TO FORMALLY WORK TOWARD BECOMING A NOH PERFORMER. BUT...THE RESPONSE WAS OBVIOUS. MY GRANDFATHER SHOOK HIS HEAD, SAYING IT WAS IMPOSSIBLE, AND MY BROTHER CONTINUED TO PLEAD WITH HIM, CRYING. EVEN WHEN I TOLD HIM IT WAS ENOUGH, TO STOP HIM, HE DID NOT WITHDRAW. HE WAS PUSHED ASIDE BY OUR OLDER BROTHER, WHO ALSO HAPPENED TO BE THERE...AND THEN THERE WAS AN ACCIDENT.

"Acci...dent?"

UI> KYOYA FELL ONTO THE FLOOR, AND ON TOP OF HIM...THE LARGE MIRROR OF THE MIRROR ROOM FELL ON HIM. THE MIRROR SHATTERED...AND THE SHARDS... Utai's fingers stopped again.

But Haruyuki could easily imagine it. Utai had said that at the time, her older brother Kyoya had been eleven, just a year older than she was now. If that enormous mirror fell on a child like that, the kind of disaster it would invite—yes, in fact, the *worst* result had indeed happened. Three years ago, Kyoya Shinomiya/

Mirror Masker had lost his young life in that room. That was what Utai was saying.

At some point, she had dropped her head again, and her hands were clenched into tight fists. He saw that those small hands were shaking, and Haruyuki felt like he had to say something. But no matter what he said, it would just be a shallow, superficial comfort, and his mouth remained glued shut.

Instead, he reached his right hand across the desk and touched the fingers of Utai's left hand. Her tightly clenched fist shook, loosened, and finally opened to let the slender fingers gently wrap around Haruyuki's. Like this, Utai inscribed words one by one with her right hand alone.

UI> Kyoya's last wish…I myself ruined that in the end. Even as a *kokata*, I will never be able to stand on the stage again. Two transparent droplets fell soundlessly to the top of the desk, beautiful seams running through the wood. UI> Because ever since that day, I have been unable to speak even a single word. My condition cannot be treated even using a BIC.

Utai had told Haruyuki the day they met that she couldn't talk because of expressive aphasia. But until today, he had never once even wondered why she had ended up like this. He had simply imagined that, like a cold, it would naturally get better one day.

Tortured by the desire to punch himself in the face for being so thoughtless, Haruyuki just bit his lip hard. The Burst Linker abilities of the girl known as Utai Shinomiya had reached terrifying heights, so perhaps he should have realized sooner that it was possible that she had lost something of equal importance in the real world. Although there was probably nothing he could have done if he had, but…even still, he should have given thought to it.

"Sorry. I'm sorry…I…I didn't…" He managed to somehow squeeze a hoarse voice from his tight throat, and Utai once more gently gripped his hand.

UI> You have nothing to apologize for. In fact…I'm

GLAD YOU WOULD LISTEN TO MY STORY. UNTIL NOW, I'VE NEVER TOLD ANYONE THE DETAILS OF MY BROTHER'S ACCIDENT...NOT FU, NOT SACCHI EVEN...

"I think...Master and Kuroyukihime, they would...they'd be able to say the right thing, but...I can only listen..."

UI> THAT IS A WONDERFUL TALENT YOU HAVE. Utai smiled, although her eyes were still a little teary, so Haruyuki also managed to loosen his mouth slightly.

With that, he mustered up just a little courage and asked, "Um... So maybe Hoo being taken care of at Matsunogi Academy...was there some kind of situation...?" It was a fairly sudden question, but knowing how hard she had worked to find a place that would take Hoo, Haruyuki couldn't believe that it was unconnected with her "scars."

Utai blinked once and then nodded, a faint smile on her lips. She removed her fingertips from Haruyuki's hand and began to type again with both hands.

UI> THAT'S EXACTLY RIGHT. THIS IS A GOOD OPPORTUNITY, SO I'LL ALSO EXPLAIN THIS TO THE PRESIDENT OF THE ANIMAL CARE CLUB. ARITA, DO YOU KNOW THE REFORMED ANIMAL WELFARE ACT?

"Uh. Um. The duty to microchip all pets...right?"

UI> YES. ALTHOUGH, MORE PRECISELY, PETS LARGER THAN A CERTAIN SIZE. AT ANY RATE, BY MAKING IT MANDATORY TO INSTALL MICROCHIPS, THEY MADE IT SO THAT PEOPLE COULD NO LONGER EASILY ABANDON A PET SIMPLY BECAUSE IT HAD BECOME A HASSLE, LIKE THEY COULD IN THE PAST. THE NEW CHIPS HAVE A FUNCTION THAT CONNECTS THEM TO THE GLOBAL NET, SO IT'S ALSO NOT POSSIBLE TO SECRETLY DISPOSE OF A PET IN YOUR OWN HOME.

As the characters advanced in the chat window, the look on Utai's face grew pained. But the fingers of both hands continued to tap resolutely on the desk.

UI> BUT THERE IS ALSO A LOOPHOLE THERE. HOO WAS MOST LIKELY LEGALLY SOLD IN A PET SHOP, BUT...AS YOU KNOW, IT IS

NO SIMPLE TASK TO TAKE CARE OF A WHITE-FACED OWL. YOU
NEED A CAGE LARGE ENOUGH FOR THE OWL, AND THE FOOD IS
ALSO SPECIAL. ALTHOUGH THE PREVIOUS OWNER PURCHASED
HOO, THEY LIKELY COULDN'T TAKE CARE OF HIM PROPERLY. IN
THAT CASE, YOU EITHER HAVE TO PAY THE SHOP A CONSIGNMENT
FEE TO HAVE THEM TAKE THE ANIMAL BACK, OR FIND A NEW
OWNER YOURSELF.

After taking a deep breath, Utai typed out the rest.

UI> BUT HOO'S PREVIOUS OWNER CHOSE THE EASY LOOPHOLE.
THEY REMOVED—NO, DUG OUT THE MICROCHIP EMBEDDED IN
HOO'S RIGHT LEG AND RELEASED HOO OUTSIDE.

"That's..." Haruyuki murmured, dumbfounded.

The smile on Utai's face grew sad, and she nodded. UI> BIRDS
ARE NOT GOOD WITH BLEEDING, AND GIVEN THAT HOO HAD
NEVER CAUGHT HIS OWN FOOD BEFORE, HE COULD NOT SURVIVE
ON HIS OWN IN TOKYO. WHEN WE FOUND HIM WEAKENED AND
COWERING ON THE PREMISES OF MATSUNOGI'S ELEMENTARY,
THE ANIMAL CARE CLUB TOOK CARE OF HIM. WE TOOK HIM TO
THE VETERINARIAN RIGHT AWAY AND GOT EMERGENCY TREAT-
MENT, BUT IT WAS TRULY A MIRACLE THAT THEY MANAGED TO
SAVE HIS LIFE. AND...PERHAPS BECAUSE HE HAD SUCH A TER-
RIFYING EXPERIENCE, HE BECAME EXTREMELY CAUTIOUS OF
PEOPLE.

"Well, of course, with his owner doing something like that
to him."

UI> THE VETERINARIAN SAID THEY WOULD HAVE NO CHOICE
BUT TO PUT HIM TO SLEEP. BUT I...I SIMPLY COULDN'T ABAN-
DON HOO. IT WAS TOO ABSURD THAT HE SHOULD HAVE TO DIS-
APPEAR FROM THIS WORLD SOLELY BECAUSE THEY SAID NO ONE
NEEDED HIM.

Although Haruyuki could imagine Utai's state of mind as
the characters popped up in the holo window, he wouldn't dare
give voice to that. Instead, he put his own feelings into words.
"Like, lately, I've been thinking that even if a hundred people say
they don't need you, if there's just one person who does, that's

plenty of reason to stay in this world. I wonder if maybe it's not like that for Hoo, too."

Utai turned damp eyes on Haruyuki and finally nodded sharply. UI> FORTUNATELY, HOO FINALLY ATE THE FOOD I KEPT OFFERING HIM. FROM THEN, HE GOT BETTER BIT BY BIT. ONCE THE WOUND ON HIS LEG HAD HEALED, WE GOT A NEW MICRO-CHIP, AND I THOUGHT HE WOULD LIVE FOREVER AT MATSUNOGI ACADEMY. BUT THEN THE ISSUE OF ELIMINATING THE ANIMAL CARE CLUB WAS BROUGHT UP, AND YOU KNOW THE REST OF THE STORY, ARITA.

"Huh. I'm gonna work to make sure that Hoo can finally relax and find a home at Umesato."

UI> I'M COUNTING ON YOU, MR. PRESIDENT, she typed, a slight smile on her lips. Haruyuki could basically guess at that expression. They weren't dueling or even accelerated, but that look said that the purpose for which Utai had invited Haruyuki to her house had been accomplished, that he had been told everything he needed to know at the present stage.

Several mysterious, quiet metallic noises sounded in succession somewhere in the house. *What?!* he thought, but Utai said, IT'S ALREADY SEVEN THEN, so he assumed it was some kind of clock.

Indeed, the clock in the lower right of his field of view read 19:02. If the noise before was a clock, it was a little late, but he decided not to worry about it and started to stand from the floor cushion. "S-sorry. I didn't mean to stay so long. I should…"

Utai cocked her head as if considering something, and then quickly typed, UI> ARITA, WILL YOU BE GOING DIRECTLY HOME THEN?

"Um…I might just duel a little somewhere."

UI> THEN MAY I JOIN YOU?

"Huh? Th-that's, well…," he mumbled, and then finally he realized that the evening sky beyond the window had basically disappeared. Although it was midsummer, he did hesitate to bring an elementary school girl out onto the streets when it was past seven. "Actually, you know, it's already dark, so I'll give up on that for today. Your family will get mad at me."

Utai's slight smile turned sad. UI> AS LONG AS I RETURN HOME BY NINE PM, NEITHER MY FATHER NOR MY MOTHER HAVE ANY INTEREST IN WHAT I DO OR WHERE.

"O-oh." However advanced the social cameras, however dramatically crime rates had dropped in the city, this seemed to him to be too much of a hands-off educational policy. Although given that he himself didn't have a curfew to begin with, he wasn't one to talk. He shook his head resolutely one more time and smiled. "Even if your parents don't get mad at me, I know Master and Kuroyukihime will be furious. So let's duel tomorrow."

Utai blinked rapidly and smiled more broadly than she had all day before making her fingers dance nimbly. UI> YOU'RE RIGHT. IF WE WERE FOUND OUT, YOUR PUNISHMENT WOULD BE BUNGEE JUMPING FROM THE SHINJUKU GOVERNMENT BUILDING WITHOUT A ROPE.

Utai came out to the passage that faced the road to see him off with a wave, and Haruyuki selected the nearest bus stop along Kannana Street in his navigation app. He followed the line in the AR display in his field of view and started walking east through the dim residential area.

He had walked for about fifteen minutes, various pieces of the story Utai Shinomiya had told him drifting through his brain, when the dazzling light of the main road came into view ahead of him. Looking at his map, he saw that he was apparently close to the Honancho intersection. The bus stop toward Koenji was a little farther north. Haruyuki started to head that way, only to stop again.

His current location was basically on the eastern edge of Suginami Ward. If he kept going another three hundred meters or so down Honan Street, he would reach Nakano Area No. 2. Unlike Naka-1, which was controlled by the Red Legion, Prominence, Naka-2 was a blank space that was no one's domain. A so-called buffer zone bordering the Leonids to the east and Great Wall to the south, it was thus a mecca for free dueling, and even at this time on a weekday, there would be more than fifty Burst Linkers connected.

"M-maybe I'll just go," he murmured, and since no one objected, he took the crosswalk across Kannana Street at a trot.

Since the Suginami area was currently Nega Nebulus territory, even if Haruyuki left his Neurolinker connected to the global net, he could refuse incoming challenges from other Burst Linkers. But the instant he took even one step into the empty area of Nakano No. 2, that privilege disappeared. He straddled the ward border line that floated red in his field of view. The current location address in the edge of the navigation map changed from 2-choume Honancho, Sugiyama Ward to 6-choume Yayoi-cho, Nakano Ward. The majority of people were likely unaware of crossing borders between the twenty-three wards while they were in transit, but for a Burst Linker, they held basically the same meaning as national borders. These days, Haruyuki could roughly fill a blank map of central Tokyo with the shapes of the twenty-three wards off the top of his head.

In that moment, the name Silver Crow was already appearing on the matching list for Nakano Area No. 2. He could be challenged at any time, so he walked along the edge of the sidewalk, ready for the automatic acceleration. Although it would only be for 1.8 seconds of real world time, he wanted to avoid stopping in the middle of traffic.

Spotting a small park for children about fifty meters ahead of him, Haruyuki decided that if he wasn't challenged by the time he got there, he would challenge someone himself, and kept walking. He would choose an opponent who used powerful red-type light attacks, in order to give shape to the image of a mirror that was being born in him thanks to Utai showing him the mirror room and telling him the story of her brother.

A true mirror was not just a panel that repelled light. It was actually maybe similar to an entrance that took in light. Now that he was thinking about it, despite the fact that the Destiny, the Enhanced Armament Haruyuki had owned until just a few days earlier, was a mirrored armor with the property of nearly total resistance to light, it also had the capacity to factor in the user's attributes. The armor was somehow gentle and warm, which was exactly why it hadn't been able to reject Chrome Falcon's rage and despair, its own shape in the end being warped by those...

Considering all of this, Haruyuki was about ten meters from the park when *Skreeeeee!!*—the familiar roar of acceleration filled his hearing, and his back straightened. His consciousness would be cut free from the real world and carried off to the Accelerated World, where time was accelerated a thousand times.

However, the flaming text that burned red in his field of view was not the expected HERE COMES..., but rather A REGISTERED DUEL IS BEGINNING!!—somewhere in Nakano Area No. 2, a duel he had registered to watch was starting.

It wasn't his own duel, but the Gallery was fun, too. Excitedly wondering who the duel was between, Haruyuki slipped through the rainbow-colored gate opening up beneath his falling self.

9

Silver Crow's hard feet stepped onto a metallic floor. At the same time as he stood himself upright, he first checked the two health gauges shown in the upper part of his field of view. The player challenged was on the left, and it was a name he knew well: Frost Horn, level five. An ice user who belonged to the Blue Legion, Leonids, he was the one for whom Haruyuki had registered on his automatic Gallery list. Unusually, he wasn't in a tag team with his partner Tourmaline Shell that day.

And the name of the challenger on the right side was one he was seeing for the first time. The roman letters below the gauge spelled out WOLFRAM CERBERUS. Level...one. In other words, a newbie—who had just not too long ago become a Burst Linker—had challenged Horn—who was getting into the veteran range.

"W-wow...When I was level one, I could barely challenge someone one level higher," he murmured to himself, and then focused his attention on the avatar name again. "Um...W-Wallfram... Kerberus?" When he had managed to read it out somehow, someone spoke from directly behind him.

"It's pronounced Wolfram Cerberus, with a soft C."

"Oh! Th-thanks—Wait, what?!" He looked back and bowed his head, only to then leap back nearly a meter straight to one side.

Standing there was a girl warrior avatar clad in heavy, deep-blue armor—the person who had threatened him so cruelly at close distance only two days earlier. Belatedly, he regretted not setting a dummy avatar for Gallery use in case this sort of thing was going to happen, but it took time to manually go back to your duel avatar when you were challenged. He gave up on his flailing and rubbed the back of his head as he bowed neatly.

"Oh! G-g-g-good evening. Uh, um, Mangan— No, Cobal— No, wait, actually, M—" The reason he couldn't immediately settle on a name was that, also unusually, she did not have her partner in tow. When they were together, he could distinguish between them as the bluer one and the greener one, but with just one of them in the gloom of a Purgatory stage, it was hard to immediately decide which one it was.

The warrior narrowed her sharp eye lenses and stared at Haruyuki, whose head was cocked far to one side, before growling, "If I were your duel opponent, I would send your head and your body home separately. I'm Manganese Blade. It's not just our armor color; Cobalt's head has two horns. Remember that."

"O-oh! Right!" Now that she mentioned it, the helmet of the warrior before him had only one decorative part stretching out from the back of it. "I-I'll remember that. Cobalt's got pigtails and Maga's got a ponytail—"

"Who has a ponytail?! And the only one who can call me by a nickname is our king! I'm going to challenge you once this duel is over, so be ready!!"

"Ee-eep! I-I-I-I'm sorry!" The instant Haruyuki shrank back, a loud cheer rose up from a place a little ways off.

"Hooooooooorn! Fiiiiiiiiiight!"

"Don't let the newb do you in. Show us what you're maaaaaaaade of!"

Taking advantage of this to turn away, Haruyuki found nearly thirty members of the Gallery outlined along the tops of buildings lining the thoroughfare. Although it was Naka-2, there still weren't too many duels where this many people came together.

"Wow…Just like Horn," Haruyuki said. "He's pretty popular, huh?"

Stepping up beside him, Manganese Blade, the senior executive of the Leonids and close aide of the Blue King, changed her tone slightly as she said, "No. Over half of the Gallery here are registered to watch Cerberus's duels."

"Huh? B-but Cerberus's level one?"

"You lack education, Crow. These last few days, Cerberus…," the girl started to say, and then she closed her mouth before turning her gaze quickly to the south of the big street. "He's here. You'll understand the reason a newbie can get this many spectators when you watch the duel."

"Oh…kay," he replied uncertainly, and once again checked his surroundings.

The place was a fair ways from Honan Street, where he had accelerated. At basically the northern edge of the stage was the area around the Chuo Line at Nakano Station. The wide road that stretched out to the north and south immediately before him was Nakano Street. The large, multi-use building standing on the other side of the road was Nakano Sun Plaza, and the building beyond it was the Nakano Ward office. Similarly, the shopping mall rising up on his right was probably Nakano Broadway.

The three buildings had all been transformed into the twisted organic figures characteristic of the Purgatory stage, but since Haruyuki came to hang out in this area every so often, he could tell them apart somehow. There was a shop specializing in old video games on Broadway that had a good selection. *Right, maybe I'll just stop in there on my way home. No, wait, my real body's way south of here…*So his thoughts were running when—

To his right, from the north on Nakano Street, he heard a powerful roar, and then a large figure charged into sight. Chunky armor like cubes of ice, a fairly transparent ice-blue, and the characteristic horns stretching out from the forehead. Mr. "Go for Broke" from the Leonids himself, Frost Horn. He wasn't running; rather, he was sliding along at high speed, hips lowered.

Apparently, he had the ability to make a thin layer of ice just on the road around his feet and slide on that.

When they had fought near the government building at the beginning of that month, Horn hadn't been using that mode of transportation. It looked fairly staid at first glance, but it was a good technique to cover a large avatar's weakness of dulled movement speed. *He's a real fighter, develops fast.* Haruyuki was quietly impressed.

But while a few members of the Gallery were watching Horn's movement—call it a skate-dash technique—together with Haruyuki, the remaining thirty people of the Gallery were staring intently toward the south of the road, all of them wrapped in an electric air. Thinking this strange, Haruyuki also turned to face left.

In the south, he saw the overhead Chuo Line cutting across the road and the pagan shrine–like form of Nakano Station. One of the two double-axis guide cursors that told the Gallery the locations of the duelers was pointing toward the darkness under the train bridge, so Haruyuki focused his attention there and spotted a single silhouette strolling out of the thick darkness.

He was small and slender, almost the opposite of Horn. There were no noticeable protrusions on his limbs, and he didn't have any sort of weapon. The color of the armor illuminated in the weak light of the Purgatory stage was a slightly brownish, frosted gray.

"Huh?" Haruyuki cocked his head once more. According to Manganese next to him, the name of this avatar was Wolfram Cerberus. In line with the rules of Brain Burst, "wolfram" should have been an English word expressing a color. But Haruyuki didn't know any such color, and he didn't even understand the meaning to begin with. He made a mental note to look it up in a dictionary app after the duel as he continued checking out the newbie avatar for the first time.

If he were forced to list the avatar's distinguishing features, the list would have basically had one item: he had a face mask reminiscent of some kind of dog creature. From between the jagged helmet pieces with the motif of upper and lower teeth, dark goggle lenses peeked out. It was a tough design, but animal-type avatars were not that rare. Prominence's Blood Leopard, whom Haruyuki knew well, had a face patterned after a leopard, and Great Wall's Bush Utan was primate-ish, as the name suggested. In short, Wolfram Cerberus was in color and form a fairly staid duel avatar. What was tripping Haruyuki up was the "wolf" in "Wolfram." If it came from his wolfish appearance, then that would mean the second part of his name, "Cerberus," was the color name, which was the opposite of the normal rule.

Wait. I feel like I've seen the word cerberus *somewhere before. I'm pretty sure a monster in some game had a name like that.* Haruyuki started to dig into his own memories, but at that moment, the clear voice of a boy filled the stage.

"Thank you for this opportunity!!" The voice belonged to Cerberus; after emerging from beneath the bridge, he was standing still in the center of the intersection that lay before the Nakano Ward office. He put both hands against his legs and bowed neatly. The angle and his form were the perfect demonstration of manners.

"Uh...Oh?" Haruyuki said involuntarily. When he was level one, he was constantly, always aiming for a surprise attack for his first hit; he had never once greeted his opponent like that. Actually, even now at level five, he still felt the same way. "He's really got it together. I wonder who his parent is." Haruyuki looked around at the Gallery. It wouldn't be strange for the parent of a level-one rookie to watch the duel—it was, in fact, normal for a parent to take advantage of the right to get within ten meters of the duelers and even offer advice.

As Haruyuki whirled his head back and forth, the murmur of the blue warrior beside him reached his ears. "His parent's not here. Their identity is unknown."

"Un...known?" Unconsciously, he looked to his side.

Manganese returned a sharp look from beneath her forehead protector. "Cobalt and I suspected you, but...from your confusion, it seems we were wrong..."

"Huh? Me? Wait! Whaaat?!" He barely managed to keep himself from shouting. "M-me, his parent?! A-a-a-a-as if! That's not happening! It's about a hundred years too early for me to have a kid! And I mean, why would you suspect me?!"

"Well—" Manganese tried to say something, but before she could, there was a fierce roar from the street below.

"Not even tryin' for a surprise attack! You got some nerve!!" This was, of course, Horn in the middle of his skate dash. He leaned even farther forward and picked up speed. "But!! It's not just my imagination, is it!! That attitude of yours is condescending to sweet little me!! Getting too full of yourself just 'cos you beat Tori!!"

"Y-you're so mean, Hooooorn!!" Horn's partner, Tourmaline Shell, shouted from the roof of a building.

Haruyuki was stunned. "Huh? He beat level-four Tori?!"

During this time, the distance between the duelers was rapidly closed. The instant it was down to twenty meters, Horn readied both his hands tightly at each side of his body. The horns on his forehead and shoulders emitted a pale glow. "Getting things off to a good start...Frosted Circle!!"

Fwsh! Together with a crisp sound effect, a ring of light spread out with Horn at the center. The ground and structures within it were quickly covered in a white frost.

In his surprise, Haruyuki forgot about his conversation with Manganese and leaned forward. What shocked him was not the effect of the technique. It was that Frost Horn had already charged his gauge fully for his special attack. Filling your special-attack gauge before you met your opponent was the most basic of duel techniques, but since hiding and smashing terrain objects as soon as the duel began actually looked pretty small-minded, it wasn't something higher-ranking Burst Linkers usually did with lower-ranked opponents. And Horn's motto was supposedly "go hard." Did this mean, then, that he was sending a powerful warning to this level one?

"Ngaaaaah! Eat this, right in the faaaaaaace!!" With this battle cry, Horn adopted a tackling posture with the horn on his right shoulder thrust out. Haruyuki, in the Gallery, could see the battlefield clearly, but Cerberus, in that Frosted Circle blanketed in white fog, shouldn't have been able to see his opponent. Without the time to see the trajectory of the tackle and dodge it, his only choice would be to gamble in the early stage and pick a direction to leap in.

Or it should have been, but the gray level one didn't so much as flinch. Instead, he slowly lowered his body and thrust out the head patterned after a wolf. He brought his fists together in front of his chest, and the top and bottom of his visor came together with a clang, completely hiding his goggles. This sight stirred something in Haruyuki's memory, but before he could figure out why, Cerberus was also shouting out:

"Ooo...aaaaaah!!" The dignity of the boy and the ferocity of a beast mixed together into a war cry that was almost beautiful. The air of the stage crackled electrically, and the Gallery pulled themselves upright. The frozen earth at Cerberus's feet cracked. With almost the force of a bullet, the small avatar started into a dash, his trajectory perfectly matching the line of Horn's charge.

"No...way. From head-on?" Haruyuki croaked, hoarsely.

"That...fool." Manganese groaned at the same time.

The sharp roar of an impossibly hard crash filled the duel stage. The impact generated at the epicenter of the intersection in front of the Nakano Ward office was so enormous that all the windows in Sun Plaza Hall next to it shattered. The ice generated by Frosted Circle was pulverized and became pale smoke blanketing the road. The thirty or so members of the Gallery watched with bated breath until the wind blew it away.

"Wh-whoa...," someone said.

What appeared when the ice-smoke cleared were two completely static duel avatars, a distance of zero meters between them: The horn on Frost Horn's right shoulder and Wolfram Cerberus's tapered jaw were touching at a single point. The metal road surface was cracked in every direction at their feet, conveying the true enormity of the impact.

...*Snap.*

The faint noise reached Haruyuki's ears. *Snap, snap.* The hard sound was colored with a faintness like glass breaking. It was obviously not the sound of the stage being destroyed, but a duel avatar.

"So he can't handle it after all." Haruyuki sighed. Though, wait—the scene below his eyes was already a miracle. Wolfram Cerberus had met the full-fledged charge of level-five Horn—a heavy, close-range type on top of that—square on and not been sent flying; Cerberus, at level one, should have been amply praised for the feat. Manganese's "fool" was too harsh of an assessment.

One of the two health gauges in the upper part of Haruyuki's field of view was instantly dyed red, dropping below 30 percent in one go. The instant he checked the name beneath it, Haruyuki gasped, dumbfounded. "Wha...?"

At the same time as he returned his gaze to the battlefield, Frost Horn's right arm shattered into pieces from the shoulder down to the fingertips. Staring dubiously at the enormous blue form as it lost its balance and went down on one knee, Haruyuki belatedly understood the true meaning of Manganese's words.

They had been her assessment of a midrange member of her own Legion, as given by a senior executive. In other words, she had been expecting this result before the impact.

"Th...at's why...this is...?!" *Impossible!* Haruyuki groaned internally.

In Brain Burst, there was the basic principle of "same level, same potential." Put another way, different levels had different powers. To meet the tackle of someone not just one or two levels higher, but four, and a close-range tackle to boot—it was hard to believe you could beat that. If the sight before his eyes wasn't some kind of trick, it meant that Wolfram Cerberus's close-range

attack and defense power was so great that he could overturn a four-level difference.

"An Enhanced Armament? Or...It can't be an—" *Incarnate attack?*

Just as Haruyuki was on the verge of letting this slip, Manganese stopped him. "No. This is the basic performance produced by his—by Cerberus's own color."

"C-color? Cerberus, what color is that?" Even while Haruyuki asked the question in a trembling voice, the battle on the road was beginning again. But perhaps from the shock of losing one arm and having his greatest special attack ruined, Horn's movements were dull. His health gauge was steadily carved away by Wolfram Cerberus, who came at him resolutely, not flinching in the slightest before his enormous opponent.

"His color name is 'wolfram,' of course," Manganese murmured, as she looked down on the battlefield with hard eyes.

"Huh. So then it's not connected with wolves or anything? Wolfram is...the name of a color?"

"Aye. Or...more precisely, maybe the name of the armor material, *like us.*" Here, Manganese Blade turned her head and looked directly at Haruyuki. "Wolfram is an English word meaning a kind of metal. In Japan, we usually use the Swedish name. Incidentally, Cerberus is similar; we mainly use the Greek name in Japan. In other words, if you translate his name...it's this."

On the street, Frost Horn's enormous body, finally exhausted of strength, shattered into pieces. Haruyuki's vision was filled with the shining winner display with Wolfram Cerberus's name inscribed in it. As the sound effect signaling the resolution of the duel played, Manganese's voice carried to him quietly.

"Tungsten Kerberos."

Because his own duel avatar was a metal color, Haruyuki had looked into the main characteristics of the metals. For instance, gold was heavy and chemically stable but so soft that you could bend it with your hands. Magnesium was extremely light, and although it was sufficiently strong when forged, it bonded easily with oxygen. Aluminum was light and soft, but it was surprisingly strong when tempered as an alloy. And silver was stable, albeit not as stable as gold; it was the most electrically conductive of all the metals; and, according to the information Takumu had added the previous day, it was also apparently the most reflective of visible light. Naturally, not every little characteristic that metals had in the real world was applicable to the metal-color avatars in the Accelerated World. But at the very least, you could assume that the biggest characteristics would be reproduced.

So then, if there was a duel avatar with the name Tungsten, what kind of characteristics/performance did it have? In the real world, tungsten was used for the armor plating of tanks, the armor-piercing ammunition to shoot through that, or in drills and blades for processing other metals. In other words, it was hard. This hardness went beyond the realm of metals, approaching even that of a diamond. In which case, naturally, the tungsten—Wolfram, in English—avatar would have inherited this feature.

"...The hardest metal color...?" The words slipped unconsciously from Haruyuki's mouth.

Next to him, Manganese Blade nodded. "Currently, that assessment is correct."

In the intersection before the Nakano Ward office below them, the small avatar with the tungsten armor faced Frost Horn, already gone from the stage, and bowed deeply once more. His clear voice rang out. "Thank you very much!" At this display of politeness, rare in the Accelerated World, the Gallery, who normally didn't do anything like this, showered him with appreciative applause.

Haruyuki moved to clap his hands together as well, but Manganese continued to speak, so he stopped himself and looked at her.

"It's only been three days since Wolfram Cerberus appeared in the areas of Shibuya Number One, Shinjuku Number Three, and Nakano Number Two here. Given that you had your hands full with purifying the armor, it's no wonder you didn't know."

"R-right. I hadn't even heard his name before today."

"But the impact he's having is even bigger than when Dusk Taker was rampaging in Shinjuku and Shibuya two months ago. His strength, though, was understandable when you saw the combo of his long-distance firepower and the flight he stole from you, but…"

"Th-that—I'm sorry about that time," Haruyuki apologized without thinking. Hearing the name of the Twilight Marauder in this unexpected place had that effect.

Manganese looked at him with exasperated eyes and snorted. "You were a victim of that, too. At any rate, unlike Taker, you can't see the bottom of this strength of Cerberus's."

"Huh? Isn't it just that he's super hard because he's the metal-color tungsten?"

"He's hard. But his way of fighting isn't really hard. Normally, a level-one chick insists on their own abilities and has a narrow field of view, so their fighting style is stiff. Like how you used to focus just on your flying and always get shot down by Red snipers, Crow."

"R-right. I really am sorry." Reflexively, he apologized once more, and Manganese responded with another snort before continuing her explanation.

"But Cerberus there only uses the hardness that is his greatest strength in places where it's most effective. The reason this duel was resolved in such a short time is because that impulsive idiot Horn suddenly charged him head-on. But…a normal level one in that situation, no matter how much they believed in their own hardness, I doubt they would have been able to meet him in earnest without even hesitating."

"It's true, he did meet Horn's powerful shoulder charge with his own head butt without so much as flinching. When I was level one, I would have been running around for twenty-five minutes."

At his own words, he suddenly became concerned and checked the timer in the lower center of his field of view. It had started at 1,800 seconds, and he was a little surprised that there were still nearly 1,000 seconds left. Looking around him, he saw that more than half of the Gallery had already left the stage, and Cerberus, the issue at hand, appeared to be operating his own Instruct menu on the road. This space would not disappear until the time ran out or he burst out.

Also turning her eyes down to the road, Manganese narrowed her eye lenses fiercely and lowered her voice. "...He doesn't appear to be accompanied by a parent or belong to any Legion. So then where did he learn that duel sense? Or if he was able to fight like that on his own right from the start, then his true power isn't the hardness of tungsten, but..."

"...But...?" Haruyuki gulped the throat of his avatar and waited for her to continue.

"...But maybe that he's a genius. A natural talent who's been given everything necessary for the duel—no, for a Burst Linker—right from the start."

Genius. The instant he heard that word, Haruyuki felt a soft part of his heart wither suddenly. Because, for the human being Haruyuki Arita, this was the word most unconnected with him. At every opportunity, Kuroyukihime told him that his speed was a talent no one else had. But he knew better than anyone that this speed—his reaction speed in a VR environment—was absolutely not something he had been born with.

Ever since he was little, Haruyuki had fled to the virtual world to forget about his unpleasant reality and spent a great deal of his time with a variety of VR games. His reaction speed was nothing more than something polished and refined through that. His high score in the squash game corner in the Umesato local net that had drawn Kuroyukihime's eyes to him was also nothing but a number built up because he hid in that place to escape his bullies.

It was a fact that that speed had given his Accelerated World duel avatar the unique flight ability. However, the reason Haruyuki had been able to overcome all kinds of crises without losing all his points up to that day was exactly because of the many, utterly many people who had helped him. There probably wasn't one problem he had solved alone under his own power. The current mission to obtain the Theoretical Mirror ability was the same. Even though Niko and Utai had been kind enough to diligently show him the path, he had finally only been able to see a single hazy hint—

"Honestly. This and that all at once, it's too much!" Manganese exploded abruptly, interrupting Haruyuki's negative thoughts.

"A-all at once?" he asked, jerking his head up.

"That's right. You have the creepy generation of the ISS kits, the transfer of the Archangel Metatron, and now the appearance of Wolfram Cerberus. All these things have happened in the last week."

"R-right. That's true."

"Given all this, I should actually say it's fortuitous that we took care of everything concerning the issue of your Armor of Catastrophe yesterday. I don't even want to imagine the situation where you have a bounty on your head and we have to send a team to subjugate you. Not that I'm thanking you or anything, though!"

"W-well, of course, no." As he bowed his head, the thought suddenly popped into his mind: He could maybe say that he had only fought just the slightest bit under his own power to purify the Armor of Catastrophe aka the Disaster. It wasn't a problem to have a lot of people helping him, but there had to be one or two situations where he stood firm on his own. Even if he didn't have a natural talent, he was growing bit by bit, for sure. With that thought, he managed to cheer himself up just the tiniest bit, and Haruyuki bowed his head unconsciously to Manganese once more. "Um. Th-thank you."

"…You have no reason to thank me."

"Oh, I—I guess so. Ha-ha-ha!"

Perhaps Cerberus on the road had finished with his Instruct while they were talking; he suddenly looked up at the Gallery, down to ten or so people now, and called out in a voice that carried, "Well then, I'll take my leave of you here! Thank you so much for watching!!"

Normally, the Gallery was for having fun watching duels or gathering information on an opponent you would fight one day, so there was really no need for a thank-you here, but with Cerberus's too-fresh attitude, everyone responded unthinkingly with another round of applause.

Finally, the gray metal color bowed neatly once more and raised his voice. "Burst O—"

He stopped halfway through.

Haruyuki realized the wolfish face mask was looking in their direction, and he unconsciously tried to hide behind Manganese. But before he could, the clear voice of the boy reached the roof of the building.

"Um, please excuse me if I'm mistaken! Standing up there...are you perhaps Silver Crow of Nega Nebulus, by any chance?!"

Gah! He threw his head back. If it had been just the two of them, he surely would have shaken his head swiftly back and forth and said, "You've got the wrong avatar." But starting with Manganese, all the other remaining members of the Gallery would certainly have been aware that it was Silver Crow standing there, so he couldn't even come close to pulling that off.

He had no choice. In a relatively smooth voice, he replied in a mumble, "Y-yes, well...I guess, yeah."

Cerberus immediately ran up to the spot directly below him at street level and shouted even more forcefully, "It's a pleasure to meet you! I've wanted to meet you for so long! When I reach level two, I was thinking about coming to visit the Suginami area. I never dreamed I'd see you here today. I'm overwhelmed!"

"Th-th-that's very nice of you..." Although he had been told many times that "it was a pleasure to be able to shoot you down," he had never gotten "I'm overwhelmed to meet you," so Haruyuki simply pulled his head in, unsure of how exactly he should respond. He couldn't decide whether he should he run away right then and there, or if he should continue the conversation a little longer.

The words that Cerberus uttered next stabbed right through him.

"I have a request, Crow! Please duel with me now!!"

10

There were two ways in the system to connect directly with the next duel rather than ending a duel. One was to switch into battle royal mode to bring the many members of the Gallery into a one-on-one duel as duelers. Because this only worked if all the members of the Gallery agreed to the switch, it didn't happen very often.

And the other method was that the winner could immediately start the next duel by challenging a member of the Gallery once the regular duel was over. Since there wasn't the added work of quitting acceleration and then reaccelerating, it seemed to be quite convenient, but this too almost never happened. The reason was the fact that the challenger's side using up a Burst point remained unchanged—and the fact that a series of duels was mentally hard on a person.

Fights in the Accelerated World inevitably brought a fairly deep exhaustion compared with general full-dive-type duel games. It wasn't because time was accelerated by a thousand, but rather because of the diverse duel stages and overwhelming freedom of movement, along with the strategizing to go up against duel avatars that never had a single thing in common. Even when they were not in contact with the enemy, the duelers had to intently rack their brains and concentrate with everything they had for when they did cross swords again. It had already been eight months since Haruyuki became a Burst Linker, and if he fought for a full thirty minutes, he ended up almost slumping down to the floor upon his return to the real world. Even the successive Chrome Disasters, feared as the most extreme berserker, had been unable to withstand the exhaustion of endless battles in succession and been dispersed.

Thus, the majority of Burst Linkers disconnected their Neurolinkers from the global net immediately after finishing a duel and took a break of at least a few minutes. Although he was level one, Wolfram Cerberus couldn't have been unaware of this, given that this was not his first duel. And yet, without showing even a hint of hesitation, he had challenged Haruyuki. It wasn't just about winning or losing, either; the small avatar was spilling over with the pure desire to fight Silver Crow and was waiting for Haruyuki's response.

In this situation, do I have the right to say, "No thanks"? I don't really.

Muttering in his heart, Haruyuki glanced at the health gauge in the top left of his field of view. The name inscribed below it was Silver Crow. The right side was Wolfram Cerberus. The timer in the middle had a full 1,700 seconds remaining. In other words, Haruyuki had accepted the challenge from the newcomer prodigy with the super-hard tungsten armor, praised as a "genius" by the senior member of the Leonids, Manganese Blade.

He had actually come to Nakano Area No. 2 to duel, and when he connected his Neurolinker to the global Net, he had resolved to fight whatever opponent came at him. But given that this opponent was a nonstandard Burst Linker who, at level one, had pulverized a level-five opponent head-on, it was a different story. At the very least, he wanted to fight him after watching in the Gallery two or three—no, five or six—times...

"Don't chicken out now!" he scolded himself quietly and stared at the guide cursor in the center of his field of view.

From Cerberus's attitude, even if they hadn't run into each

other on this stage, there was a strong possibility that he would have challenged him the instant he found Silver Crow on the matching list. Given that, Haruyuki should feel fortunate to be in this situation instead, in which he knew, albeit if only slightly, the characteristics of his opponent. He would forget about the level difference and fight with everything he had. This was a matter of courtesy toward Cerberus, who had stood tall and challenged him directly.

After about a hundred seconds, Haruyuki succeeded in getting the restless train of his thoughts onto a new track, and once again took a look at his surroundings. The buildings, which had until a few minutes earlier had organic shapes, were now transformed into structures made of straight-lined iron skeletons and flat steel panels. With the start of the Crow-versus-Cerberus duel, the stage changed from Purgatory to Steel. The characteristics of this stage were that all terrain objects were more or less hard, that the effects of electricity and magnetism were enhanced, and that footsteps echoed strangely. Silver Crow was weak against electricity, so when his opponent was that kind of avatar, he had to be careful of electric shock attacks through the terrain, but there was no need for that now. Probably.

Actually, what required his attention was probably the footsteps. Metal-color avatars had the weak point of making more noise when moving than normal colors. It was impossible for both Haruyuki and his enemy to run in this Steel stage without making any noise. Given the complexity of the terrain, the sound of movement would no doubt be a key point in the contest. The members of the Gallery—more than thirty people once again—likely understood that since, unlike the previous Horn-versus-Cerberus fight, they were looking down from the roofs of the surrounding buildings at the battlefield in silence.

At that moment, the guide cursor disappeared from his field of view. "…Oh, there," Haruyuki muttered to himself. At the start of the duel, the two of them had been randomly relocated. Haruyuki's current position was basically the northern edge of the stage, on the east side of the road to Nakano Broadway. Cerberus had originally been coming straight at him from the west, but because the large shopping center rose up in the compass direction, he had no choice but to come around from the north or the south. Entry into buildings was permitted in a Steel stage, but that didn't mean anything since there was no entrance along the eastern wall of Broadway.

North or south? Murmuring in his head, Haruyuki focused the entirety of his attention on his ears.

The strategy Haruyuki had come up with was extremely simple: wedge himself in between the indestructible edifices and limit his enemy's path of movement to two options. And then, by further narrowing that down to an attack that created sound, he was aiming for a surprise first attack. His own footsteps would also make noise, but Silver Crow had a weapon called a Long Jump, which made use of his wings. It should be just barely possible for him to glide soundlessly to the southern or northern corner of the building.

So then…which way are you coming?! He pressed his back up against the wall of the building, made up of thick iron plates, and waited for the sound of metal against metal to reach his ears.

A few seconds later, he heard it. But the direction wasn't north or south—it was east. In other words, right behind Haruyuki.

Skreenk! Together with an ear-splitting sound of destruction, a gray fist ripped through the iron plate and shot into Silver Crow's right shoulder. The shock was like being hit with a large-caliber bullet. He was sent flying forward, spinning, and his back slammed into the road.

Shooting sparks as he came to a stop, Haruyuki stared, dumbstruck, as the fist protruding from the exterior wall of the building was quickly pulled back. Before he even had the chance to recover from his shock, a second, even more intense roar of destruction shook the air. This time, the steel plate, likely five centimeters thick, ripped open in concentric waves, and an entire avatar came flying out.

The buildings of the stage should have been indestructible, and yet Wolfram Cerberus had torn through this one with a single head butt. He slowly pulled himself upright in front of Haruyuki, and his visor, so like fangs meeting, opened with a creak that exposed his dark gray goggles.

Haruyuki couldn't see the light of the eye lenses that should have been beneath them. However, he could feel the laserlike gaze, so directly focused on him that it was almost painful. A voice brimming with youthful passion flowed bright and clear, tinged with the peculiar echo of the stage.

"This is my second time in the Steel stage. It really is hard, though! My head is still spinning!"

At this cheerful line, Haruyuki finally managed to wake up from his daze. He checked that his opponent didn't appear ready to attack him and then quickly got to his feet.

Seen from up close for the first time, Cerberus, while having an orthodox form and color, radiated a particular kind of presence. The reason for that was the pattern of thin striations running along the armor of his entire body. It was almost as if a hard-to-process material was machined to the point of exhaustion, so there was just nothing left to finish the surface—it was that kind of roughness. Despite the fact that he was also a metal color, Wolfram Cerberus was the polar opposite of the smooth-mirrored Crow.

"Maybe you could tell me: How did you know my position with such accuracy? You didn't just guess at it, did you?" It was very much not a question a level five should be putting to a level one, but Haruyuki felt compelled to ask. Even if Wolfram Cerberus had seen through to Haruyuki's plan to ambush him, there was no way he could have seen his position on the other side of the thick steel plate.

Cerberus stood up straight again and bowed his head, for some reason. "I do sincerely apologize for the surprise attack! It isn't that I measured your position, Crow. It's simply that this is the middle of the wall of the building. I like the middle."

At this response, even the members of the Gallery, quiet thus far, stirred. Haruyuki also stared in mute amazement at the wall behind Cerberus. The large hole that he had plunged through did indeed seem to be precisely equidistant from the north and the south. After all, Haruyuki had readied himself in the middle so that he could respond whichever direction Cerberus came from. If he had been even a meter off to either side, then perhaps he wouldn't have had the first attack taken from him.

Glancing up at his own health gauge, he saw that the one punch he had taken to his right shoulder had carved away nearly 10 percent. He really couldn't underestimate the close-range attack power generated from the hardness of Cerberus's armor.

But to put it another way, he just had to not get hit. "I get it. I have to apologize, too. I'm more experienced, and yet I was going for an ambush." He returned the apology with his own apology and slowly raised his hands. He brought his left hand forward and pulled his right back. "I won't run and hide. Let's settle this with hand-to-hand combat, as two close-range types."

"Yes! This is just what I want. Thank you very much!!"

In contrast with Haruyuki's lowered stance, Cerberus faced forward and crossed his arms in front of his body before pulling both hands back with a high-pitched sound. Silver Crow was slightly taller, but Cerberus, with his straightly lined armor, was probably heavier.

Because Haruyuki had watched him one-sidedly defeat Frost Horn in the previous duel, his request for hand-to-hand combat definitely did not mean that he looked down on his opponent. But Haruyuki was confident that when it came to a contest of fists and feet, he was no slouch. Because his speed—which even the swordmaster Kuroyukihime had acknowledged—was Silver Crow's greatest strength.

The tension between the two as they faced each other grew and grew until finally, it was so strained the air itself was almost electrified. The instant this fighting spirit made the steel panels at their feet creak, Haruyuki moved.

"*Shi!*" With a sharp battle cry, he dashed forward. In a single breath, he closed the distance between them, and his right hand shot out in a long punch.

Cerberus didn't move to dodge the fist, but rather raised his left arm to block. So he really did place absolute faith in his defensive power. The armor with the rough notches on it did seem intensely hard, and if he forced his fist through it, he might actually end up taking damage instead.

But when his punch was on the verge of hitting his enemy's arm, Haruyuki braked suddenly and instantaneously with his right wing. His body spun around, yanking his fist back. Using this vector, he went for a motionless low kick with his left leg. He was aiming for the place where Cerberus's armor looked thinnest on his lower body, the side of his right knee.

If he had tried to pull off the combination of a feint with a right straight going into a low left with just his body, that intention would inevitably bleed into his movements, but it was impossible to read his movements when he controlled his posture with his wings. And yet Cerberus reacted spectacularly, lifting his right leg to block—but Haruyuki's kick landed a moment before he could.

Metal collided with metal. The screech of collision. Countless scattering sparks cast dazzling illumination on the steel plates of the ground.

His upper body angled to one side, Cerberus shot off a counter of a right hook, but by that time, Haruyuki had already dashed back more than two meters. Of course, he had also used the thrust of his wings for a few tenths of a second to retreat.

Glancing up, he saw that this one blow had reduced Cerberus's health gauge by about 5 percent. For a clean hit, that wasn't very satisfying, but at any rate, if he aimed for gaps in the armor, he could do damage. As long as he was sure of that, then...

The only thing to do is rush him!!

"Urrr...Aaaah!!" Roaring, Haruyuki charged once more.

The high kick, normally out of range, got a boost from the

propulsive power of both wings. His curved trajectory abruptly turned straight, and the tip of his foot, stretched out into a silver lance, slipped past Cerberus's crossed-arm block to explode into the thin armor at his throat. Robbed of just under 10 percent of his health gauge, Cerberus reeled backward.

Normally, Haruyuki also couldn't move after completing a big kick until that leg hit the ground. But as he bent his extended right leg, he vibrated his left wing with everything he had. Using the propulsive force generated as a stepping stone, this time, it was a middle kick with his left leg. He drove his foot into Cerberus's undefended right flank, and his opponent staggered and dropped to one knee. Haruyuki rotated diagonally in midair and brought the heel of his right foot down perpendicularly. This landed sharply on Cerberus's neck, knocking the small avatar's head to the ground.

Using the reaction force from the heel drop, Haruyuki flew backward through space and landed three or so meters away. Here, the members of the Gallery on the rooftops erupted once more.

"What was that movement?! I couldn't read him at all!"

"You didn't know? That's Crow's Aerial Combo."

"It's been a while since I've seen Cerberus go down."

Without actively listening, these comments made their way to Haruyuki's ears as he exhaled a long-held breath.

With the three clean hits of the succession of kicks, Cerberus's health gauge had dropped to 70 percent. However, for damage done by a level five to a level one, it was comparatively small. Normally, he wouldn't have been surprised to see that his opponent's gauge had dropped into the yellow zone with hits like that.

It would be fairly tough to cut away the remaining 70 percent in this fashion—that said, he saw a chance at victory. He might be outmatched in defensive abilities and probably attack power, too, but he excelled at speed. As long as he kept his guard up and didn't lose focus, he could push ahead with his Aerial Combo.

"But this is charging Cerberus's special-attack gauge, too. The real contest starts now," he heard someone in the Gallery say.

Haruyuki once again glanced up to the right. Indeed, with the bonus from object destruction when he ripped that hole open in the wall of Nakano Broadway and the series of blasts from Haruyuki, Wolfram Cerberus's special-attack gauge was more than half charged. It couldn't be that on top of the super hardness of tungsten, he also had a special attack? Haruyuki swallowed hard as Cerberus slowly pulled himself up from the steel ground where he lay.

"Wow…" He shook his wolflike head two or three times, and his usual bright voice rang out. "Just what I expected, Crow. I'd heard about you, but you're much faster than I even imagined."

"You're a fair bit harder than I expected."

At Haruyuki's retort, the gray avatar bowed his head. "Thank you so much for the compliment. But…I'm sorry, it's still not there."

Unable to immediately grasp what he was saying, Haruyuki parroted the words back, "Still not there…? Not where?"

"I'll show you now," Wolfram Cerberus replied, not boastful in any way, and then he clenched his hands into fists before slamming them together in front of his chest.

Perhaps the movement was some kind of switch; the visor above and below his face bit into each other with a sharp metallic sound, hiding his goggles. That was the whole of the phenomenon—the open-and-close motion of the armor he had shown off several times up to that point. But his body didn't transform; no weapon appeared.

"What exactly…?" The answer to Haruyuki's murmured question was a sudden and fierce dash.

With Cerberus charging him head-on without the slightest feint or artifice, Haruyuki was slightly confused. But his mind quickly switched to battle mode. If Cerberus was going for a big finish, that was exactly what he wanted. He deployed the wings on his back with a *gashk* and started forward.

First, he'd stop Cerberus with a low kick, and then set up another combo. With that intention, he shot his right leg out

sharply. The spot he was aiming for was the place he had gotten damage before: the side of the knee. Adding in the propulsive
power of his wings, the lightning-fast kick dug into Cerberus's
left leg.

Up to this point, the situation was unfolding just like his first
attack. But in the next instant, Haruyuki's eyes opened wide in
surprise.

The tip of his right foot should have gotten a perfect clean hit,
and yet it was repelled like it had slammed into an absolutely
impenetrable wall. And that wasn't all. His silver armor was
deeply dented, and a crimson damage effect like blood carved
out an arc in the air. As proof that this wasn't just appearance,
Crow's health gauge was cut away by nearly 10 percent.

"Wha...?" Groaning, Haruyuki lost his balance in midair,
while in front of him, Cerberus's tapered helmet closed in.

Desperately, he crossed his arms and took a defensive posture.
Immediately after that came a tremendous shock. The pressure
was like taking the charge of a Beast-class Enemy all by himself, and his arms were helplessly knocked back. The tip of the
thick tungsten armor touched—no, buried—itself in Haruyuki's
exposed chest.

"Ngh...Gaah!!" he cried out, all the air in his lungs being
pushed out, and flew backward.

In the blink of an eye, he was on the other side of the
five-meter-wide street, his back slamming into a mid-size building. The impact was such that the tough exterior wall of the Steel
stage was dented several centimeters, and his field of view went
white for a moment.

With the damage from having a large hole opened up in his
chest armor and the secondary damage of colliding with an
object, Haruyuki's health gauge, previously up around 90 percent, was abruptly colored yellow. This was a fearsome—actually,
he wanted to say it was impossible—explosive attack power. And
this decisive, full-power head butt should have caused some

recoil for Cerberus as well, but he dug in to forcefully put a stop to it before charging again without a moment's pause.

If I take this here, I can face him down!

Judging this instinctively, Haruyuki peeled his avatar off the dent on the steel plate and plunged forward. He focused all of his mental powers on the incredible force of the right straight punch that Cerberus was swinging at him. The power contained in that fist was apparent from the effect of the air scorching around it, but compared with the punch Great Wall's Iron Pound had launched at him, it was slow; he could read its trajectory.

"Hngaah...!" His voice leaking out from between clenched teeth, Haruyuki let his left fist fly from down low. As he knocked away Cerberus's punch from the inside with the armor of his arm, he'd hit his opponent's head—basically, he was aiming for an irregular cross-counter.

The gray fist came flying at him, carving out more or less the arc he had expected. He aligned his left punch with the inside of that trajectory like a hook. The outside of Silver Crow's forearm (the hardest part of his body) and the inside of Cerberus's elbow (the part where there was only a thin overlay of metal panel) came into contact, and sparks flew.

Krrnk! A collision that rang through his bones. All the joints of his left arm creaked.

And what bounced back was once again Silver Crow. His full-body counterpunch was easily beaten back as though it had never even existed, and Cerberus's fist slammed into the left side of his face. Once again, the impact was so great that not only his vision but his consciousness threatened to go flying. He worked hard to keep himself from flying off by utilizing the instantaneous thrust of his wings.

Why?! Haruyuki shrieked in the back of his mind, catching sight of his health gauge being cut away nearly 30 percent. Why would the kick or punch he launched with perfect timing be repelled this easily? His opponent's armor might indeed have been the super-hard tungsten, but Silver Crow was a metal color with an armor hardness bonus. He had hit a brittle part; he just couldn't process this result.

No, not yet. Don't give up yet. Even if you lose in armor hardness, I still have speed...and the wings on my back! If this is how it's going to be, then I'll use up all of my special-attack gauge. It's fully charged now from the successive serious damage. I can win this with a full-power dive attack from a super high altitude. Let's see whether you can send even that bouncing back, Cerberus!!

"Urrr...aaaah!!" Haruyuki howled, mustering up the last of his will to fight.

He jumped into a back dash, whirling around and very narrowly avoiding the left hook his opponent threw his way after the right straight. He sank down, turning around to the rear, deployed the wings on his back, and flapped the metal fins with every bit of power he had. With his drawn-in right leg, he kicked hard off the ground and took off straight into the air like a rocket.

"—?!"

But in that instant, Haruyuki saw something that again went beyond all expectation. Cerberus had bent down slightly at exactly the same time as Haruyuki and kicked at the steel plate of the road with both feet, legs bent so much they creaked and squealed.

Whaaaam! The sound was an incredibly loud echo; the surface of the road rippled like a wave. The small avatar became a bullet shooting up vertically, twisting in midair, chasing after Haruyuki. He had no sooner flipped his body around with all his might than his helmet, visor still closed, hit the helmet of Silver Crow.

Haruyuki heard the sound of Silver Crow's mirrored visor shattering and the sound of his own remaining health gauge being carved away to zero at the same time.

You lose!!

In his field of view robbed of saturation, the flaming letters popped up, burning relatively weakly compared with

when he won. This was followed by the results screen being displayed—both of which Haruyuki stared at in a complete daze.

He had lost to an opponent four levels lower, so his reserve of Burst points dropped with alarming speed, but he wasn't even aware of that. His duel avatar had already turned into polygons and scattered, so his consciousness alone hovered in a ghost state in the coordinates where he died, while he turned vacant eyes on the stage where the battle had ended.

A few meters away, Wolfram Cerberus, his visor closed once more, stood up straight facing Haruyuki (or in his general direction). He bent deeply at the waist and bowed before offering up a cheerful greeting without a hint of unpleasantness. "Thank you very much! I had a lot of fun!"

Haruyuki, the defeated, could leave the stage whenever he wanted once the results screen was shown, as long as he shouted the "burst out" command. But he didn't even have the energy to utter those words; all he could do was stare at the young Burst Linker, his mind frozen.

Naturally, he had lost any number of duels. He had even been taken out by a lower-level opponent, had the whole fight flipped on its head when the enemy's health gauge had less than 10 percent left once or twice. But those times hadn't given him anywhere near the shock that this did.

There were two reasons that Haruyuki was hit so hard that he didn't even have the energy to get depressed. First, there was Wolfram Cerberus's overwhelming hardness. Of all the Burst Linkers Haruyuki had fought up to that point, the one with the greatest defensive abilities had been the Green King, aka Invulnerable, Green Grandé. Even though Haruyuki had at the time been fused with the Armor of Catastrophe, the Disaster, he had only been able to make the tiniest crack in the great shield the king carried, one of the Seven Arcs, the Strife.

However, Cerberus at level one normally couldn't be compared with a level-nine king, but his hardness in a certain sense exceeded even that of Grandé—or rather, it was something *different*. In the first half of the duel, even with that hardness, Haruyuki had been able to do damage by aiming for the gaps in the armor. But in the second half, after Cerberus's visor closed, his hardness was such that his entire body seemed impenetrable, including his so-called weak points. Haruyuki's full-powered attacks had been in vain, repelled each time by Cerberus's armor, and he couldn't help feeling a despair that went beyond amazement.

And then there was the second, larger reason that knocked Haruyuki off his feet—his speed. In the final stages of the battle, he had abandoned the idea of hand-to-hand combat on the ground and wagered his hope of a reversal on a sudden drop kick after flying up to the limits of his altitude. Watching for an opening to take off, he tried to fly up in the shortest time, immediately after he had dodged his opponent's big attack. That had been the plan.

But in that instant, despite the fact that Cerberus clearly kicked off the ground after Haruyuki, he'd gotten the jump on Crow after he'd taken off. The fact that his vertical ascent had been beaten down from in front of him was proof of that. In other words, although it was only in the last moment, Cerberus was also superior to Haruyuki in speed. He had lost in hardness as a metal color, and in speed, his greatest ability. On top of that, it was to a newbie opponent who had only become a Burst Linker a few days earlier.

Even after more than ten seconds had passed since the end of the duel, he still couldn't believe the results screen before his eyes, and he continued to float, dumbfounded, in the place where he'd died. Through the light-purple, semi-transparent window, he could see the small gray avatar moving away from him. He was heading over to where several members of the Gallery were standing, and it looked like they were saying something—probably an invitation to a Legion—but he couldn't hear what.

As he watched Cerberus from behind conversing with the

more-senior Burst Linkers without seeming the slightest bit shy, Haruyuki's ability to think finally recovered—however slightly—and he let fragments of vague guesses run through his mind.

The fundamental rule of same level, same potential. Had this finally been broken? Had Wolfram Cerberus been given power practically impossible for a level one right from the start? It was hard to believe, but that was really the only thing he could think of. Or rather, that's what he wanted to think. He had lost because his opponent was a deviation from the rules of the Accelerated World, an exception—a violation of the rules. He couldn't think of another reason for his defeat.

"—Silver Crow." Abruptly, a low voice called his name from behind, and Haruyuki jumped and shrank back into his invisible body. Ever so timidly turning around, he saw a female warrior avatar standing there, with blue armor that had a hint of green to it. It was Manganese Blade.

Her sharp eye lenses quietly gleaming, the senior member of the Leonids continued. "I'm under no obligation to show you any kindness, but...considering the Metatron attack, it would be an issue if you were to collapse for a few days. I'll offer you a word in the guise of advice." Even though she shouldn't have been able to see the form of the loser, Manganese's eyes caught Haruyuki's directly. Like her voice, they cut into his mind like the tip of a sword.

"First, acknowledge Cerberus's strength. Unless you start there, you'll do nothing but struggle. It's true, his power—his ability, Physical Immunity, is overwhelming. You probably want to think it's against the rules. But that is what a lot of Burst Linkers thought eight months ago—when the unique Aviation ability was before their eyes."

"...!!" Haruyuki held his breath.

Manganese's tone eased slightly as she murmured, "Go back to your starting point, Crow. A strong power is born from an equally deep wound—you should already know that. That's all

I can say…Ask Cyan Pile about the rest." She finished with this fairly cryptic suggestion, and then the woman warrior turned around, somewhat dashingly. As she walked, she likely gave the command to stop the acceleration; her tall form soon disappeared without a sound.

His thoughts were still half-paralyzed, but Haruyuki carved Manganese's words into his brain before staring at the gauges in the top of his field of view once more. Wolfram Cerberus's health gauge actually had 70 percent left in it. The duel had taken a mere eleven minutes. He clenched formless fists and squeezed his eyes and his mouth shut before he quietly called, "Burst Out."

The instant he returned to the real world, he naturally traced out the same movements with his real body. With his eyes closed, he forced open trembling fists and held down the global disconnect button on his Neurolinker. The circuit disconnection was shown in his field of view, and once that had disappeared, he lifted his eyelids.

Unlike when he was accelerated, the evening scene of Honan Street looked slightly blurry. Haruyuki wiped his eyes with his fist and muttered, "…Dammit."

Still standing stock-still on the dim sidewalk, one more time: "Dammit!"

With the passage of time, the shock at his unilateral defeat was steadily replaced with regret. He couldn't use the excuse that Cerberus was an illegal avatar. If Physical Immunity was real, then it was indeed an incredibly powerful ability, but…if he was going to say that, then Silver Crow's flight was the same thing. He was the only one in the Accelerated World who had the wings he had just used, and he lost completely to a level-one opponent.

The memory of Manganese Blade telling him to acknowledge his opponent's strength came back to life in his mind. But it didn't look like he'd be able to do that right away. Acknowledging Wolfram Cerberus's strength would mean also acknowledging Silver Crow's weakness, and he didn't want to do that. Even though he had broken through the guard of the super-class Enemy, the

God Suzaku; had returned alive from the depths of the castle; had even won against the control of the Armor of Catastrophe... he couldn't bear to throw away the self-confidence he had built up little by little.

At that moment, the last thing Manganese had said echoed in a corner of his brain: *Ask Cyan Pile about the rest.*

Why had she said that before leaving? Why had she brought up Cyan Pile—Takumu—out of the blue? It was true, he had originally been a member of the Leonids, but he had left after the battle with Haruyuki, eight months ago—

"Oh...!" The instant his thoughts reached *that*, Haruyuki cried out with a realization. He staggered slightly and pressed his back up against the exterior wall of the building on the left side of the sidewalk.

The defeat by a level-one opponent with an "illegal" power. That was how the situation must have looked from Takumu's perspective in the hospital battle when Silver Crow and Cyan Pile fought for the first time. Level four at the time, Takumu had had the chest of his avatar pierced by the fist of Haruyuki, who had awakened the flight ability, and been carried high up into the sky like that. And then he had been pressed by Haruyuki.

Do you concede, Taku?

That you totally cannot beat me in this Accelerated World. Do you concede, Taku?!

There was no way Takumu couldn't have hated that. And yet he had acknowledged his defeat, and to atone for his actions, he even withdrew from the Blue Legion. After that, he had carefully guided Haruyuki, who was still very much a newbie; he had worried alongside Haruyuki, when he made a careless mistake and was on the verge of losing all his points; and he continued to firmly support Haruyuki even now, eight months later.

"...Taku..." Still leaning against the building, he closed his eyes tightly once more and said his friend's name.

All this time, I forgot there's something more important than getting the Theoretical Mirror ability, than purifying the Armor of Catastrophe, than anything, something I should do first. Losing badly to a level one, I finally realize it—or maybe I lost because I forgot...

He took a deep breath, his chest trembling, let it out again, and pulled his back away from the wall. Upon reaching the road he originally came down, his pace quickly changed to a trot toward Kannana.

11

He jumped onto an EV bus near the Honancho intersection, headed north, and got off at the Kita-Koenji bus stop, the one closest to his house. It was 7:50 PM. It had been after seven when he left Utai Shinomiya's house, and given that he had taken a detour into the Nakano No. 2 Area, sat in the Gallery once, and fought one duel, he was home relatively quickly. This was one of the good things about Brain Burst, but dragging the regret at his loss back to the real world made the acceleration technology meaningless, so he had to do his best to switch gears—that's what his master, Kuroyukihime, had told him, quite severely.

However, that day at least, he couldn't do that. The whole time he was on the bus, Haruyuki intently examined every angle of the fight against Wolfram Cerberus. And then he did the same for the fight against Cyan Pile eight months earlier. The two battles were similar in a way. In which case, this time Haruyuki's regret had to be the same as Takumu's from back then. Whatever the reason they fought, at the very least, Haruyuki shouldn't have said that. Those words had no doubt left a wound inside his friend that wouldn't disappear.

Go back to the beginning, Manganese Blade had told him. He had no doubt that one beginning for him was that fight with

Takumu. He'd have to start there, or he'd never reach the Theoretical Mirror.

Racing through the entrance hall of his condo, Haruyuki launched his mailer and sent a short text message to Takumu, who should have been home already. The answer that came back to him a few seconds later was a brief GOT IT.

"—I'm sorry, Taku!!"

Standing next to the dining table in the Arita living room, Haruyuki bowed his head deeply.

Takumu—Takumu Mayuzumi—sat in his chair, blinking rapidly. He put the tip of his finger to his sharply tapered jaw and appeared to think for a while. "What did you do now, Haru?" he asked timidly, when he finally lifted his head. "You couldn't have leveled up without any margin again, right?"

"N-no, it's nothing like that. I mean, level six is still a ways off and all."

"So then...does it involve Chii? Did you do something to make her mad and you want me to go apologize with you or something?"

"N-no, it's nothing like that. I mean, if it was that, I'd run around for a while," he answered, stammering, still bent at the waist.

His friend offered him a broad, wry grin. "No matter how good I am at this, I can't tell from just a 'sorry.' Well, anyway, sit down, Haru. Let's talk while we eat. You haven't had supper yet, right?"

On the table were six neatly packed rice balls arranged carefully on a square plate. There were also plates full of Japanese-style side dishes, like *chikuzenni* stew and sablefish pickled in Kyoto-style miso. It was the Mayuzumi evening meal, all delivered for two at Takumu's request to his mother. Naturally, this had not been Haruyuki's intention in mailing Takumu, so he was at maximum apologetic. But all he had eaten was the *mizuyokan* at Utai's house, so his stomach was also at maximum hunger, and it ignored his earlier intent and continued to complain one growl after another.

"…Sorry, Taku." The words contained a different kind of apology from before, and Haruyuki sat down across from Takumu.

"It's fine. It's more fun to eat with you. The only things my family ever talks about over dinner are developments in global finance and my recent grades," Takumu said, laughing brightly. He was wearing a plain T-shirt and a pair of jeans, the ultimate in simple looks, but even still, his appeal was not reduced in the slightest.

Really, I have to rethink a bunch of things. Including the sense that a guy like this is friends with me even now, Haruyuki told himself, as he picked up his chopsticks. He joined Takumu in saying, "Let's eat," and first brought some of the chikuzenni, which included a bit of taro root, to his mouth.

Since both parents worked in the Mayuzumi house, he had been told previously that the food on the dinner table was as a rule half-prepared frozen foods. Even so, it was much more an actual meal than Haruyuki's basic supper of frozen pizza. He ate a rice ball, some stew, and half of the grilled fish in a trance before his stomach finally settled down.

"…I lost." The words spilled one by one from Haruyuki's mouth. He glanced at Takumu—his hand had stopped with dinner and he was staring intently at Haruyuki—and said once more, "Earlier…I stopped by Naka-Two on my way home from school…and I completely lost there to a new opponent. The duel time was a mere eleven minutes, and he still had seventy percent of his gauge left."

His hand dropped to the table, still clutching his chopsticks. The instant his empty stomach was sated, the regret that welled up once more naturally turned his hands into fists. "…And my opponent had just become a Burst Linker…he was level one…"

For a full ten minutes thereafter, Haruyuki explained the events of Nakano Area No. 2 without leaving anything out, from the part where he joined Frost Horn's Gallery. He spoke in great detail, from the appearance and abilities of the miraculous genius newcomer Wolfram Cerberus, to how he himself had lost against him.

Even after hearing everything Haruyuki had to say, Takumu remained silent. Finally, without saying anything, he reached out his left hand and firmly grabbed Haruyuki's fist, which was clenched upon the table. "Just one fight doesn't decide anything, Haru."

Reflexively, he lifted his face, and Takumu relaxed his grip. He patted Haruyuki's hand before pulling his arm back. "I mean, even if you fight a hundred times and lose a hundred times, you don't know how the hundred-and-first time will turn out. That's the game of Brain Burst, right? It looks like you're totally focused on the fact that you're higher level, Haru, but you completely lost the information war. I mean, even though your opponent knew that Silver Crow is a flying type, you knew nothing about…Wolfram Cerberus's Physical Immunity." Takumu's words were filled with a warm, deep compassion.

But the more compassionate he was, the sharper the thorn of guilt stabbing into Haruyuki's heart felt. Because Haruyuki had once thrown the very opposite words at Takumu. Words a Burst Linker must absolutely never say, no matter what the situation.

"…I'm sorry, Taku," Haruyuki murmured once more, head hanging deeply. This time, he didn't stop there, but earnestly put the feelings filling his heart into words. "I…I don't deserve to have you saying that to me. I mean…that time, I said that to you, right? Even though I only won the one time…" He took a deep breath. "I said, you totally can't beat me in the Accelerated World. I made you concede." He managed to somehow voice the words that made him want to get a knife and cut out his tongue just reproducing them and jerked his head up.

Hearing this, Takumu's smile did not disappear from his face. But Haruyuki felt like he did see a pain that hadn't been there before, bleeding into his light-colored eyes. He opened his mouth, closed it, and opened it again. And the words that came then weren't ones blaming Haruyuki. "Haru, that time, you had the right to say something much, much harsher than that. I mean, I was targeting Master—your precious and only parent—with illegal means, and I lost to you desperately defending her. If you had thrown me down to the ground that time, you could have made me lose all my points. But you didn't; you forgave me. When I think about it, what you said wasn't even enough."

"No, no, that's not it, Taku." Haruyuki hurried to interrupt Takumu's words of self-reproach. He didn't need to be reminded of the fact that Takumu still seriously blamed himself for the backdoor program incident when Cyan Pile, his Burst points starting to dry up, had targeted the Black King, who was in a state of hiding.

But this crime of Takumu's was already being erased. He had taken on the role of guiding Haruyuki, to the point of changing Legions, and after that, he had fought hard, sustaining many injuries, in the Chrome Disaster incident, and then in the Dusk Taker incident as well. Nega Nebulus already couldn't exist without him, and more than anything, Kuroyukihime herself had long ago forgiven Takumu.

It was actually Haruyuki's crime that hadn't gone away. Reflecting on this awareness once more, he changed the swirling vortex of feelings in his heart into words one by one.

"What I want to apologize for…It's the fact that I said that to you, but it's also the fact that I forgot about it until now. Way, way sooner, I should have—when you quit the Leonids and joined Nega Nebulus, I should have apologized for saying anything like that to you and asked to take it back. Manganese Blade told me to go back to my starting point…And that's when I finally realized it. It's because I'm the kind of guy who can say something like that to a good friend and then forget about it. It's that, on top of losing to Cerberus, I'm sure of it."

There, once again, he stood up, the chair clattering, pressed his hands against the table, and bowed his head deeply and forcefully. "Taku, I'm really sorry. That...I said something that hurt your pride as a Burst Linker, that I looked down on you. And then I forgot about it this whole time. Please forgive me."

I'm hopeless, a guy who only sees himself. I act like my problems, my struggle, my pain are the only ones that exist...I just sulk and get jealous. Without even considering other people's feelings, I hardened the shell of my heart, made it thicker, made it so that everything would bounce off it...

Right, just like Silver Crow's imperfect mirror armor. Even if it can bounce back a certain degree of physical attack or heat or light, it can't repel a truly powerful attack like Cerberus's head butt or Niko's laser. A totally lukewarm existence, that's me...

"I forgive you. On one condition."

Hearing these sudden words, Haruyuki ever so timidly lifted his gaze and found there Takumu's gentle smile, the same as always.

His friend set his chopsticks down, stood up, and went around the table to stand in front of Haruyuki. His large hand, calloused from his wooden kendo sword, clapped down firmly on Haruyuki's slumped shoulder. "A jumbo parfait from Enjiya. How's that work for you, Haru?"

"..."

Desperately swallowing the things welling up in his heart, Haruyuki asked, "...All you can eat?"

"Ha-ha-ha! Just one's good. I'm not as big of a challenger as Chii is." After laughing cheerfully, Takumu's expression grew stern, and he put his hands on both of Haruyuki's shoulders. He tugged on them to make Haruyuki face him square on and continued in a serious voice. "Haru, I said this before, too, but back then, you had every right to say whatever you wanted to me... But I won't argue about it with you now. It doesn't seem like that's what you want. So instead, let's make a promise. Someday, when we both make it to level seven, when we join the high rankers, we fight one more time with everything we have, no holds barred."

"...Taku." A little surprised, Haruyuki opened his eyes wide. Above him, Takumu's eyes were nothing but serious.

"You've made it through so many trials, and you're gradually getting stronger. But I'm working hard to beat you next time with my own power. How about it, Haru?"

Right, Haruyuki finally realized. This was Takumu's kindness. It was a declaration that he would render those words that Haruyuki had given voice to—*you can never beat me*—invalid. It was a vow to aim for tomorrow's victory as a Burst Linker, rather than shrinking at one defeat.

"Got it," Haruyuki replied. "It's a promise, Taku."

"Okay then." Takumu grinned and nodded sharply before removing his hands from Haruyuki's shoulders. "Let's hurry up and eat. Somehow, I can already see that the next plan is homework, since I'm here anyway, huh?"

"Y-you got me. Just like you, Professor Mayuzumi."

Takumu jabbed Haruyuki's shoulder one final time before returning to his seat on the other side of the table. Inwardly, Haruyuki spoke to Takumu's back:

Thanks, Taku.

Almost as if he had heard these words, his friend turned around and said something unexpected. "Haru. About what Manganese Blade said before—'Go back to your starting point'... If that's it, then I think there's a starting point you should go back to more than the duel with me."

"Huh? Wh-what?"

"You'll have to figure that out yourself...But it was pretty great of Manganese to give you that advice, huh? Haru, you do always get the older ladies—"

"N-no! It's not like that!" He hurriedly cut Takumu off (with a protest he had recently heard elsewhere) and settled back into his seat. He picked up a rice ball, opened his mouth wide, and started chewing, before speaking with his mouth full, ever so impolitely. "But I mean, you too, Taku. Do you know Manganese

Blade? Like, maybe you were pretty friendly back when you were in the Leonids?"

"As if. She's an executive of the executives, the close aide of the Blue King. Although there *was* a little 'thing' when I left the Leonids," Takumu mused with a faraway look in his eyes, and Haruyuki unconsciously leaned forward.

"A little thing? Like what?"

"Okay, if you finish your homework by eight, I'll tell you."

"Ngh…Th-then I'm gonna start while we're eating."

Even more impolitely, Haruyuki started tapping away at his virtual desktop with his right hand while holding a rice ball in his left; it made Takumu click his tongue with a wry smile. Looking at that familiar expression through a holo window, Haruyuki once again was deeply grateful that he had a friend like this by his side. The pain of being utterly defeated by Wolfram Cerberus also seemed to recede just a little at that moment.

12

A bright Wednesday on June 26, 12:30 PM.

After polishing off a lunch of pork cutlet sandwich and milk at maximum speed, Haruyuki dived into the squash game corner in the Umesato local net. Accepting Takumu's advice that there was a starting point further back he should return to, he had examined various avenues and decided that maybe this was that place.

There was also the idea of making his dive location the stall in the boys' washroom on the third floor of the second school building, but he decided that there was no need to go so far as to bring back all those sad memories, so he was using a viewing booth in the library. Besides, no matter where you connected in the school, it didn't have the slightest effect on the local net response anyway.

Stepping into the squash corner in the form of a pink pig avatar, Haruyuki touched the holo panel to start the game and tightly gripped the racquet that appeared. He swung it a couple times to test out the feeling that he remembered all too well. He hadn't actually played this game since last fall, a full eight months earlier. In other words, he hadn't played once since becoming a Burst Linker, so he was a bit astounded at how self-interested he was, but still, he also felt this had to be done.

Because back then, this had been Haruyuki's lone place of

shelter at Umesato, the place he fled to nearly every day. He had probably shed liters of virtual tears onto this polygonal floor. His desire to never return was joined by his wish to let this place rest quietly after protecting him for such a long time, and the two had kept him at bay.

But when he set foot on this game court for the first time in so long, the same feeling hung in the air, no different from eight months earlier. A game as unpopular as this didn't get updates, so it was only natural, but it made him happy somehow. "I'm home," he murmured absently, as he touched the start panel once more.

The countdown started in the center of the court, and the instant it hit zero, a ball fell from the sky. He hit it lightly with the racquet in his hand; it hit the floor and the wall ahead of him, and then bounced back. Haruyuki hit it a little harder the next time. While a light sound effect echoed, the ball came back about a meter to the left, and he returned it with a backhand.

Although he just barely returned it any number of times in the beginning, his instincts quickly returned, and Haruyuki sent his little pig avatar flying up and down and side to side, totally focused on chasing the ball. Each time the game went up a level, the speed of the ball increased, and its reactions became irregular. That said, this was still a game approved by the Ministry of Education, installed on the local net of a junior high school. It was slow compared with the bullets fired by red-type duel avatars in the Accelerated World, and it also didn't use any feints like the strikes of blue-type duel avatars.

More than ten minutes had passed from the start of the game, and the ball was already just a trajectory of light zigzagging about, but even still, Haruyuki continued to pursue it on basic instinct alone. He could have perhaps played to the end of time like this...And just when he started thinking that—almost as though the game system had read the arrogant thought—it went up another level.

"…Whoa?!" Without thinking, Haruyuki stopped his avatar's feet.

The ball had suddenly split in two. He couldn't manage to decide which half of the ball flying off to either side he should go after, and so in the end, he let them both go by. As if lying in wait for this, the eight letters GAME OVER dropped from the sky and bounced around on the court.

"…Th-that's really something…," he murmured, and he glanced at the score that was then displayed. Since it was the first time he had seen the number of balls increase, he had no doubt he had set a new record, but there was no high-score mark next to the results HAL LV160 SCORE 2806900 that were displayed.

"Huh…?" Cocking his head to one side, puzzled, he poked at the panel and called up on the court a list of the high scores. The number at the very top of the window that displayed the best five of his own scores was the impressive level 166, with a score of over three million. But he had absolutely no memory of hammering out a score like that.

"Oh…Ohhh, right!" he cried out, finally remembering the incident eight months earlier.

That high score was not Haruyuki's. When he had been disconnected with an abnormal link out, another student had kept playing his game and neatly taken the highest score. And that student had been the student council vice president, the object of adoration of all students at Umesato, Snow Black aka…

"Don't you want to go further, boy…to accelerate?"

He had suddenly heard this voice behind him and jumped up. He rotated his avatar ninety degrees in midair and landed as he turned around.

Standing at the slightly elevated entrance to the squash corner was a single silhouette looking down on Haruyuki. The long dress, hem reaching to the floor, and the long hair swinging slightly were both a sleek jet-black. Hands covered in similarly black long gloves held a folded parasol. And more striking than anything else were the large spangle butterfly wings that stretched out from her back. With light shining through them from behind, the scarlet pattern at the base shone like fire.

"If you do, come to the lounge tomorrow at lunch."

Haruyuki saw a vision of the avatar saying this and then disappearing, but of course, that wasn't what happened. Instead, she came down the short flight of stairs, heels clacking, and stood on the game court.

She looked around the dim space and smiled. "Such sweet memories. It's already been more than six months since then, hmm..."

"...Yeah. To be precise, it's been eight months and one day. It was last October, the fourth Tuesday...when you spoke to me here."

"You remember it well." She let out a short laugh and came over to him. The spangle butterfly avatar—Kuroyukihime—glanced at the high-score window floating in the center of the court and laughed once more with satisfaction. "It seems my high score is still intact."

"B-but you said you used acceleration to get this score."

"Mm. Was that it? Well, it's fine either way, isn't it? It's more fun for you if you have a goal, right?"

"H-huh? ...Are you telling me to break that record under my own power?!"

"Mmm. If you can, I'll give you a hundred butterfly points."

The strangely named points could be collected in all the apps Kuroyukihime made—catching one of the butterflies that appeared earned one point. Haruyuki still hadn't made it to three hundred points, so being told he could get a hundred all at once was definitely intriguing. Although he had not actually been informed of what would happen when he saved up the target thousand points.

"...I-I'll do my best." Still, Haruyuki clenched his pig hoof.

Kuroyukihime nodded with a solemn look on her face, and then her mouth relaxed. "It's been a while since I've seen you in that form, too. I said this before as well, but I am fairly fond of it. You haven't been on the local net too much these days, so

it's been a little lonely." Through some gesture, the parasol in her hands vanished in an instant, and she walked over to him briskly. While he was unable to respond, her hands grabbed his pig avatar's big head and pulled it up.

"Huh? Um, uh…" He twitched his ears and tail, but naturally, movements like that proved to be no resistance. The instant he was squeezed tightly in her arms, he felt a softness and warmth that seemed impossible for two polygon avatars, and his thought clock decelerated to less than 30 percent of normal.

…*Huh? I was pretty sure avatars couldn't touch on the local net…*, he thought, ideas drifting vaguely about. *But, well, a rule like that, I guess it doesn't apply to her.*

A surreptitious voice rolled into the large left ear of his pink pig. "…You came here to confirm your own starting point, yes?"

"…Huh…?!" After a few seconds, he grasped the meaning of what she said and opened and closed his eyes rapidly a few times. From this close, Kuroyukihime's eyes glittered with a radiating scarlet light that they did not have in the real world, almost like onyx wrapped in flames. Staring intently into these beautiful jewels, he asked in a small voice, "D-did Taku tell you…?"

"No, he didn't. I just happened to hear a rumor. About a duel you had in the Nakano Area last night."

"—!!"

Although his avatar's entire body stiffened reflexively, Haruyuki soon relaxed again. In addition to the fact that there had been more than thirty people in the Gallery in that stage, Wolfram Cerberus was currently an up-and-comer drawing widespread attention, so it was actually only natural that the news would travel far and wide through the Accelerated World.

But that said…

"W-word travels fast, huh?" he said, filled with surprise, given that it hadn't even been twenty-four hours since that duel.

"Naturally." Still holding his piggy head to her chest, Kuroyukihime patted it and smiled. "When it comes to you, I know everything," she boasted matter-of-factly, as she moved to the stairs at the edge of the court, high heels clacking. After sitting sound-lessly on the lowest step, she set Haruyuki on her knees, which tilted to one side.

"...Did you find some kind of hint in this place? To attack the opponent who defeated you," she asked, somewhat suddenly, smile still on her face.

Haruyuki blinked hard once more. *Right, that reminds me. I came here to find my starting point...and more than that, to get some clue to a strategy against Cerberus*, he remembered belat-edly. He had been totally caught up in playing virtual squash, and while he did succeed in setting a new personal record, he unfortunately couldn't believe that that was his hint.

"Um...I feel like I've maybe taken some steps forward when it comes to speed, but...but..." The super-premium situation of being held on Kuroyukihime's lap—although they were both avatars—also disappeared from his mind, and Haruyuki turned his pig snout downward. Around his solar plexus, the shock and regret at his complete defeat throbbed back to life. "But he might be faster than I am now. And to begin with, speed might be meaningless in a duel with him. I mean, he's almost impossibly hard. Silver Crow can only do physical attacks. No matter how fast I move, I can't actu-ally do any definitive damage, can I?" He had ended up sounding like he was whining, and he glanced up at his Legion Master.

But Kuroyukihime's expression was unchanged. She nodded once before replying. "I see. Was he that hard, this rumored Wol-fram Cerberus or whatever it is?"

"Yeah. Manganese Blade said it was the ability Physical Immunity."

"Hmm. If that's true, then he is indeed a strong enemy."

"And Manganese told me to go back to my starting point, so I saw Taku after I got home last night. And Taku said that there was a starting point further back, so I tried the squash game here, but..." He sighed and hung his head.

Kuroyukihime pinched his pig cheeks with both hands and once more made him face her. What he saw there was not the gentle smile from up to that point, but the clear, taut face of the swordmaster. "Very well. So then, I shall offer another piece of advice."

"O-okay. Please do!"

"You've gone too far back. Your starting point is one step ahead of this place."

"O-okay? One step...to where?" He whirled his head around, surveying his surroundings, but the squash court had walls in front, and on all sides, so there was nowhere he could go. Just as he was cocking his head to one side—

"This one's on me. I'll take you there." After saying this, Kuroyukihime uttered a phrase that was completely unexpected: "Burst Link!!"

...*O-okaaaay?!* Already reeling as the *skreeeeee!!* filled his hearing in the next instant, Haruyuki's consciousness was suddenly cut even further free from the virtual world.

When you accelerated during a full dive to a VR space, including the Umesato local net, the objects that were there around you in the real world were all colored blue, transforming into the so-called virtual Blue World of the initial acceleration space. Although it varied by the type of VR game, the movement speed here decreased by a relative thousand times, which was precisely why it had been possible for Kuroyukihime to drum up a score of three million in the squash game.

However, this time, Haruyuki was only able to look at the frozen blue game court for an instant. Immediately, his field of view was blacked out, and in the center, flaming text appeared, burning red. They were, of course, the familiar HERE COMES A NEW CHALLENGER!

As he transformed from his pink pig avatar to his silver duel avatar, he slipped through a rainbow-colored ring and landed on the battlefield beyond it. Stretching, he quickly looked at his surroundings and cried out, "Huh?!" What he saw was not the deserted squash court, but rather a room with several desks lined up in it. He thought for a second.

"Right, I guess so..." He soon nodded. This was the library on the second floor of the second Umesato school building, where the real-world Haruyuki was sitting in a chair in a viewing booth. As long as the stage did not prohibit entry into buildings, the starting point of a duel was always the coordinates where your real-world body was.

"So then...where's Kuroyukihime?" he murmured. He looked around for her, but he caught no sign of the swordmaster who had been holding him only moments earlier. Which meant that she had dived from somewhere in the school other than the library. The places that came to mind were the ninth-grade class-rooms, the cafeteria lounge, and the student council office. When he checked the guide cursor in the center of his field of view, the point of it was motionless, facing south by southwest. Given the connection with her position within the school, there was a strong possibility she was in the student council office.

Finally, he turned his eyes toward the health gauge in the upper right of his field of view. The avatar name inscribed there was, of course, Black Lotus. Staring at this name, the English text of which alone emitted a powerful sense of presence, he murmured to himself, "Why a duel all of a sudden? Although she did say she would take me there..."

Where exactly? As he thought, he unconsciously took a few steps, and a bright red light reflected dazzlingly from the surface of his avatar. Through the window, he could see the enormous sun sinking into the horizon. When he checked again, the desks and floor of the library were not their original synthetic wood, but had changed into cracked marble that had lost its luster. This was a lower-ranking sacred-type stage, the Twilight stage.

As soon as he was aware of this, a certain scene came back to life in the back of Haruyuki's mind, and he lifted his head with a gasp. Umesato Junior High in the Twilight stage. This sight was nothing other than what he had seen the first time he visited the Accelerated World with her, his parent. In other words, Kuroyukihime was saying she'd take him—

At that moment, a beam of red light, thin as a thread, moved upward. It was sitting below him, about a meter to the left of where he was standing stock-still. And then, a little after that—*shrk!*—a sharp sound reached his ears.

"...?"

What was that just now?

Blinking rapidly, Haruyuki went to step toward the place the light had passed. But then, with a weighty vibration, the school building shifted before his eyes. The marble floor and columns separated, upward and downward, revealing a smooth cross-section. And apparently, the side that dropped was the one Haruyuki was standing on.

"Wh-whooaaa?!" Crying out, he desperately ran along the inclined floor. He made it to the glassless window and didn't hesitate before jumping. In midair, he opened the wings on his back and glided in the direction of the first school building. In the next instant, the red light again—

Shrk!

The first school building was mowed down vertically. This time, without a moment's pause, a second, then a third beam of light glittered diagonally, slicing into the marble like it was tofu. The building began to crumble in all directions.

"Wh-wh-whooaaa!!" Haruyuki shouted again. If his special-attack gauge had been charged, it would have been possible to ascend to any height, but since he could only glide diagonally downward at the moment, he would be forced to plunge into the crumbling school building. His ability to turn either way while gliding was also limited, so he pulled his head in, drew his limbs back, and somehow managed to dodge all the enormous chunks of rubble pouring down. Once he had broken away to the grounds side, he let out a huge sigh of relief.

He landed on the grassy field colored in the evening light and timidly looked back to see all the school buildings of Umesato collapse with a roar. As to whose work it had been, that was obvious when he saw the special-attack gauge in the upper right of his vision become fully charged all at once. And since this person normally only had close-range attacks, the red light that gave rise to this incredible damage would have to have been a forbidden Incarnate attack.

"Now the view is much better." A cool voice reached his ears as he stood there in a trance. "Big buildings in the Twilight stage are too unromantic. You have this lovely sunset, but you can't see it...Don't you think?"

Together with this statement, a duel avatar came strolling toward him from the direction where the student council office had been. Her four limbs were sharply tapered swords, her armor skirt a water lily design, her semi-transparent armor reminiscent of black crystal. All of it was fiercely beautiful—this was the Black King, Black Lotus.

Once more, Haruyuki looked in turn at the ruthlessly destroyed school buildings on the right and the sunset burning redly on the left, and nodded slightly. "Y-yes. That's probably true. But still, why go this far...?"

"Mmm. Well." She lowered her voice a little, and it became sharper. "Because I'm just the teensiest bit angry."

Th-this kind of destruction was "just the teensiest bit"?! He resisted the urge to shout this out and instead stood at attention. In this situation, if Kuroyukihime was angry, then the only possible reason was him. Because he had lost to Wolfram Cerberus? Because he couldn't acquire the Theoretical Mirror ability? Or...

"Haruyuki," Kuroyukihime said, her voice quiet, severe, and just a little sulky. "The moment you were told to go back to your starting point, the first thing that should have come to mind was me. It's not that I don't forgive you for going to Takumu, but... why would the squash court be next?!"

"Huh? No! That! It's—!"

She snapped the sword of her right hand up and pointed at him as if to say, *No excuses!* "If you thought for a millisecond about it, you would know that your starting point as a Burst Linker could be nothing other than your parent, me!" the Black King shouted. "I understood that in a nanosecond! If you had come straight to me, I would've given you special training in easy mode, but now I consider hard mode inevitable given how you took the long way!"

"Ea— Uh! Easy mode…Wh-what training…?"

"It goes without saying." Her right hand cut horizontally with a sharp whine. Haruyuki's parent and Legion Master said, "The strategy for Wolfram Cerberus, obviously!!"

There was no doubt had he not asked for this. But even so, once they had moved to the center of the grounds, Haruyuki couldn't help but ask first thing, "Um…Even if I went to you for help, I thought you'd just tell me to figure it out myself. I mean, I'm already level five, and my opponent's still level one, so. Um, wh-why?"

"Does a parent need a reason to help their child?" Kuroyuki-hime stated calmly, before shrugging and adding, "But, well, perhaps this is a little overprotective. If this was Fuko, she'd definitely tell you to 'please figure it out yourself ♡,' and that would be the end of it. But…your opponent this time's caught my interest."

"Interest? Do you mean his strength?"

"There's that, too…but also his timing, I suppose." Kuroyuki-hime stopped speaking, and then her bluish-purple eye lenses shone quietly behind her smoked-mirror goggles as she came back with a question: "Haruyuki. After the meeting of the Seven Kings three days ago, you said to me and Raker that the Quad Eyes Analyst Argon Array is a core member of the Acceleration Research Society."

Haruyuki swallowed his breath and then nodded slowly. "Y-yes. Just like I said at the time, I have no visible proof you can see. I just have that dream from when I was parasitized by Chrome Disaster, which is a super vague foundation anyway, but even so, I'm sure of it. She's been friends with Black Vise of the Acceleration Research Society for a long time, and she was involved in the birth of the Armor of Catastrophe."

"Mmm. I and Raker both believe you. Right, Fuko?"

"Yes, Corvus would never speak irresponsibly."

"Th-thank you very much. But…is there some kind of connection between that and Cerberus?"

"Allow me to explain."

At this, Haruyuki turned to his right. Standing there was a sky-blue duel avatar, with flowing metallic-type hair parts—unusual for the Accelerated World—the hem of her snowy white dress fluttering slightly in the breeze. Haruyuki bowed neatly. "Oh, yes, plea— Whaaaaaat?!"

He leapt up nearly two meters and then flapped his wings to descend slowly. And yet despite all that, he felt like something like this had happened before, too. Well, might as well confirm it, at any rate. "Uh, um…M-master? It's you, right?"

"Of course. If you think you're seeing a ghost or some such, you can go ahead and touch me to be sure."

Although he started to reach an unsteady hand out at these words, he felt waves of murder from the left, and he quickly pulled it back. He didn't need to confirm; standing there before his eyes could have been none other than the deputy of Nega Nebulus, "Strong Arm" Sky Raker.

Here, he finally realized that she was connected with this stage as a spectator. But still, it didn't quite make sense. Because Raker's real self, Fuko Kurasaki, went to a high school in Shibuya and should have been there at present in the middle of a weekday afternoon. But to be in the Gallery of this duel of Lotus versus Crow, she would have to move to the middle of Suginami.

"Oh. N-no, right. This duel's not happening through the global net, but the Umesato local net instead, so even if you came to Suginami, you couldn't watch it. So then, Master, are you actually in the school?"

"Unfortunately, you're wrong. Although I understand your

desire to see me." The vacuum-destroying Raker Smile exploded onto her face. Unconsciously, Haruyuki staggered, but here, Kuroyukihime cleared her throat.

"We don't have a lot of time, so I'll fill you in on the spoilers. I opened a long-distance access gate for the Umesato local net, had Fuko connect from Shibuya, to be on standby as a spectator."

"O-oh, I get it— Wait, long-distance access to the in-school net?! I-i-if anyone finds out, it'll be—"

"To secretly make a gate that won't be found out is quite the challenge, even with the privileges of student council vice president. I only implemented it very recently. If I had completed it in April, I could have taken care of Dusk Taker directly. Or rather, considering that incident, I aimed to implement this gate, I suppose."

"O-oh. So then, even when you're away and we get attacked, we can be totally secure…"

"The issue is that the gate can't be opened if I'm not in the school, but what's more important right now is the Analyst."

His relief snatched away again, Haruyuki stiffened. Kuroyukihime patted his back lightly with the flat of her sword.

"I told you this before, but Raker and I have complete faith in your story. To start with, that Argon Array has just too many unknowns. She's always been an opponent requiring a certain level of vigilance."

"Yes. She's undoubtedly more of a veteran than we are, she's never joined a Legion, and her parent is also unknown. And I have only the fewest memories of her normal duels. I really have no idea how she made it to the high-level region."

Here, Haruyuki rapidly shook his head, setting aside the shock of Raker's appearance and the long-distance gate. "R-right. But if she *is* a member of the Acceleration Research Society, then pretty much all those questions are taken care of, right? Those guys seem like they've been researching dubious ways to earn points."

"Mmm. And dubious power-ups as well," Kuroyukihime said, and turned her face mask toward the static sunset. After a brief silence, a slight logic leap slipped from her mouth: "What exactly is a metal color? Haruyuki, have you ever thought about this?"

"Huh? Metal colors?" Reflexively, he looked down at the silver armor enveloping his own body—glittering orange now with the reflection of the sunset—before answering. "You mean metallic color names, right? Like my silver, or the Leonids' Manganese and Cobalt, or GW's Iron Pound? Basically, they have high defensive abilities and are striking attack types. But they're weak against acid or electric shocks and stuff."

"The characteristics are exactly as you say." Sky Raker nodded, her wide-brimmed hat shaking slightly, but she soon connected that with a "but."

"But, you see, if we're talking defensive types, there's already green. Actually, in a group battle, metal-color and green-type duel avatars often end up playing similar roles. Taking up more specific specs, it's not as though there aren't metal colors softer than green types, and green types harder than metal colors. So then...why do you suppose the metal colors, a separate lineage from the normal colors, exist in Brain Burst?"

"The reason...metal colors...exist...," Haruyuki parroted back before slowly shaking his head. "I'm sorry. Even though I'm a metal color, I've never thought about that before. I'm not sure what to say. Me being silver, too...As to a reason, I just thought it was randomly chosen."

"Mmm. Well, there's no doubt that there are a lot of random elements in determining color name. I also would prefer insofar as possible not to think about the fact that I'm black. However, the 'kind of reason' you just mentioned...A theory that attempts to explain that existed once. Although it was limited to the metal colors."

"Th-theory?"

"Exactly. It's called the Mental-Scar Shell theory. Its proponent is Argon Array."

"—!!" Haruyuki gasped beneath his mirrored surface. It was partly because of the Analyst's name coming up in an unexpected place, but more than that, it was because he remembered hearing the term "Mental-Scar Shell" sometime before.

Right. In the scene carved into the memory of Chrome Disaster, a shadow looking like Argon Array had said those words. She had muttered them at the meeting three days earlier while looking at Haruyuki, too. And then last week, he had blurted those words out when overflow from the Armor of Catastrophe had overcome him in the rear courtyard of Umesato—at which point, Utai Shinomiya had reacted strongly to hearing them.

"Wh-what exactly is a Mental-Scar Shell?"

"Just like it sounds. A shell that envelops your mental scars... apparently," Fuko replied after taking a step forward. She turned the madder red of her eye lenses on Haruyuki and spoke to him in a kind yet clear voice. "All of us Burst Linkers have scars in the depths of our hearts. My scar is that I was born missing the lower half of both legs. That mental scar produced the duel avatar Sky Raker, who seeks the sky—and space beyond it."

Haruyuki stood stock-still. Never averting her eyes from him, the sky-blue avatar continued.

"Corvus, you no doubt already know the wounds that are the sources of your childhood friends' avatars, Cyan Pile and Lime Bell. In many cases, the color and appearance of normal-color avatars is a direct materialization of these mental scars. My child Ash is also like this. Rin, having been hurt by her brother's racing accident, or perhaps Rinta himself, having lost his dreams, created the avatar with the motorcycle Enhanced Armament. It's almost too obvious." Fuko laughed faintly.

Kuroyukihime stepped forward beside her and picked up the explanation, also speaking quietly. "But there are also Burst Linkers for whom the mental scars that are the template for the avatar are not so readily obvious in their color or appearance. I'm sure you already know this, but...those are the metal-color avatars. Almost all of them are orthodox human forms, and they have no symbolic Enhanced Armaments. Their mental scars are, so to speak, wrapped in a thick, *impermeable metal shell*. Long ago, the Analyst proposed that we call this shell the Mental-Scar Shell."

"A shell…wrapping mental scars…"

"Exactly. This shell, for exceptionally strong children—children with shells so thick that they themselves can't see their scars—are thought perhaps to produce metallic duel avatars. This is the gist of the Mental-Scar Shell theory."

They themselves can't see their scars.

Kuroyukihime uttered these words in a tone that was kind and calm to the utmost. Even so, Haruyuki's heart, wrapped in metal armor, throbbed painfully.

It's true, I don't really understand why I ended up as Silver Crow, as a duel avatar with the ability to fly.

But…that's…It's not that I can't see my scars; it's that I don't want to, so I've always turned my eyes away. The truth is, that time…the time when Dad and Mom told me they didn't want me—

Abruptly, feeling his body gently enveloped, Haruyuki opened his eyes, only to discover he had closed them at some point. When he did, Black Lotus and Sky Raker were directly in front of him, both of them gently holding him. In his ear, he heard their voices alternate.

"I'm sorry, Haruyuki. Both Fuko and I understand that talking to you about this was likely to cause you great pain. But this…is a path you cannot avoid."

"Given that you are a metal color, at some point, you will have to face your own shell, Corvus. Before some malicious opponent pulls that door open. Sacchi and I discussed it and decided we should talk about it."

Hearing this, Haruyuki finally grasped why Kuroyukihime had gone to the lengths of using the drastic move of a long-distance access gate to call Fuko into this stage. It was to ease the shock the Mental-Scar Shell theory would give him by using not just her own power as his parent, but also borrowing Fuko, who Haruyuki adored as his Master. The warm pulsations coming to him through the arms of the two duel avatars holding him was proof of that.

I'm so lucky. Even if I fail to get the Theoretical Mirror, even if I'm beaten black and blue by a level one, and no matter what scars are buried beneath the shell of my heart, that's the one thing I can never forget. Forcefully reminding himself of this, Haruyuki took a deep breath. "Thank you, Kuroyukihime, Master. I'm all right. My 'Mental-Scar Shell' doesn't even shake at a little tap like that."

"That's a strange kind of confidence, Haruyuki."

"Shall we consider this a promising outcome?"

Kuroyukihime and Fuko offered their impressions as they pulled away from him, and the three laughed together for a moment.

"This is just roughly speaking, but that's the basic idea of the Mental-Scar Shell theory. At the time it was proposed, many Burst Linkers accepted it as a theory that could explain to a fair extent the reason for the existence of the metal colors. But...after a certain time, everyone stopped saying it. It became a forbidden word, as it were."

"F-forbidden? But it only explains the reason metal colors are born, right? There's no particular harm..." Haruyuki cocked his head to one side, and neither of the girls moved to answer him right away. The slight breeze of the twilight grassy plain made Black Lotus's sharp swords clink faintly.

Kuroyukihime crossed those swords before her, as though crossing her arms, and said in a more severe tone, "The truth is, well, there's a corollary to the Mental-Scar Shell theory. Rather than something anyone proposed, this spread as a spontaneous rumor, the idea that if the theory is correct, then perhaps it would be possible to apply it."

"Apply? To what exactly?"

"The deliberate birth of a metal color."

"...!!" Haruyuki threw his helmet back in his total shock.

"If children whose mental scars are wrapped in a thick shell become metal colors, then," Fuko explained, also sounding a little more tense, "if you make a Burst Linker after creating that shell first, perhaps you could purposely make that child into a metal color. That's the idea. As a specific instance of this, you seal away the scars the target child bears through some means—for instance, through hypnotherapy or, in the extreme case, with a brain implant chip—and then install the Brain Burst program. The existence of this so-called 'artificial metal-color plan' was a whispered rumor of the early Accelerated World."

"W-was that plan ever carried out?"

"Unknown. To begin with, we don't even know the source of the rumor, so..." Kuroyukihime shook her head slightly, but then continued almost at a whisper. "But it is a fact that a while after that, a metal color appeared in the Accelerated World. His name was Magnesium Drake. An avatar with hard metal armor and a dragon head that came with a powerful flame attack. He immediately went up levels and was revered by a great number of people."

This was the first time he'd ever heard the name. But Haruyuki felt a spark in the corner of his memory and furrowed his brow. "'Was?' Does that mean he's gone now? Even though he was that strong?" he asked ever so timidly, and the other two nodded together.

"But, you see, he didn't simply lose all his points and vanish from the Accelerated World."

"He was the target of a concentrated attack by countless Burst Linkers, undergoing one fierce and bloody battle after another. As a result, he was subjugated."

"Huh. Th-that—was he maybe—you talked to me about him before?"

"Exactly. Even though he was a noble leader, Drake suddenly became the second Chrome Disaster."

It wasn't that he had a memory of this. When Haruyuki became the Sixth Disaster, he had used the ability Flame Breath any number of times, spilling white-hot flames from his mouth. This was the ability left behind in the armor by the Second Disaster—in other words, the originator of that skill had been none other than Magnesium Drake.

"So, then." Haruyuki pushed a hoarse voice from his throat, somehow taking in the shock that was large enough that he forgot to breathe. "This Magnesium Drake was an artificial metal color created by applying the Mental-Scar Shell theory—is that it? Is that the reason he became the Second Disaster?"

Given the flow of the conversation, it was only natural he'd want to make that assumption, but neither Kuroyukihime nor Fuko assented immediately.

"This is all in the realm of rumor, Corvus. All that is certain is the fact that Drake appeared in the Accelerated World and astonished everyone with his strength, but then at a certain time, he fused with the Armor of Catastrophe. After much blood was spilled, he was subjugated and disappeared."

"And one more thing: As of that incident, Mental-Scar Shell became a taboo term. Though, from what Haruyuki said, Argon Array appears to be the only one not concerned by this."

"...So that's what happened..." After he had finished listening to the long story, Haruyuki glanced at the timer as he let out a sigh. The time remaining was eight hundred seconds—a little over thirteen minutes.

Now that he was thinking about it, why exactly had they gotten onto the subject of Mental-Scar Shell to begin with? He rewound his memory. It was Argon Array who had coined the phrase, and she was probably a veteran member of the Acceleration Research Society. Kuroyukihime had said she was concerned about the timing of her appearance, and that timing was—

"...Oh!!" Here, Haruyuki finally remembered that the main point of this duel was not a meeting, but rather special training. Kuroyukihime had invited him to this stage to instruct him in a means of attacking the new level-one metal color with the super-hard tungsten armor whom he had lost to so completely and utterly. "Huh? Wait. H-hold on a second, please..."

Having had a large amount of information stuffed into him

in a short time, Haruyuki held his head up with an index finger on either side. It felt like his head was reaching the limits of its memory capacity.

"The thing you said you were worried about before, Kuroyuki-hime. Is it that the timing of the appearance of Wolfram Cerberus and Argon Array coincide? So then…that means, you think…" He lifted his face and stared at the black lotus avatar. *"Cerberus may be an artificial metal color. Is that it?"*

Haruyuki had worked his mental circuitry to the limit to come to this hypothesis.

"No idea!" was Kuroyukihime's quick response.

"S-sorry?"

"How could I know? Not only have I not dueled him, I haven't even been in a Gallery. I'd like to see him just once. I'd actually very much like to try fighting him, but he appears near the territories of the Leos and GW, so I can't do that."

"R-right."

"And given that our opponent is level one, Uiui and I hesitate a little to challenge him," Fuko added.

Kuroyukihime nodded. "So there, Haruyuki. You will study him in the guise of a revenge match. The full, unexaggerated power of your opponent. In other words, you have to draw out a feeling of desperation that goes beyond planning and strategies. The preamble to this has gotten quite long, but we are here for special training to that end. We won't get any hints with a half-hearted approach. I'll go full power as well!!"

H-huh?! Holding in the urge to scream, Haruyuki shrieked, "Uh, um, but, we only have like ten minutes left, and I mean, like, it doesn't have to be actual battle style; a demonstration would be—"

"It's okay. We have plenty of Burst points left over from spring break!"

"B-b-b-but when I really think about it, before I get revenge, I should really get the Theoretical Mirror ability—"

"No problem. All efforts converge on a single eventual point!"

"If push comes to shove, I'll also help out. ♡"

Looking back and forth between the level eight and the level nine, Haruyuki gave voice to the only thing he could say in that situation:

"...Th-thank you for this opportunity..."

Five consecutive duels spanning thirty minutes, with the last one in battle royal mode with Fuko joining in.

After somehow managing to finish the special training time—the most serious fighting he could remember doing for the last little while—Haruyuki couldn't immediately stand up after awakening in one of the library's viewing booths. The vision of little yellow chicks circling his head continued for a while, and his body trembled on the reclined chair.

After about thirty seconds, the dizziness finally subsided, and he let out a long sigh. "I-I'm so hungry..." His stomach felt empty—as if he really had used up all the energy in his body from battle, which had taken up more than two and a half hours of subjective time—but it was a false sensation. He had just had a cutlet sandwich in the real world less than an hour earlier, so he couldn't exactly refuel again now.

Staggering out of the booth, he made it to the fountain in the hallway and drank from it to distract his stomach. He was extremely uneasy about whether or not he could make it through his afternoon classes in this condition, but he had to, if he wanted to take back the pride that had been ripped away from him. If the alternative was clutching his knees and losing his nerve after his stunning defeat by a level-one newbie, then being knocked down to the point of dizziness by grueling training was by far better.

Or rather, perhaps understanding his extreme, foot-dragging nature, Kuroyukihime and Fuko had been kind enough to beat him black and blue. Maybe they did it while inwardly crying, but he couldn't be certain of that.

Standing at attention in the deserted hallway, Haruyuki first turned toward the student council office, and then to distant

Shibuya Ward, where he bowed his head before murmuring, "Thank you, Kuroyukihime, Master. Next time, I'll definitely—I don't know if I can beat him, but I'll give him a good run for his money."

Exactly.

It didn't matter if his opponent was a genius or if he had the Physical Immunity. He would also forget new things like the Mental-Scar Shell theory and the artificial metal-color plan. Give what you get: this simplest obstinacy was precisely the first principle of Brain Burst—and of the fighting game genre.

Haruyuki now finally felt like he could accept both his unsightly defeat of the previous day and his own weakness. He would take it all in just as it was and move forward from there. If he did that, the road would surely spread out infinitely before him.

"...All right!!" Clenching his fists once more, Haruyuki started to run toward his own classroom.

13

Battling drowsiness, he managed to get through his two afternoon classes and the short homeroom after that. When he stepped outside after it was all over, a drop of rain hit him smack on the nose.

He looked up at the sky to see thick gray clouds hanging there, as dense as any in the Thunder stage. The weather report on his virtual desktop said 2.5 millimeters of rain every hour starting at three thirty PM. It was enough rain that outdoor practice for the sports teams would be canceled, but of course, that had no bearing on the work of the Animal Care Club.

Moving at a trot to the rear yard, Haruyuki first said hello to Hoo before getting to work on the hutch cleaning at 1.2 times his usual speed. Unfortunately—he supposed—his colleague Izeki had sent him a colorful text saying that she had to get ready for the school festival, so she couldn't come to the hutch that day; she *definitely* wasn't just skipping because of the rain.

Around the time he had finished washing the water bath, he heard light footsteps behind him. When he turned his face that way, a girl approaching him at a trot, carrying a red umbrella, came into his field of view. It was the Animal Care Club super president Utai Shinomiya, but something was different from usual. He squinted his eyes and realized that her feet were in red boots.

"H-hello, Shinomiya," Haruyuki greeted her, still carrying the bath, and accidentally stared at the boots, which were made of breathable, waterproof fabric. *That reminds me—I used to wear boots like that when it rained. When did I stop, I wonder...* His thoughts drifted away.

UI> HELLO, ARITA. IT'S A LITTLE EMBARRASSING TO HAVE YOU LOOKING SO CLOSELY. The words popped up in the semi-transparent chat window, the two boots squirming on the other side of it.

"Oh! S-sor— I'm sorry!" he cried out, slightly panicking at the possibility of him getting tagged a leg fetishist. "Um! I—I just thought your boots were cute!"

Silence.

Quiet filled the rainy courtyard. Utai's face turned bright red, and she hung her head. Belatedly realizing what he had said, Haruyuki froze, until he was finally rescued by the protesting flapping wings of a hungry Hoo.

After polishing off one of the thin slices of meat from Utai's hand, the white-faced owl gave them a little show of flight around the hutch to improve his digestion before returning to his perch.

Haruyuki watched as Hoo instantly switched to nap mode, and said, quietly, "Looks like he's gotten pretty used to this hutch, huh?"

Utai removed the protective glove from her left hand and nodded, her fingers flashing. UI> YES. I ALSO NEVER IMAGINED HE WOULD SETTLE DOWN TO SUCH AN EXTENT IN ONLY A WEEK. IT'S THANKS TO EVERYONE IN THE ANIMAL CARE CLUB WORKING SO HARD FOR US.

"Oh, no, I mean...All I do is clean...And Hoo seems to like Izeki better and all."

Maybe because he sounded somewhat jealous, Utai giggled as she typed, UI> THAT'S NOT TRUE AT ALL. HOO TRUSTS YOU QUITE A BIT, ARITA. A LITTLE LONGER, AND I WAS THINKING THAT I'D ASK YOU FOR YOUR HELP IN FEEDING HIM.

"Huh? But you said Hoo would only eat from *your* hand," he began reflexively, only to snap his mouth shut. A second later, he changed his tone and asked, "Shinomiya, is the reason for that… because Hoo was hurt by his previous owner?"

Utai's hands stopped cleaning up the feeding kit, and she looked straight at him. She nodded slowly, blinking her large eyes. UI> IF YOU LOOK CLOSELY AT HOO'S LEFT LEG, THERE IS STILL A SCAR FROM THE MICROCHIP BEING GOUGED OUT.

Haruyuki read this and lifted his gaze with a gasp. He focused on the left leg of the owl—whose ears were flattened and who had both eyes closed—and indeed, there was a horizontal scar about two centimeters wide that looked like it had been sliced opened with a blade.

"…So awful…Such a big cut." He bit his lip and clenched his hands.

It was true that keeping a northern white-faced owl as an individual was hard. The food was special, and a fairly large cage was required. But all this would have naturally been explained at the stage of buying him in the pet shop. And no matter what the situation, gouging out the microchip with a blade and then tossing the injured pet outside like that, all to avoid additional expenses, was inexcusable.

The fact that Hoo had not lost his life and was here now, safe and sound, was something of a miracle. Recognizing this all over again, Haruyuki murmured, "I just know it was because you were so serious about taking care of him that you saved him."

After a moment's pause, the cherry-colored font was falteringly displayed. UI> I NEVER AGAIN WANT TO SEE ANYTHING LOSING ITS LIFE IN MY HANDS.

After a few seconds, he grasped the meaning of this and swallowed his breath. That meant that a life had been lost in Utai's hands. And it hadn't been a pet like Hoo. A person—no doubt her own older brother and her parent as a Burst Linker, Kyoya Shinomiya.

According to what Utai told him the day before, Kyoya had lost his life in an accident in the mirror room of the Noh stage after being caught under the enormous three-paneled mirror there. Utai said she had been there with him, but that probably wasn't all of it. Maybe the young Utai had tried to stop the bleeding from the wound inflicted by a fragment of the broken mirror with her own hands. But it had been useless. Kyoya had passed on.

Envisioning this tragic scene in the back of his mind, Haruyuki suddenly realized something, and his eyes flew open.

Utai Shinomiya's duel avatar, the Shrine Maiden of the Conflagration, Ardor Maiden. That figure, upper body white as snow, lower body clad in true scarlet. That pure, yet heavy, deep red, perhaps...

He took his eyes off Hoo and looked at Utai standing beside him. At her small form wrapped in the snowy white uniform of Matsunogi Academy, wearing the red boots.

Perhaps reading all the thoughts in his mind through his eyes, Utai smiled slightly and nodded sharply. UI> Ever since that day, the saturation of the *hakama* trousers of my duel avatar changed, albeit slightly. From a pale pink... to a deep scarlet. Perhaps it is the color of my brother Kyoya's blood.

After that, they continued to work wordlessly for a while. Once they had finished cleaning the hutch and dealing with the garbage, Haruyuki submitted the log file. But even after all their duties were complete, Haruyuki couldn't really bring himself to open his mouth.

Every duel avatar was clad in a color symbolic of their nature, and more than a few had a design with a two-tone color. In fact, Haruyuki's Silver Crow was split into the silver armor elements and matte-gray body elements.

So even given an avatar with a white upper body and a pink lower body, no one would think that level of color difference strange. Categorizing them on the color wheel, they would fall into the "slightly long-distance white type."

What was unique about Ardor Maiden was that she had two

very different colors of unbleached cloth and scarlet. The previous day, Utai had explained it as being because of the two aspects of herself, the original her and the Noh *kokata* her. But that definitely wasn't the whole story. Ever since that day when she had held her deeply injured brother in her young hands, desperately trying to stop the flow of blood, Utai's lower half had been dyed a deep red.

So the color of her duel avatar's hakama had changed—and that was probably also why Utai had lost her physical voice.

"I'm sorry, Shinomiya," Haruyuki apologized suddenly, and Utai turned around, pulling her backpack on in front of the bench, cocking her head to one side. "Yesterday, you told me so much. All so that I could learn the Theoretical Mirror ability. But my head's been full of other things since last night..."

If only he had gone straight home from Utai's the night before. If only he hadn't thought of dueling a little in the Nakano Area. If he hadn't, he wouldn't have encountered Wolfram Cerberus, he wouldn't have been defeated in such an ugly way, and he *would* have been able to focus on the mirror again that day. In order to repay Utai's feelings after she had sincerely shared what was likely her most painful and sad memory—her brother's death—he had to learn the mirror ability as soon as possible. And yet, ever since his loss the previous evening, Haruyuki had only been able to think about that.

"I'm really sorry. But...But I..." Unable to say anything more, Haruyuki hung his head deeply.

After setting her backpack neatly on her back, she stepped in a pool of water with her red boots and walked over to him. She stopped in front of him and grinned as she typed. UI> THERE'S NO NEED TO APOLOGIZE. BECAUSE I'VE BEEN SO LOOKING FORWARD TO IT, I CAN HARDLY STAND IT, YOU KNOW?

"Huh? Looking forward to it? To what?"

UI> TO MY BOX SEAT FOR YOUR REVENGE MATCH WITH THIS WOLFRAM CERBERUS, NATURALLY.

"...S-sorry?"

UI> It's getting to be time. Now then, shall we hurry in that direction?

And then she opened up her umbrella before a now-speechless Haruyuki. Half on autopilot, he picked his bag up from the bench and pulled out his folding umbrella. He opened it with a *shk*, and almost as if that were a signal, the drizzle turned into real rain.

"Um, that's— Did Kuroyukihime tell you about Cerberus?" he asked, speaking slightly more loudly so as not to be drowned out by the louder sound of the rain.

Utai nodded as if it were obvious. UI> Yes. It was decided that on behalf of Sacchi and Fu, I would carefully watch over your fighting style.

"O-oh, really..."

So then, if I don't put up a good fight all the way today, the special training tomorrow will be double—no, triple. Tremors of fear shook his heart, while the reluctance that still hadn't disappeared made his feet heavy. When Haruyuki made no move to start walking, Utai looked up at him from under the brim of her umbrella, and the fingers of her right hand danced.

UI> Arita, this is what I think. That perhaps you met Cerberus when you were supposed to meet him, C.

"When I was supposed to?"

UI> Yes. The Theoretical Mirror ability, with the absolute resistance to light-type attacks, and the ability Physical Immunity, which completely repels all physical attacks, are very similar powers, due to their extremity. It feels that way to me. In which case, fighting Cerberus is surely necessary for you to reach the mirror state of mind.

"I...guess so...," Haruyuki murmured, and in that moment, Hoo—whom he had thought was sleeping after filling his stomach—flapped his wings loudly in the hutch, and added a bonus cry of "Gwee!"

And of course, Utai noted, UI> See? Hoo is wishing you luck.

Haruyuki could only grin wryly at this. He looked first at the white-faced owl in the animal hutch and then at Utai beneath her red umbrella. "Right. If I don't go now, it'll be like I'm running away from another fight with him, using the Theoretical Mirror as an excuse. Kuroyukihime said I had to concentrate my whole self, too."

UI> THAT'S EXACTLY RIGHT!! Hitting her virtual enter key with force, Utai took that hand and squeezed Haruyuki's left wrist once. Then she turned around and stepped out into the rain falling at her booted feet.

They departed the rear yard for the front, slipped through the gates, then turned left. After they'd walked a ways, the wide street of Oume Highway spread out before them.

The day before, Haruyuki had entered Nakano Ward from Honan Street far to the south, but since Nakano Area No. 2 bordered their current location of Suginami Area No. 2 along the north-south edge, if they just went east, they would reach it from some point or another.

As he walked in that direction alongside Utai on the sidewalk of Oume Highway, Haruyuki opened a navigation map on his virtual desktop. He adjusted the magnification and made it show him the area around Nakano Station where he had fought Cerberus the previous day. Half to himself, he muttered, "If we just keep walking this way, we'll get to Naka-Two in about a kilometer and a half. But if we're going to Nakano Station, maybe it's better to take the train from Koenji. But then that's the opposite direction from your house, Shinomiya."

Then he heard a relaxed voice from behind. "It might be faster to get a bus on Oume Highway rather than the train. There's one coming in three minutes for Nakano Station."

"Oh, there is? So there's a bus on this road, too...I don't usually use it, so I forgot." Scratching his head, his eyes still on his map, he now heard an exasperated voice.

"Now, look here. You see any number of these buses on your way to school every day. Honestly, Haru, you've always been like this. It's like you don't even see things you're not interested in."

"Th-that's not true! I already know about eighty percent of the faces of the people in the same class— Wait."

Here, Haruyuki finally realized that he was having a conversation with people with his real voice and jumped up into the air. The umbrella in his right hand spun around a hundred and eighty degrees on its axis, and he looked back and forth at the two very familiar faces there.

"Huh? Takuchiyu?! Why are you here?"

"Look, Haru. I won't say don't stick our names together, but shouldn't you at least do ladies first?"

"O-okay, then Chiyutaku...But that kinda sounds like *tsuyudaku*." At his own words, he started to imagine the *gyudon* pork bowl with extra miso soup before abruptly shaking it off. "S-seriously! Why are you here?!"

The tall boy carrying a wooden sword case over his left shoulder and a blue umbrella in his right hand—Takumu Mayuzumi—replied, in the most matter-of-fact way, "With this rain, Chii and I got out of practice early, so we figured we'd come cheer you on. We were waiting for you at the gates."

The girl with the short hair walking next to him, large gym bag slung across her chest—Chiyuri Kurashima—grinned as she opened her mouth to speak. "While we were waiting, Taku and I made a bet. About whether or not you'd notice us when your head's so full of the duel. And the result is a clean pass without stopping! See, told you, you didn't even see us!"

"Uh! S-so then who won the bet?"

"Obviously, Taku and I won, and you lost, Haru! Treat us to a soy milk banana au lait with tapioca on the way home!"

"Hey—wh-what's this, so one-sided..." Haruyuki was flustered.

Chiyuri turned her eye beam on him lightly. "You totally ignored your two best friends when we were trying to come and cheer you on in this rain. That's the least you could do!"

He was forced into silence here, and Utai, having listened, grinning, to the exchange thus far, struck the killing blow.

UI> NATURALLY, I NOTICED BOTH OF YOU.

"I'm so sorry." Haruyuki pressed his hands together and rubbed them up and down as he apologized when Takumu, with his usual impeccable timing, sent out a life raft.

"Look, the bus is here, guys."

"Oh! It is! Run! Run!" Haruyuki started running toward the bus stop straight ahead without a moment's delay.

"Don't you go running away!" Chiyuri shouted out behind him.

They scrambled onto the EV bus, where, happily, the last row was completely empty. They sat with Haruyuki on the right, then Utai, Chiyuri, and Takumu, before letting out a collective sigh. Compared with the deeply uncomfortable June rain, the air-conditioned interior of the bus was basically heaven.

"That reminds me, did you guys hear about this from Kuroyukihime? That I was going to Nakano today?" he asked Chiyuri, who was sitting on the other side of Utai.

"No." His childhood friend shook her head slightly. "I heard from Taku. And Taku…"

"Maybe a guess from knowledge and experience. Judging from how down Haru was yesterday, I figured he might get back to his feet sometime today and go get revenge," his other childhood friend said, pushing his glasses up with a fingertip.

UI> You really are quite the combination, Utai typed with an admiring look on her face.

"Haru's just easy to figure out!" Chiyuri commented bluntly.

While this exchange was going on, the bus soon passed the Koenji Rikkyo intersection—where Haruyuki dueled Ash Roller every other day—and approached the border with Nakano Ward. Two more traffic lights until the area change.

Chiyuri composed her poker face and quietly checked with Haruyuki. "What do you want to do? Should we find somewhere to sit near Nakano Station? Or…"

"It's raining and all. Inside the bus like this is good. We'll start as soon as we get into Nakano."

His friends all nodded at this from Haruyuki. Together, they leaned back in their seats and got ready. The bus, racing along

Oume Highway slick with rain, passed the first light, and when it was approaching the second, Haruyuki took a deep breath. He had come this far; no point in kicking and screaming now. All that was left was to do everything he could.

After waiting a second, Haruyuki whisper-shouted the command with all the fight he had in him: "Burst Link!"

14

The categories of stages randomly generated by the Brain Burst program had no links to the time or season or weather in the real world. Thus, when Haruyuki dived into the Accelerated World as his duel avatar Silver Crow, he was a little surprised when he saw that the Oume Highway on this side was also slick with pounding rain.

The bus had, of course, disappeared, so he landed on the road surface from the height of the seat, sending droplets of water scattering.

He quickly glanced at the sky. Although the thick gray clouds blanketing it as far as he could see were the same as in the Thunder stage, the swirling clouds were flowing from west to east at a fairly high speed, while droplets of water fell without stop. This was a Storm stage.

Its characteristics were the fact that the strength of the rain changed periodically, the fact that gale-force winds sometimes blew through, and the fact that terrain objects would, rarely, be destroyed by those winds. Thin buildings would snap in half, so it was essential to keep an eye on the surroundings.

Having finished confirming the specifics and characteristics of the stage in the span of two breaths, Haruyuki then stared at the enemy gauge in the upper right of his field of view. The avatar name inscribed there was, of course, Wolfram Cerberus. Haru-yuki had accelerated on the bus, and no sooner had he found the name at the top of the matching list in ascending order, than he had challenged him to a duel without a moment's hesitation.

What was a little unexpected was that Cerberus was still at level one again today. The day before, he had beaten the level-four Tourmaline Shell, the level-five Frost Horn, and the similarly level-five Silver Crow. And those were only the ones Haruyuki knew about. Considering the compensation for the level differ-ence, he had probably earned a relatively large number of points. Unlike the Haruyuki of old, he should have been able to go up to level two with plenty of a margin left over.

"But that doesn't matter now," Haruyuki murmured, and lastly looked at the guide cursor. The triangle was indeed indicating the northeast, the direction of Nakano Station. From the fact that there were no members of the Gallery around him, he knew there was a fair bit of distance between them. The moment his friends riding the bus with him had dived into this stage, after their automatic registration had been activated, they would have been sent flying to the central point between Crow and Cerberus along with the other members of the Gallery.

He shook his helmet, knocking off the drops of water stick-ing to it, and then once again spoke out loud: "All right...Here we go!"

In the pounding rain, he began to run toward Nakano Station. Quickly reaching top speed, Silver Crow left a trail of water drop-lets swirling into a mist.

The day before, he had tried to use the terrain for a surprise attack and had instead had the first attack snatched away from him, so today Haruyuki decided to attempt to make contact head-on, no tricks. But even so, the instant he spotted the silhouette standing boldly in the center of the street, Nakano Station at his back, he couldn't help but feel a little nervous.

No, I should actually be ready. I should go at him with that mindset. Because I was totally crushed by him yesterday. Today, I'm the challenger.

As he told himself this, Haruyuki slowed to a stop in the center of Nakano Street, about fifteen meters in front of Cerberus. Unlike the day before, they were on the southern side of the station, and there were basically no tall buildings here. Inevitably, the members of the Gallery, about thirty occupying the roofs of the buildings alongside the road, were also much closer than they had been the previous day.

Among the Gallery, out of the corner of his eye, he caught sight of the massive Cyan Pile, the slender Lime Bell, and the even smaller Ardor Maiden. Haruyuki concentrated his strength in the pit of his stomach and began speaking to his duel opponent, standing beyond him in the pouring rain.

"I'm sorry, today on the heels of yesterday. I'd like to have a revenge match. I don't like to let a loss sit." For Haruyuki, these were challenging words, and the Gallery reeled slightly.

"Not at all." Silencing this was the response of Cerberus's ever cool and clear voice. "I'm glad. There are few people who are kind enough to duel with me again so soon after fighting me."

These too could have been fairly challenging words, depending on how you took them. The Gallery stirred once more, and the temperature of the battlefield rose the slightest bit.

"Okay then. If I lose today, I'll declare here and now that I'll come again tomorrow for revenge...Although I don't think it'll come to that," Haruyuki replied, and Cerberus giggled. Or that's what it felt like, at any rate.

"You really are *good*, Crow. Just as I'd heard—no, more than that. I would like to fight you any number of times."

"Is that maybe a declaration that you'll turn the tables no matter how many times I come?"

"No. It means that if I lose, I will quickly ask for a rematch. Although I don't think it will come to that."

On the surface, this was a cool and polite exchange, but Haruyuki was keenly aware of the fact that with each riposte, the air in the field grew tenser. The feeling of that tension bursting and crackling spread out, a much different sensation from the vibration of the raindrops hitting his body.

Perhaps feeling the same way, Cerberus glanced down at the gray armor covering his body before lifting his head again. "Well then, shall we get started?" He raised up both arms and snapped them out to the sides. "Thank you for this opportunity!"

The previous day, Haruyuki had mumbled a response to the impressive greeting, but now, he raised his voice to the same level. "I also appreciate it! Now…here we go!!"

He sank down, stepping out onto the wet asphalt with his right foot. The sole of his lead foot had no sooner bitten firmly into the road surface than he was dashing forward ferociously.

At the same time, Cerberus charged straight forward. Silver and gray, the two metallic armors pulverized the raindrops on the road the instant they touched them, transforming the water into a minute spray. Drawing out white trajectories, the two metal colors instantly crossed the fifteen meters between them.

"Haah!" Cerberus launched a right long hook, the entirety of his kinetic energy riding on it.

"*Sheh!*" Haruyuki shot forth the exact same punch.

At that moment, neither of their special-attack gauges had been charged even a pixel. Thus, Cerberus was unable to use his ability, Physical Immunity, and Haruyuki couldn't do his Aerial Combo, which required the thrust of his wings.

Their fists closed in on the other's helmet, sending droplets of rain scattering. However, Cerberus showed no sign of trying to get out of the way. He had probably determined that even before his ability was activated, evasion didn't matter, given the fact that the difference in their armor hardness was a draw.

And that was correct. If both of their punches hit their targets, then Haruyuki would take nearly double the damage. However, he wasn't aiming for a direct attack with his fists.

His right fist, on the trajectory of a right hook, suddenly opened up wide. He collected as much rain as he could in his palm and five fingers, and with a snap of his wrist hit Cerberus's face with that moisture.

The water splashed up against the dark gray goggles. Cerberus reflexively turned his face away, and the trajectory of his punch deviated very slightly.

"Nngh...!" Gritting his teeth, Haruyuki intently twisted his head to the left. The super-hard iron fist grazed the left cheek of his helmet, sending white sparks scattering everywhere. His health gauge decreased by a few dots, but he ignored that. He used the vector to rotate his body to the left and launched a low kick with his right leg.

Skreenk! A sharp metallic noise rang out, and he saw a damage effect, a beam of light jetting out from Cerberus's left knee joint. Cerberus's health gauge decreased 5 percent. A perfect first attack.

I got it today! Haruyuki shouted out in his heart. He still hadn't gained any distance, but while Cerberus reeled, Haruyuki now used his water attack with a left palm strike. After blocking his opponent's vision, he connected this with a left-middle kick. He got a clean hit on the thin flank of the armor and took another 7 percent off Cerberus's gauge.

Here, Cerberus crouched down low. He leapt far back in a big jump—pushing off with both feet at the same time—as he had the previous day. Getting out of the close-range situation for a moment rather than aiming to pointlessly resist it—he definitely had good duel sense.

Haruyuki also had the option to close the distance between them with a dash. However, with just the smoke screen of a normal strike combo, it was impossible to cut away all at once the more than 90 percent remaining in his opponent's gauge. And his opponent had Physical Immunity, which changed even his weakest parts into absolutely impenetrable armor. The real contest would start when he brought that out.

Thus, rather than chasing Cerberus, Haruyuki also stepped back. He opened up a dozen or so meters between them, and a quiet commotion rose up from the rooftops of the buildings on either side.

Not seeming to pay any mind to the voices of the Gallery, Cerberus slowly rose up from his landing position and, without taking his eyes off Haruyuki, he said, "I had absolutely no idea this rain could be used like that."

"It's actually hard to collect the rain in your hand, though, instead of having it bounce off," Haruyuki responded.

Cerberus opened his right hand and sliced it through the air, palm up. But the raindrops all scattered, and none of the water pooled in his hand like the water Crow had thrown. In truth, Haruyuki had applied a secret technique Kuroyukihime had taught him.

"I see. It doesn't look like I'll be able to imitate it so easily."

"It'd be a problem for me if you could. I had to seriously train before I could do it."

Hearing this, Cerberus lowered the hand he had offered up to the sky and clenched it into a fist. Haruyuki thought he might have been a little daunted, but... "I'm happy to hear that. So there are still things in this world to study and train in!"

Hearing this clear voice, Haruyuki felt that, while Cerberus was the hardest Burst Linker he'd ever fought, he might have also been the most refreshing. It was almost like there wasn't a shred of negative emotion beneath that armor.

But that, unfortunately, was not possible. Great power was born from equally deep wounds. Just as Manganese Blade had recounted the previous day, that was the basic principle of the Accelerated World. Behind Cerberus's strength were the mental scars he was carrying inside. Even if he himself was not aware of those scars.

The instant he had this thought, the words "Mental-Scar Shell theory" throbbed painfully in the back of Haruyuki's mind. But he quickly shook them out of his head. He couldn't be thinking about anything but the duel right now. He had to muster all his strength and face this powerful enemy. For that reason alone, Haruyuki was standing in this place now.

As if in sympathetic vibration with Haruyuki's thoughts, Cerberus also changed his attitude slightly. After his right hand, he clenched his left and stood taller, the armor of his body clanking. From beneath the somehow wolflike helmet came a somewhat more severe voice. "Well then…this is a bit soon, but I'll take my leave to begin!" He slowly raised his fists and turned his body forward. It was the form to activate his ability.

"Yeah. Come at me, Cerberus!" Haruyuki shouted, and crossed his own clenched fists in front of his chest.

Cerberus slammed his right and left hands together, and on cue, the top and bottom of the helmet visor clamped down on the sparks generated. When his goggles were nearly completely hidden, the area that had been his face up to that point looked almost like fangs. As a phenomenon, it was simple, but the system changes behind it were nothing to laugh at. He was now under the protection of Physical Immunity, which would repel punches and kicks, of course, but also probably even attacks with close-range weapons like swords and hammers. Haruyuki hadn't noticed it the day before, but when he focused on Cerberus's special-attack gauge, it was decreasing slightly, and he saw that the ability was not the nonstandard defensive power from the Incarnate system.

At the same time as Wolfram Cerberus activated his ability, Silver Crow snapped the arms crossed in front of his chest back to his sides. The metallic fins folded up on his back deployed with a slight rasping sound. It was the movement to ready his flight ability, but his special-attack gauge did not decrease yet. He used that up only when he was actually flying, but the mileage was a bit worse than Cerberus's Physical Immunity, so if they both fought with their abilities at full power, the consumption rate would be basically synchronized.

The timer that had started at 1,800 still had more than 1,000 remaining, but this appeared to be the climax of the duel, and the dozens of spectators fell silent. If calculated into the system, the heat contained in their gazes would have locally evaporated even the ceaselessly pounding rain.

Haruyuki didn't take his eyes off Cerberus for even a second, but even still, he was keenly aware of the feelings of his three friends in the eyes focused on him. He even felt the encouragement of the two who were not there arriving deep in his heart.

Taku, Chiyu, Shinomiya...and Master Fuko and Kuroyuki-hime, please watch. I'm going to give it everything I have right here, right now!

"Aaaaah!!" Roaring shortly, Haruyuki moved.

Stepping forward with his right leg: a dash riding on the thrust of his wings, almost twice as fast as his previous charge. The raindrops in the air scattered from the wind pressure alone, and he closed ten meters in the blink of an eye. A ramming attack—or a feint of one; he slid to the right immediately in front of Cerberus and tried to spin around behind him.

But the young prodigy also responded immediately to this Aerial Combo move. Even though he hadn't been able to follow Haruyuki's movements in three dimensions for a while after the start of the duel the day before, today he quickly spun on the axis of his left foot and continued to confront Haruyuki directly. Additionally, he even used the centrifugal force from this to launch a right middle kick.

This development was something Haruyuki had anticipated. In the back of his mind, the voice of Kuroyukihime, from his Spartan-style training over lunch, came back to life.

"Know that the techniques you showed him in the duel yesterday won't work on Cerberus today!

"But it's pointless to keep them locked up forever! With planning and application, all techniques are endlessly changeable—no, evolving!"

Right, Kuroyukihime!

Shouting in the back of his mind, Haruyuki roared and blocked

Cerberus's right leg, closing in on him, with the armor of his left arm. The instant metal touched metal, pale sparks shot out, and his forearm squealed sharply.

If he simply guarded like this, the basic differences in hardness and weight, together with the effect of the Physical Immunity ability, would simply shatter Silver Crow's armor and cause him massive damage.

But as Haruyuki took the mid-kick with his left arm, he didn't try to push it back, but rather attempted to diminish the force of it by synchronizing their rotational inertia. This required control of his entire body and his wings on par with trying to pass through the eye of a needle, but he summoned every ounce of concentration and made it through.

This guard, which nearly cracked the armor of his arm, lasted for about half a second in reality, but to Haruyuki it felt like an eternity. His brain cells threatening to burn out, he made it through the tightrope walk and somehow managed to absorb just the amount of lethal force contained in that kick. And then he moved to the next stage.

"Hah!" Expelling a sharp breath, he generated a new spiraling vector with the left arm that was still touching Cerberus's right leg. The axis of the kick targeting Haruyuki's torso slipped off to the outside from the interference. If he pushed like this, Haruyuki could probably ward off Cerberus's kick without taking any damage.

He hadn't had the leeway to use this in the duel the day before. Or rather, he had forgotten, to be honest. This technique, Kuroyukihime's teaching, the Way of the Flexible. The way Haruyuki had caught the falling rain in his palm and thrown it before was also an application of this. And today at lunch, through five consecutive duels, Kuroyukihime had beaten the technique into Haruyuki anew. In the back of his mind, her stern voice rang:

"Haruyuki, your Way of the Flexible has basically passed the first level. But, of course, with every technique, there is always something more!

"If you're going to simply block an attack and ward it off with no damage, then dodging without making contact to begin with is far less risky. The essence of the Way of the Flexible is not defense. It can change that into an attack, and then for the first time, the technique comes alive!"

Right, Kuroyukihime!

Responding in his mind, he further focused his concentration. With a strange *skree* sound, the sense of super acceleration came over him, and the world changed color slightly. For Haruyuki, even the pounding rain appeared frozen in midair.

Haruyuki had secretly given his own Way of the Flexible the name "Guard Reversal." But when he thought about it, this was too arrogant a name. What Haruyuki had been able to do thus far was simply interfere with the momentum of his opponent's attack and ward it off; that clearly was not a reversal. If he couldn't actually send it back to his opponent, he had no right to give it that name.

At that moment, the axis of rotation had been taken from Wolfram Cerberus's own body to the point of contact between his kick and Haruyuki's arm, and his posture was crumpling as his kick flowed to the outside. Like this, he would simply be knocked back to the other side of the road, and without falling, he would stop himself and then instantly be readying his next attack. Just as Kuroyukihime said, this brought risk, and there was no point in having defended with the Way of the Flexible.

"Ngah!" With a brief battle cry, Haruyuki took decisive action with absurd control, ascending with his right wing and descending with his left.

Naturally, his entire body listed to the left. Or rather, not listed—he generated intense enough torque to almost knock him over sideways on the spot, and his avatar's body squealed. He poured this energy, all of it, into Cerberus's right leg where it intersected his left arm.

"…!!"

An aura of shock leaked out from beneath the wolf-shaped helmet with its closed visor. It was only natural that he be surprised at Silver Crow's body suddenly rotating like a propeller, sucking his own feet in. But it didn't end there.

"Saah…yaaah!" Spinning to the left one time before standing again, Haruyuki yanked both arms up. The momentum of his spin was released—and with the force of his own kick combined with all of Haruyuki's rotational power, Cerberus's body was knocked flying spectacularly.

He crashed into the road nearly ten meters away and bounced hard, scattering a mist of water. He continued to tumble along until he crashed into the guardrail on the side of the road and finally came to a stop.

"Yaaaaaaah!!" The dozens of members of the Gallery cried out all at once in amazement. This surprise was not aimed at Haruyuki's Guard Reversal. It was for the fact that Wolfram Cerberus's health gauge had decreased nearly 20 percent.

"Wh-why'd it go down?! He's using Physical Immunity right now, right?!"

"D-don't ask me! Maybe it's 'cos of the rain pooling on the road?"

"Obviously! He might be a metal color, but, like, submersion damage!"

The Gallery clamored, but then abruptly fell silent. Cerberus nimbly got to his feet and was readying himself for another attack.

"We're only just starting!" His voice was crisp and clear as usual, and he dashed forward, ripping through the wall of rain.

About five meters ahead, Haruyuki sank gently down and jumped. He had repelled the first attack with a circular movement perhaps because he had determined that it was a curving middle kick, and now he was faced with a flying kick without any kind of rotation in the body. The speed at which he made the judgment and switched was nothing short of impressive. The jump kick was like a missile, with plenty of force. It looked like it could crash through two or three of the cracked buildings of the Storm stage.

And yet...

"Too soft!" Haruyuki shouted, and this time took Cerberus's kicking leg with his right palm. He immediately vibrated his wings and rotated horizontally on the axis of his body. The intense spin that was generated swallowed up his enemy, knocking him once more onto the road on his back.

Perhaps because he crashed at a more acute angle than the first time, Cerberus's small body made a *wham!* and cracked the asphalt beneath him. A moment later, a powerful impact wave dispersed the water on the road and in the air into a semisphere. His health gauge dropped by about 20 percent again. The accumulated damage had already surpassed 50 percent, coloring Cerberus's gauge yellow.

"H-holy crap, he seriously pushed Cerberus into the yellow zone..."

"Is Crow seriously gonna get revenge?!"

"But...why is the damage hitting him?! I mean, the road surface's totally a physical thing, right?!"

"...I see." The quiet but fully menacing voice of a girl cut through the shouts of the Gallery. "The difference between a strike and a throw, then?"

When Haruyuki glanced at a building ahead, off to the right, even through the pouring rain he could see a female warrior avatar colored a deep blue. The horn on her helmet was a ponytail, which meant it was Manganese Blade. But today, standing beside her was the pigtailed warrior, Cobalt Blade.

Just like you, Manganese, Haruyuki murmured in his head as he got some distance from Cerberus, still lying on the ground.

Just as the member of the Gallery had noted, the road and the buildings were just hard objects, so they assumed that attacks using these would be physical and thus wouldn't work on Cerberus in his current state of being physically invulnerable. And actually, making Cerberus crash into buildings or punching him with a mass of concrete made from smashing a building shouldn't have done any damage to him. But with the road, the situation was a little different.

First of all, in a Brain Burst duel stage, the ground, including roads, was fundamentally indestructible. Looking at it another way, this meant nothing other than the fact that the ground was in the same state of physical invulnerability as Cerberus.

And secondly: In essentially all fighting games since the previous century, striking and throwing techniques were in different categories. In the old 2-D fighting games Haruyuki collected, too, the majority of titles didn't allow you to avoid throwing attacks even when you had super armor activated.

Naturally, Haruyuki hadn't been sure of it himself. But during his special training with Kuroyukihime, he had realized the possibility that even if striking attacks were ineffective, he could do damage by throwing Cerberus onto the road surface, and had asked for new training in the Way of the Flexible. In the space of a day, he could not in any way reach the level of Kuroyukihime, freely reversing the attack momentum of her opponent with a single arm, but if he combined the guarding technique he had practiced with his Aerial Combo that used his wings, he thought he might somehow manage to take in his opponent's attack and return it—in other words, learn a real Guard Reversal.

To polish the technique to this extent, Haruyuki had had his armor endlessly sliced open by the swords of the Black King. After taking on the challenge of those fearsome swords—also known as World's End—even Cerberus's super-hard punches and kicks felt somehow round and soft.

The key to the Way of the Flexible was not to firmly repel anything, but rather accept it, become one with it. It absolutely couldn't succeed if your heart was simply frozen with hostility.

The me of yesterday probably couldn't have succeeded, even if I had remembered the Way of the Flexible. Thinking this, Haruyuki soundlessly watched Cerberus as he finally pulled himself to his feet. With the rainwater flowing along the notches of the design, the tungsten armor looked less hard than it did beautiful, somehow. The sharply tapered helmet and the protruding edges of the shoulders seemed like nothing but terrible weapons the previous day, but now Haruyuki felt they revealed something of his interior.

...What if.

What if that other failure the day before yesterday...happened because I was only thinking about firmly repelling? What if it was the same as this at the root? Accept it, become one with it. That's not just the key to the Way of the Flexible...something bigger... This thought flitted through the back of Haruyuki's mind.

"This...this is still the beginning!!" He was interrupted by the low cry of Cerberus, now on his feet.

At some point, he had thrown off the polite speech, and the young wolf bent over three times. *Chak!* He stepped firmly forward, almost carving out the asphalt, and came charging at Haruyuki from dead on, with no tricks or feints.

He was probably betting on settling this with his strongest weapon, the head butt that had broken Crow's helmet the previous day. It was indeed a terrifying power. If Haruyuki took a direct hit from that, the difference in their gauges would at once be reversed. But.

"*When your opponent fires off his big technique, do not flinch! Stand and face it! Because that is precisely the moment when your opponent is afraid!!*"

Right!!

"Aaaaah!!" Haruyuki roared and prepared to meet the charging Cerberus. That said, he wasn't going to fight head butt with head butt, of course. Just as they were on the verge of contact, he created negative pressure with his wings, sank down to the point where he was touching the ground, and dived under Cerberus. With his right hand, he held his opponent's neck and quickly rotated vertically to the rear.

Kawhump!

The largest impact so far shook the stage. The raindrops over a wide area turned into mist, momentarily turning his field of view white. When this faded, Haruyuki and the spectators saw the figure of Wolfram Cerberus, his head and shoulders half-buried in ground that was supposed to be impenetrable. Haruyuki had basically flung his opponent straight down in an overhead throw, and all the energy from the head butt was absorbed by the road.

Cerberus's health gauge was dyed red, a mere 10 percent remaining. The four gray limbs stretching out into air fell to the road surface. Haruyuki also flipped over and stood on his knees.

A low voice flowed out into the pounding rain. "...I give...You really did get your revenge. But...I'm happy. There must be many people in this world who are strong like you..."

Haruyuki didn't immediately reply. He stared hard at the face mask of the fallen Cerberus from very close.

The top and bottom of the visor were still biting into each other, but when he saw them from close up, they weren't actually glued together, but rather, there was a gap of about a centimeter. When he really thought about it, if there wasn't a gap, Cerberus wouldn't have been able to see, but in that gap was only black darkness; he couldn't find the light of eye lenses.

"But I won't let this loss stand. I'm going to work hard and get strong, and next time, I'll crack your technique." Even in this situation, there wasn't a trace of poison in Cerberus's words. They were sunny, clear, and full of the straightforwardness of a boy.

But—

But was that what a duel was?

Cerberus's technique, in which he had had absolute faith, was crushed, and then he'd been one-sidedly defeated in front of the large Gallery. The difference in their remaining gauges was even bigger than it had been the day before. Because the only damage Haruyuki had taken was the few dots when the side of his helmet had been lightly grazed at the beginning.

And yet the fact that he was able to cheerfully acknowledge his defeat here was more than straightforwardness, somehow...

"...Is that how you really feel?" Unthinking, Haruyuki tossed out the question.

At the same time, the rain grew even more intense, and the raindrops pressing in on them at a diagonal mercilessly pounded both of the metal colors. With this, their conversation wouldn't reach the Gallery.

But Cerberus didn't say yes or no, his body half-sunken into the pool on the road. He simply continued to be pounded by the relentless rain silently, almost as though he had turned into a simple metal statue.

Abruptly...

Before Haruyuki's eyes, Cerberus's helmet made a quiet creaking noise. The visor, with the centimeter-sized gap, now bit together completely. All that remained then was a zigzagging line thinner than a thread; he wouldn't be able to see outside like that.

Suspecting that this was some kind of intentional act, Haruyuki furrowed his brow. Immediately after that, something even more incomprehensible happened.

A clinking metallic noise also came from the armor covering Cerberus's left shoulder. When he looked there, the fine zigzagging line that he had assumed was just a pattern up to that point expanded about a centimeter.

It was like, almost...his face and his shoulder had switched places.

This was the impression he had when, in the next moment, the gap that was created on the shoulder armor shone with a sharp red light.

Staring at this in amazement, Haruyuki watched as the shoulder zigzag spoke.

"...So it's finally my turn..."

To be continued

AFTERWORD

Reki Kawahara here. I'm bringing you *Accel World 11: The Carbide Wolf*.

To be honest, when combined with my other series, this book is my twentieth. And the number twenty was my original target.

Ever since I made my debut in February 2009, I've been privileged to have a book come out every other month, so to get to this place, it's taken three years and two months. When I look back on it, it feels like a long time, but also like the blink of an eye. And fortunately, I was able to reach the number of books I was aiming for without any real trouble or serious writer's block…But as to why I set twenty as my target, it was because I thought that if I wrote that many, the end for Accel World (and my other series) would come into view. (LOL)

However, the result is as you can see: far from ending, I don't even really know at present how far the story's actually gotten. I think Haruyuki's grown a fair bit as a protagonist, but Kuroyukihime and their friends have basically not developed at all; the Legion still has a mere six members; and their territory hasn't expanded from Suginami area—none of which I expected at all by this point. And of course, in this book, I actually intended to move the story forward toward the conclusion, but I wrote and wrote, and it never seemed to be getting there, so eventually, I was faced with the predicament of ending it with "to be continued!" I'm sure all of you readers are rolling your eyes, but if I might be allowed to make the slightest excuse, when a story goes on to this extent, control is impossible, or rather, it's like the story just yanks the author along in the direction it itself wishes to go. Though, of course, that is simply my own personal case.

However, the flip side of this is that being allowed to add onto the number of volumes is, for the writer and the story, an extremely fortuitous thing, so rather than relaxing simply because I reached the target number of volumes, I would like to continue to bring you the story for as long as I'm able to write it.

To conclude: The fact that I was able to reach this number twenty is naturally and obviously because all of you have given me your support. I would like to take this opportunity to thank you once more. And I would ask that you all join me in setting your sights on the next twenty volumes.

This is a bit of a change of subject, but thank you all so much for the many, many entries we received for the first *Accel World* Duel Avatar Contest, which was held in November 2011. I let out a cry of delight at the many marvelous avatars, more than 450 of them, but after careful consideration, I am announcing the three that will be used as avatars in the novels.

First is Uraomote Yamaneko's Peach Parasol. The unified feel of the design as a duel avatar, along with the idea of the parasol Enhanced Armament (named Hopping Shoot) really hit me. I had the wild idea she was maybe a member of the Red Legion!

Next is Nagomi Kiya's Chocolat Puppeteer. At any rate, I was knocked out by the delicious-looking armor texture. (LOL) I'll have to think a little about her Legion, but on the occasion when she does appear, I want her to be licked—I mean, play a really active role!

And then, finally, Alt's Tungsten Wolfram. If, hypothetically, I were going to give a prize, it would perhaps be the Miracle Prize. And as to what exactly is the miracle, it's the fact that the avatar Wolfram Cerberus that appears in Volume 11—which I had already written a fair bit of at the time the contest was opened—and this idea have a lot of points in common! I was honestly surprised by this myself. (LOL) The design and the abilities are actually a little bit different, but from Volume 12 on, I'd like to adopt some of Alt's ideas and make Haruyuki's new rival Cerberus even cooler.

As for the avatar contest, as of the writing of this afterword—February 2012—the second application period has begun, and we're getting a great number of entries once again. I plan to adopt several additional avatars in the novels, so please look forward to seeing them!

Around the time Volume 11 comes out, the first episode of the TV anime *Accel World* will have already finished airing, I think. The staff and the cast all worked hard to really become the Burst Linkers and create this show, so I'd love to ask for your support for the anime and game versions of *Accel*, too.

Thank you again to my illustrator HIMA, who once again passionately drew our new character Wolfram Cerberus and Utai, who has an important role in this volume; and my editor, Miki, and deputy editor, Tsuchiya, for whom I'm worried about when exactly they sleep in this storm of related missions. I'll keep working hard, too!

Reki Kawahara
On a certain day in February 2012

Special guest illustrator on page 50: Tatsuya Kurusu

ACCEL WORLD, Volume 11
REKI KAWAHARA

Translation by Jocelyne Allen
Cover art by HIMA

ACCEL WORLD
© REKI KAWAHARA 2012
All rights reserved.
Edited by ASCII MEDIA WORKS
First published in 2012 by KADOKAWA CORPORATION, Tokyo.
English translation rights arranged with KADOKAWA CORPORA-
TION, Tokyo, through Tuttle-Mori Agency, Inc., Tokyo.

English translation © 2017 by Yen Press, LLC

Yen On
1290 Avenue of the Americas
New York, NY 10104

Visit us at yenpress.com
facebook.com/yenpress
twitter.com/yenpress
yenpress.tumblr.com
instagram.com/yenpress

First Yen On Edition: September 2017

Yen On is an imprint of Yen Press, LLC.
The Yen On name and logo are trademarks of Yen Press, LLC.

Library of Congress Cataloging-in-Publication Data
Names: Kawahara, Reki, author. | HIMA (Comic book artist) illustrator. |
    Beepee, designer. | Allen, Jocelyne, 1974– translator.
Title: The carbide wolf / Reki Kawahara ; illustrations, HIMA ; design,
    bee-pee ; translation by Jocelyne Allen.
Description: First Yen On edition. | New York, NY : Yen On, 2017. | Series:
    Accel world ; 11
Identifiers: LCCN 2014025099 | ISBN 9780316376730 (v. 1 : pbk.) |
    ISBN 9780316296366 (v. 2 : pbk.) | ISBN 9780316296373 (v. 3 : pbk.) |
    ISBN 9780316296380 (v. 4 : pbk.) | ISBN 9780316296397 (v. 5 : pbk.) |
    ISBN 9780316296403 (v. 6 : pbk.) | ISBN 9780316358194 (v. 7 : pbk.) |
    ISBN 9780316317610 (v. 8 : pbk.) | ISBN 9780316502702 (v. 9 : pbk.) |
    ISBN 9780316466059 (v. 10 : pbk.) | ISBN 9780316466066 (v. 11 : pbk.)
Subjects: | CYAC: Science fiction. | Virtual reality—Fiction. | Fantasy.
Classification: LCC PZ7.K1755Kaw 2014 | DDC [Fic]—dc23
LC record available at https://lccn.loc.gov/2014025099

ISBN: 978-0-316-46606-6

10 9 8 7 6 5 4 3 2 1

LSC-C

Printed in the United States of America